SECOND WIVES CLUB

RENEE DANIEL FLAGLER

Divine Write LLC

Baldwin, NY 11510

ISBN-13: 978-1-7347775-0-5

ISBN-10: 1-7347775-0-5

First Divine Write Trade Paperback Printing: May 2020

eISBN-13: 978-1-7347775-1-2

eISBN-10: 1-7347775-1-2

First Divine Write Electronic Edition: May 2020

Library of Congress Control Number: 2020940230

10 9 8 7 6 5 4 3 2 1

Printed in the United States of America

❀ Created with Vellum

CHAPTER 1

 aige Thompson

WHAT THE HELL is she doing here?

Before I got out of my chair in the kitchen, I knew that it was Maya Thompson banging on my front door. The nasal quality of her voice grated my nerves. Surely, there was no emergency. Maya was simply being her masterfully annoying self.

My husband, Rick, obviously didn't hear the commotion because he hadn't come out of the bedroom. The more she banged, the slower I walked. By the time I reached the door, Rick barreled past me mumbling his discontent. Maya's forehead pressed against the glass pane, but the frosted texture only offered a blurred view of her prying eyes. This woman's audacity could fill the Grand Canyon. Rick snatched the door open.

"Were you just looking through my door?" My neck craned to the side of Rick's arm so she could see the words come directly from my lips. I was ready to be amazed by some ridiculous response. *Who did that?*

"I wouldn't have to if you hadn't taken your time getting here," Maya spewed.

I took a deep breath—a really deep breath. By the time my lips were ready to deliver a response, Rick had both hands in the air, drawing our attention to him.

"Maya, I thought I asked you to call before showing up at my house." Rick looked at me. "Our house."

My mouth eased into the smuggest smile I could manage even though I couldn't understand why she still needed to be reminded after seven years. Maya snarled.

"Since when did things get so formal between us?" Maya snarled, responding to Rick but glaring at me.

"Since you don't frigging live here!" I yelled. My composure crumbled. I couldn't seem to still my trembling lip.

"Well, my daughter does …when she's here anyway." Her scowl made its way past Rick to me.

I narrowed my eyes. She parked a hand on her hip.

Rick took a deep breath. "You know she's not here now." His words were surprisingly even. He looked beyond Maya. "Where is she?"

"She's not with me."

Rick threw his hands in the air. "I can see that!" Frustration etched itself into the lines around his eyes.

Tension squeezed at my temples. Every muscle in my face tightened. I headed for the kitchen leaving Rick to handle her on his own. I was done. My tolerance meter had reached its peak. Who knew what would happen next if I didn't separate myself from them? I stomped circles in front of the kitchen sink, but pacing did nothing to calm me down. I flopped onto one of the stools in front of the island and forced myself not to cry.

"Rick loves me," I whispered to myself.

Once again, my soulmate was in the next room arguing with the one woman who seemed to possess the missing link to my blissful marriage. Maya was the thorn piercing my side—the constant reminder that Rick would never be all mine. As annoying as she'd always been, I truly couldn't blame her for the recent return of my insecurities. I hated it when they seeped through my composure. I couldn't count how many times it had happened since I stopped working to stay home and focus on my family. Sometimes I managed to navigate my way out of the pit of insecurity all on my own. Each bout took more effort.

Squeezing my eyes shut, I shook my head. "My husband loves me." That wasn't it. "I'm strong and smart." I was getting closer to the truth. "I'm … I have value." It came as a whisper.

Rick's grunt rumbled through the hallway. In a few steps, I was standing at the edge of the kitchen spying on their heated exchange. Maya asked for money *again*. It had become a habit in the past few months. I didn't know what was going on with her besides the fact that she refused to work. She sat around the house growing bigger by the month. At least eighty pounds had latched onto her since the day we met. She'd been evil ever since, even though Rick and I met two years after their divorce.

I left my job when Rick and I decided I would stay home until our daughter Scotland reached middle school age. But Maya had it in her head that if I didn't have to work, then she shouldn't have to either.

Rick owned an electrical contracting company and did well. He sent Maya more than enough money to pay for her mortgage and to care for their daughter, Jayden, even though Jayden spent half of every month with us.

"This is the last time." Rick's words broke through my thoughts. His tone was firm enough. I rolled my eyes. Every time was the last time—like when her car stalled the month before. Rick went out and bought her a new car.

I prayed that one day he'd recognize the puppetry. Maybe

he'd finally get tired. Perhaps his patience would run out. Hopefully, it would be sooner rather than later. Or before it was too late.

I heard Rick walk off. Moments later the sound of his footsteps brought him back toward the front door.

"Don't worry. I'll get this back to you ASAP." I could hear the slick victory in her tone.

The door connected with a slam and shorty, after Rick came to the kitchen. He sat down hard on the stool and heaved a winded sigh. As angry as I was at my husband, I also pitied him for having to deal with that woman.

I walked to the table where I'd left the cake I'd been icing before Maya showed up. Rick sat with his head in his hands. For several minutes, we maneuvered around each other silently. I finished icing the cake, cleaned the spatula, placed the cake in a carry dish, and set it on the counter. Rick went to the refrigerator, unscrewed a water bottle and downed it without closing the door. Together, we expertly avoided the eyesore in our union. We gave it room to breathe. To grow. Fester. This was our dance whenever Maya disturbed our peace. We knew it well. We had choreographed it.

"How much this time?" I broke the silence.

"Thirty-five hundred."

"Rick!" The dishtowel I'd been wiping the counter with flew from my hand and landed on the floor with a soft thud.

"I know, Babe. I just want peace. I don't want to have any problems when it comes to Jayden."

"That *is* the problem," I said, picking up the towel and snapping it.

"What's that supposed to mean?"

A sputter in my stomach dispatched heat throughout my core. Anger was a cancer spreading through my body fast. "You're always giving in to her to keep the peace or avoid getting her upset so that she won't interfere with you seeing Jayden. Can you see that she's just manipulating you?"

"No!" he said, pressing his lips together as if that couldn't possibly be true.

Inhaling gave me a moment to organize my words and regulate my rage. "You're so busy trying to keep everyone happy that you're always miserable." *And you're making me miserable.* "You need to put your foot down." I managed to speak evenly. "She'll get with the program." Taming my irritation, I walked over to Rick. "You're trying to do the impossible and it's never going to work."

Rick looked confused. "And what's that?"

"Trying to keep two women happy. Both of us can't win."

Rick looked baffled.

"It's time to pick up Scotland." I wouldn't allow my eyes to meet his as I left the kitchen. My leave was intentionally dry. "We'll see you after the birthday party."

I wondered how much longer I could remain patient in this situation. How long could I stand by while another woman handled my husband like a puppet master? Something or someone had to give.

I went into our bedroom to get dressed and Rick appeared in the doorway several minutes later.

"The only woman I'm trying to keep happy is you." He sat on the bed slowly as if his body ached. "I'm just trying to keep Maya from acting unreasonably."

"How's that working?" I slathered the words with a thick layer of sarcasm and then peeled myself out of my leggings and t-shirt. Rick followed me into the bathroom.

"What do you mean?"

"Babe." I held my hand under the shower water to make sure it wasn't too hot. "I can't do this now."

Rick leaned against the sink and folded his arms. He really didn't get it.

I stepped into the shower and concern for my husband softened me enough to try to help him understand. Taking a side seat obviously wasn't helping after all this time. "What's your biggest fear?"

"What?" he yelled over the spray of the water.

I repeated my question louder. "Hello!" I said after a few moments of silence.

"That she'll keep Jayden from me."

"Right! To avoid that, you try not to get her angry, but where does that get you?" No response again. "If you're not firm, she'll keep pushing until you have nothing left to give."

Rick didn't respond. I scrubbed, giving him a moment to absorb what I had said. When I got out of the shower, he was still standing in the same spot with his face knitted into a tight frown.

"You know I love you, right?" he asked, looking as though he really wanted me to believe him.

I sighed. "Yes, Rick." I kept the rest of my thoughts inside my head. *How long was I willing to put up with the fact that my husband's ex-wife had more power over him than me?*

CHAPTER 2

$\mathcal{L}$ yric Delaney

I JUMPED up off the couch in the sitting room and ran to my bedroom. My husband was on his way home from a weeklong business trip. That's right, I said my husband. I was going to show him how much I missed him.

I was so excited that Nate would be home soon. I planned to dote on him so much that he'd never want to leave me again—even for business. I stood in my dressing room, twisting and turning in the front of a wall of mirrors. A white negligee that pushed my D-cups up to my neck caught my eye. I paired them with black six-inch stilettos. That was too innocent looking. I shimmied out of that number and replaced the negligee with a flowing, black sheer nightgown that swept the floor in the back. I slipped on black lace panties, let my boobs hang free, and stuck my feet back in the stilettos. Yes! This was the look I needed to greet my sweetie.

I called up the restaurant to check on the food delivery

because I don't cook. Our housekeeper Gilda had set the table before I sent her home for the day. My plans for the evening didn't call for witnesses.

After double-checking everything, setting up the delivered food, and looking at the clock, I still had time to spare. I went to the bedroom, dialed my best friend Candy, and sat back against my comfortable plush headboard.

"Hey, girl! What's up?"

"Not much. Just waiting on Nate to get back from L.A. He should be here in about an hour." I heard a man's voice in the background. "Is that Jeff?"

"Girl," Candy paused and then quietly said, "No." The voice in the background became distant. Candy must have moved away from him.

"Mm hm. You're being scandalous, aren't you?"

"No. I'm. Not! Just hanging out with a friend. That's all."

"Yeah, right! Does Jeff know about this friend?"

"Girl, please. Jeff doesn't own me. When he finally divorces that no-boob cornball, then he can tell me what to do. As a matter of fact, he would need to put a ring on it to control me and even then, he can't tell me what to do."

I giggled. Candy always tickled me when she talked about Jeff's wife. The poor girl looked like a little boy. She didn't own a single feminine curve. "I hear that. You had better be careful. I know you don't want him to stop those checks. Brooklyn is nothing like Park Avenue."

"Whatever! Not everyone is as lucky as you are. I still don't know how you managed to get Nate to put a ring on your finger —especially when I have been with Jeff longer. I think I like being the side chick more, anyway. There's a lot more freedom."

"Cut the crap, Candy! Don't act as if you wouldn't marry Jeff in an instant." I hated it when she threw my marriage up in my face as if it was something foul. Why couldn't I be marriage worthy?

"What's that supposed to mean?" Candy asked as if she was really surprised by my statement.

"You wish Jeff would marry you, too. If not, you wouldn't do all the ridiculous things he asks of you. You should have never let him talk you out of having that baby. That would have given you more leverage!" The phone went silent and I instantly felt bad. "At least you got a banging Jag out of the deal." I hoped my last comment offered some consolation.

"Shut up, Lyric. I told you the abortion was my decision."

"Um-hm."

"I'm a model, remember? I need my body to be perfect."

"Candy, I know you on the inside."

"Goodbye!" The line went dead.

I shouldn't have gone there with Candy. Calling her back wasn't an option even though I felt a little bad. Groveling wasn't my way. She'd get over her feelings and everything would be as it was. No one wanted to be reminded of his or her regrets. Plus, she was right. Getting Nate to marry me hadn't been easy. He needed convincing. I just helped him see things my way. The ring surprised me. The actual marriage surprised me, and everyone else. Girls like us didn't become wives. But I did.

I heard a car and ran to my window just as the tail end of it pulled up to the house and disappeared from my view. Nate was home early. Clapping my hands, I ran to my dressing room and rubbed his favorite scent behind my ears, between my boobs and on the inside of my thighs. I was a smitten teenager when it came to Nate. I couldn't love him more. On my way downstairs, the heel of my stiletto caught on the carpet and almost sent me tumbling the rest of the way. I slowed my pace. I couldn't greet my husband with bruises.

I glanced at myself in the mirror one last time before opening the door. Pressing my lips together, I evened my red lipstick with a pop. I fluffed my hair and tossed the ends over the front of one shoulder. Rick loved it that way. Girls paid big money to add hair like mine onto their heads. Mine came courtesy of my Cajun and Trinidadian roots, which stretched all the way back to Africa and India.

When I was sure I looked scrumptious enough, I fixed a seductive smile across my lips and opened the door wide for my sweetheart. I didn't care if the driver got an eye full of my curves. Nate needed to know just how much I had missed him.

Nate was dragging his suitcase from the trunk when he looked up and noticed me. His mouth opened and he stood frozen like that for several seconds. He turned his head toward the front of the car, and I followed his line of sight right into the face of his ex-wife, Vivian. One of those identical, evil twins of his was in the driver's seat. I couldn't tell if it was Sidney or Sky.

The smile melted from my lips. Vivian's face twisted as if she smelled something foul. I turned around, giving them a full view of my ample backside and slammed the door. Nate called my name over and over. I heard him through the door but refused to answer. I made the mistake of assuming he had used his usual car service. What was he doing in the car with them?

I traipsed to the kitchen, snatched an open bottle of white wine from the fridge and filled my glass. Nate always said that was tacky—filling the glass to the rim. I didn't care about what he thought right now. Drowning my humiliation had my full attention.

Vivian again. I flopped on the couch and folded my legs under me. No matter what, she was always around. But Nate was with me now. My gulp cleared half the glass. His kids were grown—a few years younger than me. He and Vivian shouldn't have much to connect about. When she asked him for the divorce, I thought we were done with her. She hated him and I finally had him for myself. No more second rung for me. But sometime after the divorce was final, they became cordial. And then they became downright friendly. That was a new problem.

Minutes later, Nate appeared in the entrance of the den. I twisted my lips and looked the other way.

"What's the problem, Lyric?"

I rolled my eyes and took another gulp.

"Lyric!" Nate huffed. "I know you hear me talking to you."

I still faced the other way. My back was so rigid it could have broken. "Why didn't you tell me she was picking you up from the airport? I could have done that." My bottom lip quivered as it always did when I was about to cry. I bit into it to stifle the tears.

Nate walked over to me with pouted lips. He was teasing me again. I swatted his hand when he reached for me and turned my back to him. Nate hugged me from behind, chuckling.

"What the hell is so funny?"

"You're jealous! It's cute."

"Cute!" I was about to let him have it when he turned my face towards him and pressed his lips against mine. The kiss was so light and sweet.

"Sydney wanted to talk to me about something, so she came to pick me up. Vivian happened to be with her. I didn't ask them to pick me up, Babe."

Now I felt like a brat. "You could have told me. Look at how I came to the door."

Nate licked his lips and raised his brows. "Nice welcome. Let's not waste it." Nate kissed me again.

I didn't want to give in. He kissed me again—my ear, my neck, and my forehead. Nate touched the tip of my nose with his index finger and smiled. I didn't smile back but felt my irritation easing away. Nate was always my weakness. This strong, smart, important man chose me, lavished me with a wealth of money and attention, made me feel worthy. I couldn't resist him when he was married to Vivian, and once we got married, nothing changed. I didn't want to want him. But Nate knew what to do. I was clay in his hand. He made me into whatever he wanted. Just like now. I was grateful, dammit.

'They' said models like us weren't the marrying kind. Nate made me his. What else was I to do? If I didn't show my appreciation, I might be responsible for giving Vivian another chance.

Nate laid me back on the couch. I didn't fight against him, there wasn't any resistance left in me. This was Nate. My husband. I laid back and let Nate do what he wanted, and I enjoyed it and reminded myself that I was the lucky one. I'd never forgotten it.

CHAPTER 3

 erri Rhodes

I WATCHED, mesmerized, as my handsome husband shaved his head clean. We were preparing for the Brimming Nest gala. After ten years of marriage, he still set off tiny bombs inside my loins. I loved refined men. Chris was sharp. Polished. Brilliant.

"Baby...baby!"

"Yes," I said when it finally registered that he was calling me. I was looking right at him and still didn't hear him.

"You can't just stand there checking out all this goodness. You need to get dressed, too," he roared. His laughter bounced off the walls and sent my heart fluttering.

"I can check you out all I want," I said, rolling my eyes. "You're hogging the mirror, buddy. I need to put my make-up on." I bumped him with my hip. He winked and flashed the same smile that snagged my attention the day we met.

Work had been so hectic that I'd practically lived at the television station. Being home with Chris prancing around in my undies almost made me giddy.

He moved his shaving kit over, clearing space on the vanity. "There's room for you here, honey."

I started to set my make-up bag down and then snatched it back. "Oh no! I don't want any of your little hairs getting in my make-up. I'll wait."

"Suit yourself." Chris went back to shaving, and I went back to staring at him for a few more moments.

Chris aimed the tiny remote toward the television and music flowed through the hidden speakers in our bedroom and poured into the bath. I shimmied. Chris stopped shaving long enough to engage me in a two-step. Our laughter merged and danced off the walls.

Chris wrapped his arms around me. "I missed you." He stared right into my eyes.

"I missed you too, sweetie." Sliding my arms around his neck, I stood on my toes and puckered.

This kiss was sweet. I could have spent the night in his arms. I loved my job but didn't love when it took me away from my family for days at a time.

Chris picked up his razor and lifted his chin to capture the hairs under his jawbone. "Riley should be here soon."

"I can't believe she's sixteen now." I shook my head. "And she's so pretty. Those boys at school are—"

"Who?" Chris stopped moving. I turned toward him and stared into eyes that had narrowed to slits.

"Your daughter. You're going to have to get used to the idea of boys being around eventually."

"Not my daughter." Chris went back to shaving. "I told her no dating until she graduates from college…and the same thing goes for Alisa."

I couldn't contain my laughter. Chris pointed his clippers at me. I couldn't help but laugh harder.

"Bless your heart, Daddy."

"Whatever." Chris hated it when I teased him about his girls. He cleared the vanity. "The bathroom is all yours."

I went in and tried to put on my make-up the way the girl showed me at the MAC counter, then slipped on my dress. "Zip me please."

Chris came over and instead of zipping the back of my dress, squeezed my behind and wrapped his arms around me once again.

"Leave my little booty alone!"

"Correction! It's my little booty and I happen to love it."

"Zip me, buddy! Literally."

I knew the pun was cheesy. Chris twisted his lips and then laughed.

He looked scrumptious in his tailored tuxedo. We were finally ready to go. Just as we made it downstairs, the doorbell rang.

Chris headed for the door to let his daughter in.

"Hey, honey!

"Hey, Dad!" Riley gave her father a hug and a quick kiss and then turned her attention back to her cell phone. Riley's fingers popped across the screen like lightning. It amazed me that her thumbs didn't fall off. "Hey, Mama K." She came in for a tight hug, before yelling for her little sister, "Alisa!"

"She's in the den."

At the same time, Alisa yelled back, "I'm in here!"

"I've got something funny to show you," Riley said and disappeared into the den.

Chris, and I shook our heads.

"We better get going."

"Yes, sir." I saluted him. "It wouldn't be right if the keynote speaker was late." I teased him, but truly couldn't be prouder. "How often have they had a world-renowned architect among them?"

Brilliant white teeth flashed between Chris's proud grin. "Because of you, now they will."

"Well." I straightened the lapels of his suit. "You've always been the captain of my cheering squad. I love bragging about how terrific you are." Another peck.

I grabbed my shoes from the bedroom and went in search of the girls. With a wagging pointer, I instructed Alisa to listen to her big sister. I reminded Riley she was here to watch her sister, not her "Likes." Chris and I pulled the girls into a snug embrace and headed to the gala.

"No boys this time, girls. You hear me!"

"Oh. Alright!" Riley whined, playing along.

"Wait! What?" Chris's smile faded fast.

The girls and I fell out sniggering. We so loved teasing him.

"Not funny!" Chris tried to look mad but ended up laughing too.

We made it across the George Washington Bridge into Manhattan without incident. The gala was held at a fancy hotel along the perimeter of Central Park. Once there, we met up with Camilla, Chris' ex and her new fiancé.

"I picked up our place cards. We're all at table five," Camilla said to Paige and me.

Camilla and I chatted while being directed to an ornate room for the cocktail hour. I spotted a few other friends.

After we were all seated, a gentleman made a brief announcement. That's when we noticed our men had stopped talking. Their heads simultaneously whipped in the same direction. We looked at each other then followed the men's line of sight to a woman shaped like Jessica Rabbit from *Who Framed Roger Rabbit*. Long, slick hair framed the sides of her pretty face. Red lipstick looked like it had been painted onto her pouty lips and her boobs, like melons, fought to break free from the plunging neckline of her form-fitting dress.

Paige popped her husband in the head. "Close your mouth." Her attempt to whisper was an epic fail.

I looked back towards the curvaceous beauty and "Damn," slipped out of my mouth. Paige and Camilla laughed.

The three of us couldn't take our eyes off this woman. She had arrested the attention of the entire room. Scowls replaced the smiles on some of the wives. Men pretended not to look and a few more wives popped their husbands in the head much like Paige had done to Rick.

"Would you like it if I had a booty like that?" I said into Chris's ear. He nearly spat out his drink.

"I'm not sure I'd know how to work with that!" Everyone within earshot laughed.

"You two are crazy," Paige said.

The girl and her husband stopped at our table, looked at their seating card and nodded. The man pulled out her chair and she covered the entire seat with that abundant behind. They looked more like they were attending the Grammys than a benefit for a nonprofit organization that focused on blended families.

We were done laughing. Paige, Camilla and I looked at each other again. The men worked hard to act as if they weren't paying attention. Chris spoke up first, greeting the husband.

"Chris Rhodes." He nodded and shook hands with the very debonair gentleman who said his name was Nathan Delaney. The rest of the men followed suit until they were all introduced. The women sat dumbfounded until Mr. Nathan Delaney made the introduction.

"This is my wife, Lyric."

Another beat of silence.

Lyric's smile faded.

I plucked myself out of our collective trance and responded first. "Nice to meet you, Lyric. I'm Kerri Rhodes, Producer at WTBK," I said, leaning forward. My title slipped out. I was so used to attending industry events I'd forgotten how to offer a simple greeting. "Chris is my husband."

"Oh. Hi!" I'm a model."

Collectively, eyes widened. Camilla, Paige, and the other women continued introductions until everyone presented themselves. Conversations resumed around the table, but no one spoke directly to Lyric. I invited Lyric into our conversation. I wanted to ask how old she was since she looked like she could have been her husband's daughter, but I remembered my manners.

A little while later, I excused myself. Paige and Camilla followed me to the lady's room. I looked behind me before closing the door to make sure no one else was coming. Camilla checked the stalls. Once we knew we were alone, we looked at each other and laughed until we were bent over.

"Damn!" Camilla said. "She's right off the pages of some men's magazine!"

"I bet she's a video vixen," Paige said.

I sucked my teeth. "That's so stereotypical. She's probably an ex-porn star!"

The three of us hollered, cackling until the sound of our merriment reverberated off the bathroom walls.

The door eased open and the three of us swallowed our laughter as Lyric walked in.

"Hey, ladies," she said as she made her way into a stall.

"Hey!" *Awkward.* I held my smirk until I heard the lock on her stall click.

Paige covered her mouth and stared at me with wide eyes. Camilla's shoulders jerked. She tried to contain her silent laugh.

We talked about nonsense until she came out. Paige busied herself fluffing her hair in the mirror. Camilla applied a layer of lipstick she didn't need and I stood with my back against the wall. Lyric came out of the stall and approached the sink closest to Camilla. Camilla looked at me and crossed her eyes. My chuckle burst through my mouth before I could catch it, so I excused myself and cleared my throat as if I had sneezed.

"This is such a nice event," Lyric said, holding her hands inside the dryer. "Is this your first time here?"

"It's my first time," Camilla said. "She's married to my ex," she said, pointing to me.

Lyric looked confused for a second and then relaxed when Camilla laughed.

"We're actually friends."

"Oh!" For a second she looked like she didn't know what to say next. "That's cool. My husband's ex and I will never be... friends."

"Been married long?" Paige asked.

Lyric managed a coy smile. Leaning her head to the side, she held out her hand, revealing a diamond that looked like the rock Fred Flintstone had given to Wilma. "Just a few months."

"Welcome to the second wives club," Paige announced.

Lyric finally felt comfortable enough to unleash a genuine laugh. "Humph." She shook her head. "Where do you ladies live?"

"Jersey all around," I responded.

"Oh! Me too!" she said excitedly. "What part?"

"Fort Lee." I pointed back and forth between Camilla and me.

"Leonia," Paige said.

Lyric's eyes were as wide as her smile. I thought she was about to clap her hands like a seal. "That's not far from me. I'm in Englewood Cliffs."

I whistled. "Fancy!"

"Oh. My husband is in the music business," she said with her chest out and chin up. "He owns Karma Records. We met on the set of one of Seven's videos. You know who he is, right? The platinum R&B artist?"

Paige, Camilla, and I shot subtle, knowing glances at each other.

"Nice!" I said, for lack of anything else that wouldn't have been appropriate at that time.

Lyric grabbed her purse and headed for the door. "We should exchange numbers. I don't have many friends in Jersey."

"I can't imagine why," Camilla said under her breath.

"Yes, we should be friends," I said in an attempt to get past Camilla's comment. She obviously didn't recognize my sarcasm.

Little did we know, Lyric was serious. When we returned to the table, she whipped out her cell phone and saved our details. By the time dinner was served, she had sent us friend requests on Facebook and asked us if we had Twitter and IG.

Paige said, "I—what?"

"IG Paige," I said. "That's short for Instagram." Still confused, but no longer seeming to care, Paige twisted her lips and dismissed the explanation with a wave of her hand.

We were all about to be friends whether we liked it or not. As a decent judge of people, I was intrigued. Something about Lyric reminded me of women in the reality shows I produced.

CHAPTER 4

 aige

THE VIXEN, as we so endearingly named her, had already called me three times since the gala last Thursday. She wanted to make sure we weren't going to flake on her invitation to lunch, but due to Kerri's crazy work schedule, we had to wait for the following weekend.

"Lyric. Lyric. Lyric!" I forced myself to repeat her name. Kerri and I had referred to her as The Vixen so much that I didn't want to make the mistake of saying that to her face.

As I parked my practical Toyota Murano in front of the Italian Bistro, The Vixen...I mean Lyric chose, I wondered what she would look like today. I was glad Rick wasn't with me. As usual, I was the first to arrive and figured Kerri would be the last, but to my surprise, I looked into my rearview mirror and there she was pulling in behind me in her BMW. That made me wonder what kind of car The Vixen drove.

"Hey, girl!" Kerri jumped out, looking trendy and cute in a yellow leather jacket over a white shirt, jeans and black booties.

We exchanged friendly kisses and headed into the restaurant. The spring breeze was too cool for outdoor dining so we asked for a booth near the window so we could still enjoy the sunlight.

"Okay. What are we in for?" Kerri asked as she scooted into the booth. "You know she called me again this morning to make sure I was coming."

I looked towards the door and then swept my eyes around the restaurant to make sure she hadn't arrived. "She has called me every day since the gala the other night."

"Girlfriend needs a friend for real," Kerri shook her head.

Through my peripheral, I saw the flash of a red, super shiny sports car. I'm not that well-versed on cars so I couldn't tell what kind it was, but I knew it was expensive. "I think this is her," I said to Kerri.

Sure enough, The Vixen whipped that little sports car into a space in front of my crossover. When she stepped out, I swore my sight switched to slow motion as she emerged from that car like a movie star, flipped her long hair behind her shoulder and adjusted her sunglasses. I'm sure her handbag and shoes cost enough to buy my Murano outright.

Suddenly I felt underdressed in a drab pair of mommy jeans, plain shirt and flats. I felt the need for an immediate makeover. When had I become so practical?

Lyric filled the entrance of the restaurant with her presence and I waved her over.

"Hey, Ladies!" Lyric was loud. "I'm so glad you made it." She paused. "Wait!" She looked around. "This is where they sat you? Hold on." She turned away before we could return her greeting.

I wasn't sure what was happening, but I remained quiet to see how this would play out. Kerri's silence, and the look on her face, told me she was thinking the same thing.

"Emilio! Can we have our regular seats?"

"Anything for you, Mrs. Delaney."

"Come on ladies." Lyric followed the young waiter without bothering to look back to make sure we were behind her.

Kerri picked up her bag as she scooted out of the booth.

The waiter led us to a table behind glass partitions and walls lined with bottles of wine.

"That's more like it!" Lyric said as she sat. "Please bring my favorite, one white and one red. Thanks!"

When Emilio nodded and exited, Lyric turned her attention back towards us. "I wasn't sure which one you liked so I ordered one of each," she said, referring to the wines.

"I'm a red girl," Kerri said.

"I like white," I said.

"Good. You're both covered. This is one of our favorite places. Both Nate and I love it."

"I can tell you come here often. You know the staff by name I see. I have a place like that near work." Kerri said.

Somehow the conversation started with work and Lyric asked what I did again.

I wished she hadn't asked me. I was feeling a little insecure, which surprised me. I cleared my throat. "I have a master's degree in accounting." I don't know why I started with that. I guess I was suddenly feeling insecure about not working. "But, right now I'm a stay-at-home mom."

"Okay," Lyric said. I guess she wasn't impressed. "What do your husbands do?" she asked.

"Chris is an architect," Kerri said.

"Rick owns a general contracting business that mostly does work for government agencies."

"That's cool." Lyric paused as the waiter took our order. When the room was clear again, she asked. "What's up with this second wives club?"

"Huh?" Kerri and I looked at each other and then I remembered what I had said to her at the gala. "Oh. That's a joke. You thought it was a real club?"

"Yeah! That's why I wanted to meet with you ladies. I don't have any married friends and I'm new at this, so I want to make sure I'm doing this right."

Kerri burst out laughing "Girl! What's right? We are winging this thing just like you."

"Oh." Lyric looked a little embarrassed.

"It's just something we started saying after we attended our first Brimming Nest Retreat."

"They have a retreat, too?" Lyric asked.

"Yes! The gala was just one of their many events. They do annual picnics and workshops, too. Stuff for the husbands, the kids, couples. They cover the whole damn family!" Kerri said.

"Wow. I didn't know it was that deep. Well, I'm still glad we met."

"Oh! Thanks!" Kerri said, lifting her water glass like she was toasting.

"How long have you been married?" Lyric asked.

"Ten years!" Kerri said and followed that up with a forkful of salad.

"Seven for me," I said.

"I think I can learn a lot from you ladies." Lyric looked at me. "Maybe there are things I could teach you, too."

Was she trying to say something? I wanted to get annoyed, but truthfully, I did want to learn from her. Right now I was feeling like I needed to spruce up my appeal. Things were fine between Rick and me but adding a little spark to our relationship wouldn't hurt anything.

"I'm good!" Kerri said.

"Kids?"

"A nine-year-old and a sixteen-year-old stepdaughter," Kerri said.

"My daughter is five and my stepdaughter is twelve."

"I don't have any kids of my own, but I do have evil twin stepdaughters."

That got a laugh from Kerri and me.

Our lunch came and I managed to make it through without sinking further into my blossoming insecurities. By the time we were done, I decided I needed a complete makeover. I had become much too settled in my cozy little life. I needed to find my fire again.

CHAPTER 5

 yric

I LOVED everything about Los Angeles. The vibe of the city. The air. The people—everything! Nate and I were there to attend the ASCAP Expo, which for me meant shopping, parties and profiling. I shopped Rodeo Drive all day to find the right outfit for the huge party Nate's company was throwing for their songwriters. Every person of status would be there. Industry vets, newbies, and wannabes.

The cute young bellhop at the Beverly Wilshire came with my delivery just as Nate stepped into the shower. I clapped with excitement as he carried all my bags into the suite. I knew I had gone overboard, but since I took a break from modeling, I didn't get to travel as much, which meant I also didn't shop as much as I used to. By the time he was done, bags lined both couches. I ripped open the box containing my dress for tonight, put it up against my body and spun like a child.

I ran to the room, laid out my dress on the bed, and rushed

out of my clothes so I could join Nate in the shower. For a man in his forties, he looked amazing despite the few areas that had begun to grow a little soft. With his dark, creamy skin and toned body, he could compete with any dude in their late twenties or early thirties. But it was his mind I was attracted to the most. Nate was brilliant, and that turned me on.

Nate's naughty smile, curled off to one side of his lips, revealing a flash of gleaming white teeth. Rising on my toes, I kissed him softly, then turned my back and bent over to give him a wide-angle view of my behind. Nate gave my cheeks a squeeze and sucked in a breath so loud, I could hear it over the stream of the shower. I stood under the water and offered him a quick show, twisting my body as I stared directly into his eyes.

Nate pulled me to him and pushed his tongue into my mouth. His erection grew rigid against my stomach. He tasted like cognac. The steam from our bodies joined with that of the water, covering the glass walls until we could no longer see through them. Nate turned me and entered from behind.

"Yes, baby!" I shrieked. As the intensity of my screams increased so did Nate's thrusts until he was grunting and pounding me as if his life would end if he stopped.

"Oh! Baby!" he groaned.

Nate's expertise in making love was unlike that of any man I'd ever been with. Men my age never made me feel the way he did. His rhythmic maneuvers sent me into an orgasmic frenzy. My bud became so sensitive that my entire body quaked as if I were having convulsions.

Nate's pace accelerated into quick greedy strokes that made my knees week. He held me tighter to keep me from wilting and after a few urgent grunts, he howled as a hard release shot through him. As his life exploded inside of me, my own release cascaded over him. He flipped me around and kissed me until my body stopped shaking. Then we took our time washing each other's bodies, taking special care in delicate places.

I was so spent I hardly wanted to leave the hotel room. But who was I kidding? No matter how sated I felt, there was no way I was going to miss attending the coveted industry shindig on the arm of one of the most prominent men in the industry. This was my time to shine, too. This was what life was all about and I loved every second of it.

Just to taunt Nate some more, I made a sexy show of rubbing lotion on my body, modeling my lace underwear and slipping into my tight dress. I dried my hair, letting it hang straight down the sides of my face. Nate's navy blue suit complemented my electric blue dress to perfection. Who would I be if I were to wear something that was all class and no scandal? The slit in my halter dress started at the top of my right thigh. When we were all dressed, Nate pulled me against his body again and kissed me hard.

"Wait until we get back here tonight!" he said and then ran his tongue across my lips.

"Nate!" I scolded. "You're going to mess up my lipstick."

"I've got somewhere for your lipstick to go."

"You're so nasty! Let's go." I grabbed him by the arm and led him out of the room.

Lights flashed as we exited the car. The music poured through the front doors like a flood, filling the sidewalk with one of Seven's hit records. We sashayed down the red carpet. I felt like Michelle Obama on Barack's arm as we entered the swanky club with all eyes and cameras on us. Between the flash from cameras and the sudden darkness inside, I could hardly see. Strobe lights flickered and I had to shut my eyes for a few moments to adjust to the change of lighting. A personal valet met us at the door and escorted us through the thick crowd into the VIP area totally separated from the rest of the crowd. It was like 'all hail King Nate,' as we walked through. People were calling out to him, men were trying to shake his hand, and chicks were screaming his name. I even saw a few thirsty, trifling women wink at him as if I wasn't there clinging to his arm.

"Back up boo!" I said and gave this one chick 'the eye' after she shook his hand a little too long. I removed Nate's hand from hers and turned his palm up to see if she had tried to slip him her number. Then I held my hand up so she could see the ridiculous rock on my finger. "Watch it!" I mouthed as we continued as if we were on the catwalk together. She rolled her eyes, smirked, and then smiled. That was a challenge. My look told her that I dared her to try something. She walked away. These women didn't know that I had already played that game and won the prize.

Once we reached our designated seating area, our private waitress took drink orders. Nate ordered his signature cognac and I ordered a martini. I didn't love martinis, but they always looked classy, so I drank them at events like these.

As usual, women and industry folk continued fawning over Nate, so I could hardly leave his side. He wasn't the only one getting the attention. Men were casting scandalous glances at me on the sly. One even blew me a kiss and winked when he thought Nate wasn't looking.

Nate leaned over to me. He was so close I could feel the heat of his breath on my neck. I thought he was going to kiss me, but instead, he whispered in my ear. "I saw that."

I looked at him and rolled my eyes. "And I see these heifers trying to slip you their numbers on the sly." I pursed my lips and dared him to respond.

He flashed the wicked smile that caught me in the first place and I just shook my head and took a sip of my martini. Since I had to keep an eye on these tricky women, I stayed close to my husband until I had to go to the bathroom.

I looked back as I exited the VIP area and saw that the 'birds' were swarming down on my man like vultures on a carcass. I sped up, moving so fast that I slammed right into someone. We both jumped back out of the way of the liquor that swirled over the top of his glass. I checked my dress to make sure nothing spilled on me. I looked up into the face of the person that I collided with and knew immediately that this was no accident.

"Well, well, well! Look at you. Ha!" Cypher X, a former R&B favorite taunted me with his menacing laugh. The liquor on his breath assaulted my nostrils and the fact that his eyes were mere slits told me he had been smoking, too.

"It's nice to see you too!" I said and sucked my teeth as I tried to get around him, but he blocked my path. Crossing my arms, I cocked my head to the side. "Excuse me, please! I'm trying to go to the bathroom." I looked back towards Nate once again. His attention was on the big booty girl in front of him in the tacky red dress.

"What's the rush?" Cypher said. His slick smile made my skin feel as if it had come alive and tried to run off my body. "You're not happy to see me?" He licked his lips and swayed. "You spilled my drink, baby. Maybe you should buy me another one." He touched my hand and I jerked away. "I know you got the money. You're married to that big man over there," he laughed again and I clamped my teeth together to keep from screaming. "Yeah, I saw all the media coverage from your wedding. You probably sent those pictures to the magazines yourself to make sure everyone knew you snagged a big fish."

"Cypher. I can't do this with you."

"Oh, you're too good for me now? You wouldn't even be Mrs. Delaney if it wasn't for me." His menacing laugh was loud. Heads turned in our direction.

My groan was louder than I intended. "I have to pee!" I pushed past Cypher and hastened my steps, trying to get to the bathroom before he could stop me again.

"Dude done turned a hoe into a housewife!" he said.

Instead of acknowledging his callous comment, I ran the rest of the way, refusing to look back. His loud laugh haunted me the entire way. Inside the bathroom, I stood in the stall and tried to calm my heart rate. I handled my business and then looked into the mirror while washing my hands. I saw a different me than the confident one who had arrived on the arm of Nate Delaney. I closed my eyes, took several breaths, and readied myself for another confrontation with Cypher in case he was outside the bathroom door. He was unpredictable when he was drunk, and the last thing I needed was for him to cause a scene. Nate would never forgive me for that.

I peeked out of the bathroom before stepping out. When I didn't see Cypher, I tried to make my way back to the VIP area where I would be safe. There was no way they would let Cypher's grimy behind in there. His trifling ass had been black-listed for thinking it was okay to pump the daughter of one of the industry's biggest executives with ecstasy and then leak the video of their wild night on the internet. He didn't burn his bridges, he blew them to itty bitty pieces and hadn't been able to put them back together to secure a deal since.

As I approached the entrance to the VIP area, some dude asked me to get him in. I dismissed that nonsense with a wave and kept moving. He squeezed my butt and I turned around and slapped the gravy out of him. Spit flew out the side of his mouth. Security lifted him away immediately and settled the commotion as I was ushered into the VIP lounge.

"What happened?" Nate came up to me with concern creased into his face.

"Some asshole just squeezed my butt, so I slapped him."

"Where is he?" Nate's voice was smooth, calm, like a mobster.

"Don't worry, baby." I caressed his face. "Security dragged his behind out of here."

For a few moments, Nate just looked at me. Then he narrowed his eyes towards the area where the incident happened. "You stay in here until we leave."

"Don't worry baby. I can handle myself," I said. Nate responded with a scolding gaze. "Okay, baby! I'll be by your side for the rest of the evening." I didn't want to go back out there and run the risk of colliding with Cypher again, anyway. Besides, the most powerful people in the industry were in our section of the club.

The DJ threw on some old school R&B and I grabbed Nate by the hand. "Let's dance, sweetie."

Nate dropped his shoulders. He wasn't the greatest dancer, but he was used to giving me what I wanted. We stepped into a less crowded area and I closed in on Nate, turning my hips until I felt his manhood grow against my stomach. I turned around and backed up against him twisting my hips.

"You better watch it!" Nate whispered in my ear and then kissed my neck.

Getting affection from Nate in public always made me giddy. I could only imagine all of the jealous stares we were probably receiving. I decided to look around and assess the haters when my breath caught. Cypher had made it inside the VIP area and was headed straight toward us.

"Let's sit down." I grabbed Nate's hand and dragged him back to our seat.

"What just happened?" Nate asked when we sat.

"My feet hurt!" I lied and took off my five-inch heels and rubbed my sole.

When I looked up, Cypher was standing directly in front of us. I swallowed hard and almost choked.

"Nate Delaney. How's it going?"

"Cypher X, right?"

"Yeah, man. Yeah!" Cypher seemed excited that Nate remembered who he was while missing the slight sarcasm in Nate's tone.

"What can I do for you?"

"Well, since you asked. I'm working on a new project. I think you'd like it."

"Give my secretary a call next week," Nate said and turned his attention back to me. "How are your feet?"

Cypher had been dismissed and he didn't like it. His sideways glare and tight scowl told me so. I wanted to laugh but wouldn't dare do it while he stood there stewing in his embarrassment. Cypher had a mean streak, which also contributed to him being blacklisted. His ego had been bruised and there was no telling what he might have done. He stood there for another moment and took a sip from his glass before walking right out of the area.

A while later, Nate said it was time to go. He never lingered at these affairs and only stayed long enough to make a decent appearance. When we left, Cypher was outside the club talking on his cell phone. He glared at me as Nate and I climbed into the car. My phone buzzed. Cypher sent me a text.

You thought that was funny, huh? Don't forget you owe me. I'm calling in my debt soon.

When we got home, Nate undressed me at the door. We made love until he fell asleep and I waited for his snore to fill the room. When I knew he wouldn't wake up, I snuck out of the bed grabbed my cell phone, and texted Cypher back.

Do me a favor and don't ever contact me again.

I shut my phone off. The next day I had my number changed.

CHAPTER 6

erri

I PULLED up in front of Camilla's house with a hard stop, turned down the music, and tapped the horn. Camilla gave me the side-eye. I was so preoccupied I hadn't noticed her standing right at the curb.

I swung my hand, gesturing for her to get in the car fast. She was barely in when I pulled off.

"Whoa! Girl! Are you trying to kill me?"

I pointed to the Bluetooth, letting her know I was on a call. She quieted.

"Work?" she mouthed.

I shook my head and then hit the button to transfer the call to the speakers.

"This isn't right, Ms. Kerri. Who did she think she was, talking to me like that?"

Camilla scrunched her brows in confusion. "Just keep listening," I whispered.

"Ava. Where are you now?" I said in the calmest tone I could muster.

"Who, me?" Ava responded.

Camilla looked at me. I raised my brow. She understood my "see what I mean" expression.

"Yes, you! Who else am I talking to?"

"Oh! Anyway." Silence.

"Ava! You still haven't told me where you are."

"Ms. Kerri! Why you gotta be all in my business?"

"Because right now, your whereabouts are my business. I need you to get back on the set and return to that girl's conference so we can film this scene today."

"I can't."

What? I was confused. "Did you just say, you can't?"

"Um. Yes."

I groaned. "Why, Ava?"

"Because Crystal told me if I showed up today, she was going to beat my ass. Have you seen her arms? She's big as hell. One hit and I would be on the floor. I can't go out like that on TV. I have fans. They can't see me like that."

Camilla grabbed her mouth. Her entire upper body rocked as she tried her best to prevent her laugh from seeping through her fingers. Camilla didn't have to deal with crazy reality stars all day. To me, there was nothing funny.

I didn't even bother to ask Ava why Crystal threatened her. I didn't want to know why. As small as Ava was, she had a big mouth and a sassy tongue that always landed her in blistering waters.

"Ava. Need I remind you about the contract you signed? Think of your fans..." I pointed a finger in my mouth and acted as if I were gagging. Camilla continued cracking up silently. "Wouldn't you hate to disappoint them? Moreover, most importantly, no work-ee, no pay-ee, missy. That's what happens when you renege on a contract."

"Well, what about Crystal?"

"Don't worry about her. I'll take care of that. Now get back to the hotel, stat!"

The annoying sound of Ava sucking her teeth hissed through the speakers. "Alright, Ms. Kerri, but I'm telling you right now, if that cow touches me, I'm calling the police, pressing charges, and then suing her for every dime in her bank accounts and every bon-bon in her fridge."

Camille was really cracking up now.

"Bye, Ava. I'm going to call the crew and if you're not on set in the next half-hour, this will be considered a breach of contract."

"Okay. I'm going."

"Bye!"

I disconnected the call and Camilla hollered. It took several moments for her to recover. "I don't envy you at all!"

"I told you those women were crazy."

"Which show is this?"

"Society Wives."

"Oh, the reality show with the wives of all those high-profile men? I think I saw a promo for that."

"Yes, we are in our last few weeks of production, way behind schedule and these damn women are driving me crazy. Give me a second." I called the director, my right hand on the set, and told her that Ava was on her way back to the hotel where they were filming. I told her to call me when she arrived and to alert security in case Crystal decided to act out.

"We're here! I almost missed my turn." I shifted my focus to turn safely into the hotel's entrance. "Text to keep me posted," I said before disconnecting the call. We arrived at the hotel where the Brimming Nest's Women Rock Brunch was being held.

I threw the car into park, handed the valet the key, and Camilla and I rushed inside. We walked right past the fuchsia carpet into an elegantly decorated room bursting with women dressed in every shade of pink. I acknowledged a few ladies from the film and television industry.

Lyric and Paige were already inside. Lyric sat down at our table. I had helped with the seating and didn't remember placing her with us.

"I hope we are not too late," I said. Lyric and Paige stood, and Camilla and I greeted them with hugs. We pressed our cheeks together, kissing the air.

"It's Ms. Producer's fault!" Camilla said, tossing a thumb in my direction." There was a hilarious crisis on the set."

I rolled my eyes and shook my head. "As always."

"No worries. The program hasn't started yet. We've just been stuffing our faces, right Lyric?"

"Yep," she said, popping a bite-sized pastry in her mouth before clapping the crumbs away. Chewing made her plump, hot-pink lips look even larger.

As usual, Lyric's hair was styled to perfection. Her soft pink jumpsuit cascaded over her big butt like water over a fall. The purple platforms added several inches of height, giving her a statuesque, model-like appearance.

"Have you lost weight, Paige?" Camilla asked.

"Yeah. Your face looks slimmer," I added.

"Glad you noticed," Paige squealed. "Just a few pounds," she said modestly, waving away our compliments. "I joined that gym you were telling me about before, Kerri."

"Looking good." I held my thumbs up.

"I told her she looked really cute today," Lyric said and then went back to looking bored, scanning the crowd.

Small talk scurried around the table as we caught up with what was going on in everyone's lives.

"I gotta know," Lyric announced abruptly, snatching all of our attention at once. "How did y'all become so damn friendly?" She pointed to Camilla and me and then sipped from her flute.

We exchanged our usual knowing smiles before indulging Lyric's curiosity.

"We get asked that all of the time," Camilla started. "Chris and I should have never gotten married in the first place."

"What?" Lyric looked confused.

"We were friends. Close friends. We had sex. I got pregnant. We got married and one day realized we were much better at being friends than spouses. The only thing we had in common was our daughter Riley. He wanted much more stability than I was able to offer and he wanted more kids than I wasn't willing to have."

"That's where I come in. I rely on routine and being an only child, I wanted a shipload of kids," I added.

"When Chris introduced me to Kerri. I told him she was the one," Camilla said proudly.

"We've been cool ever since," I said.

Camilla twisted her lips. "Yeah, right! We became cool once I convinced you that I didn't want Chris anymore." Camilla looked at the girls and nodded her head in my direction. "This chick was like, 'What's up with your daughter's mother? Why is she so friendly?' but after that, we were cool," she said and everyone at the table laughed along with her.

"Wow!" Lyric shook her head. "Nate's ex and I could never be that cool. That chick hates me."

"Were you the other woman?" Paige asked coolly and sipped her mimosa.

"Why'd you ask that?" Lyric's lips turned up as if she smelled a skunk.

"The exes usually stay mad if the new wife is either the other woman or if she's still in love with the ex-husband."

"What makes you assume I was the other woman as opposed to her still being in love with him?"

Paige gave her a deadpan look that morphed into a sideways glare.

"Alright! Yes. I was the other woman," Lyric pled guilty and every one of us fell out laughing, including her.

"Girl! Who did you think you were fooling?" I asked. "Wives know these things—especially when the new wife is half the old wife's age." Camilla and I slapped five. "Nobody is mad at you. Well, maybe his ex." Camilla burst out laughing and then quickly covered her mouth to keep her mimosa from spraying all over the table.

"See, that's why I like y'all. You ladies keep it real," Lyric said when she finally stopped laughing. "What's your ex's story, Paige?"

"I know for a fact that she still loves him. That's why she's such a pain in the ass. You see, when they don't care, they don't act all crazy. They're cool—like Camilla," Paige added almost as an afterthought."

After another few moments of girl chat, the event host took to the podium to get the program started. To my surprise, I won a trailblazer award and certificate of appreciation for the shows I'd produced, and the work I do for the organization. Then, in a not so subtle gesture, they asked me to help coordinate the summer family fun festival. The girls laughed, so I immediately recruited each of them to the committee. That stopped the laughter.

We had so much fun together that we went out for more drinks after brunch. The fun ended when I got a call from my director telling me that Ava was being rushed to the hospital because Crystal had knocked her out cold while they were filming. According to her, 'Crystal popped her two times and then Ava was snoozing like a newborn'.

CHAPTER 7

 aige

I TWISTED from side to side in the mirror, poking and examining what I called my kangaroo pouch. Our daughter Scotland was turning six, and I still hadn't managed to get those last twenty pounds to melt away. Part of the reason was for lack of trying, but I was determined now. I wasn't sure why, but meeting Lyric made me feel like I needed to reevaluate my entire life, starting with a makeover.

From behind, Rick slid his hands around my bare waist and caressed my squishy abs.

"Don't do that!" I pushed him away and turned back to the mirror.

"Stop torturing yourself. You look fine."

"I could look better."

"What's gotten into you lately?"

I dropped my shoulders and blew out a frustrated breath. "I don't know." Tilting my head, I examined my boobs that now hung slightly lower since the last time I paid attention. "I think I'm going through a mid-life crisis."

Rick howled.

"Rick!" I swatted at him. "I'm serious."

"Okay, okay." Rick wrapped his arms back around me and nestled his chin into my neck. I pouted as he swept his eyes over my reflection from head to toe. I wanted to shrink away. "This is a woman thing, right? To me, you look even more beautiful than the day we met."

I finally managed a small smile. "You're just saying that."

Rick turned me around so I could face him. Lifting my chin, he looked in my eyes. "I meant every word."

I threw my arms around his neck and kissed him, then turned back to the mirror. "If I could just get rid of this..." I said, grabbing more than an inch of my stomach and pulled at my "hangover."

"That's your trophy for giving birth to Scotland."

"I've got her to look at every day. I don't need this, too."

I walked to the bed and pulled on the workout clothes I laid out before my shower. "I just feel like it's time for a change."

"Oh yeah?" Rick said, grabbing some jeans from the walk-in closet.

"Yeah. I want to finally get rid of this last bit of stubborn weight. I need some new clothes...I just need a makeover." I contemplated the next sentence before letting it out. I wasn't sure how Rick would take it. "And I want to get a job." I shrunk into my shoulders and waited for his response.

Rick froze while putting on his jeans. I waited for him to finish absorbing what I had just said. After a few beats, he finally pulled his pants on the rest of the way but still didn't speak.

"Where's this coming from?" he finally asked, slipping into his t-shirt.

"I need to feel like I'm doing something with my life." Part of me knew this sudden desire to feel like I was making a contribution to this world was being fueled by my new insecurities, but I needed to feel worthy again.

"You are doing something with your life." Rick walked to me and planted a tender kiss on my lips. "You're raising our daughter as we agreed."

I pulled away. "Don't patronize me!" I knew he wouldn't get it.

Rick looked confused, threw his hands up, and huffed as they fell back against his thighs. "Help me out here."

I groaned and flopped on the bed. "Sit down." I took Rick by his hand and pulled him down next to me. "I feel like I'm not contributing to making my life all it could be. I look in the mirror and I'm not happy with what I see anymore. I have all these degrees, but what am I doing with them? I feel…" I pressed my lips together, not wanting to voice the words lurking behind my teeth. "…worthless." I'd said it.

"Babe!" I put a finger to Rick's lips, silencing him.

"I'm not depressed. I'm just not happy with where I am in life right now."

"I understand about you wanting to shed a few pounds, but what about Scotland?"

"I know you aren't too keen about the idea of sending her to an after-school program because of what happened with Jayden when she was younger. I've already thought it out. I could work part-time and still be here for Scotland after school. I just need to do something. I can't continue to sit around here feeling like my brain cells are wasting away."

After a long moment of silence, Rick finally showed a sign of life when he sighed. I knew his mind had gone back to the day when Jayden came home from her prestigious after-school program and told him and Maya that a little boy tried to play doctor with her. "Can we think about this more?" he said, his face etched in distress.

"I have been thinking about it." I didn't want to sound like a spoiled brat, but that's exactly how I sounded. I checked myself so that selfish statement didn't end in a pout.

Rick twisted his lips, blinking rapidly, his go-to gesture when he's trying to work something out in his head. "This means that much to you?"

"Yes, it does," I pleaded, then batted my eyes and rubbed his chest hoping the combination worked its usual charm.

Rick turned to me. His brows lifted. "Then I guess we need to find you a job." He blew out a breath and looked at me.

I smiled and wrapped my arms around Rick's neck again and then squealed. "I need this so much." I turned back to Rick, taking in his pensive look. "And don't worry, hon, I'll make sure Scotland is all taken care of. Don't you worry about a thing! Our little princess will be fine."

"Well, you know what they say, 'happy wife, happy life.' I just want you to be happy."

I held his face in my hands and planted several pecks on his lips. "Oh, I'm happy." Heat spread between my legs when I saw how the front of his pants swelled in response.

"Oh yeah?" Wanna show me just how happy you are?" Rick pulled me back on the bed.

"Nope!" I climbed off, giggling. "I have a hot yoga class to make in thirty minutes. Maybe when I get back."

"Then you'll be all hot and sticky." Rick pretended to be in deep thought for a second. "That may not be so bad!"

"Yuck! You're nasty!" I said, laughing. After another quick kiss, I grabbed my yoga bag and headed out of the room, calling Scotland's name.

"Yes, mom?" Scotland yelled back from her bedroom.

When I peeked into my daughter's whimsical pastel wonderland, I found her lying on her stomach watching cartoons.

"Come give mommy a kiss."

"Where are you going?"

"To work out."

"Can I come?" Scotland sang.

"Not this time, sweetie, but mommy will be back soon and we can hang out when you get back from your gymnastics class." Scotland pouted, lowered her head, and cast a pitiful look in my direction with her large brown eyes. "That doesn't work with me, girly," I admonished with a wag of my finger.

"It works on daddy!" Scotland said matter-of-factly.

I shook my head. "I'm not daddy, chickadee!"

"Okay, mama!" Scotland got up from the bed and ran over to me. "Can we go get our nails done and go shopping when we hang out later?"

"We certainly can!"

"Yay!" Scotland jumped up and down and then grabbed me in a tight hug around my waist, her head pressing into my stomach. "We're having a girl's day out?"

I caressed her head. "Yes, we will."

Scotland looked up at me with wide eyes. "Daddy can't come, okay? It's just for us girls. Oh, can we invite Francesca?"

"Sure! I'll call her mother and see if I can pick her up on the way back."

"Yay!" Don't worry about Daddy. I'll talk to him so he won't feel bad about not being able to go with us. I'll promise him that we will do a daddy-daughter day and you will have to stay home."

"Okay, pumpkin. You handle that for me." The way she blatantly manipulated her dad made me smile deep in my heart. Both Scotland and Jayden had Rick wrapped around their pretty little fingers.

Scotland was back on the bed watching cartoons before I could leave the room.

Feeling renewed, I practically skipped down the steps to the kitchen to grab a few bottles of water and my car keys. My new workout regimen was off to a good start. This would be my fourth class this week. Rick encouraged me but never agreed to join me. I planned to keep working on getting him to adopt a fitness regimen himself with hopes that it would help me keep up my level of commitment.

I walked through the house swaying and humming, but all of that died instantly when I reached my front door, opened it, and stood face to face with Maya who was holding Jayden possessively. The dimmed light of Jayden's usually bright eyes clued me into the fact that something was going on that she wasn't happy about.

I narrowed my eyes at Maya but still managed a civil greeting. "Hey, Maya." She rolled her eyes. I waved her ignorant behind off and turned my attention to Jayden. "Hey, Chicca! What's the matter, sweetie?"

"We're here to see Rick. No need for you to concern yourself with our daughter," Maya answered before Jayden could open her mouth.

Jayden's shoulders dropped and she looked away.

"Maya..." I took a deep breath. I hated to let her know when she got to me. She'd only been at my door for a minute and I was already getting pretty close to being done with her. "What do you want?"

"I already said it! Where's Rick?"

Did she just roll her neck? What grown woman does that? I cleared my throat, determined not to let Maya spoil my mood completely. She'll never get to witness any sign of insecurity from me—hopefully.

I managed to muster up a small grin. Maya looked confused. "Watch your tone," I said through my smile then turned on my heel and headed upstairs to get Rick.

"Rick!" I yelled all the way up the steps, taking them two at a time.

Rick came running out of the room as if I had yelled 'fire.' "What's the matter, Babe?"

I flashed the same forced smile I'd just given Maya. "Your ex-wife is at the door. Again." I dropped the smile and replaced it with a scowl. "I wonder how much she needs today."

"Did she say what she wanted?"

"Really, Rick? Like she would tell me! Actually, she told me not to concern myself with matters about your daughter." I folded my arms and stared at him with one raised brow.

"Jayden's with her?"

"Yes. I've got to go, but Rick…" I pointed an irritated finger in his direction.

"I've got this, Babe. You're going to be late for class, remember."

I cut my eyes at him. He kissed my lips so sweetly. "I love you!" he said.

I shook my head at him before turning away and trotting down the steps. I loved how he always made sure I didn't have to question his love.

When I reached the landing Maya and Jayden were standing in the foyer, but I didn't remember letting them in. I left the words crowding at the tip of my tongue unsaid for the sake of Jayden. She was the sweetest stepdaughter a woman could ask for, despite her overbearing mother. For a moment, I thought about sticking around but decided to go ahead to my yoga class. I wasn't worried about Maya. Someone needed to tell her that being a meddling, annoying ex would never make a man come back.

"What's going on Maya?" Rick asked, but she didn't answer right away.

She was too busy glaring at me.

"By sweetie! I'll see you next weekend, okay?" I said to Jayden who reached out to hug me, but Maya snatched her back.

"She's not your mother."

"Maya!" Rick scolded and shook his head.

46

"Love you!" I mouthed, blew her a kiss and winked. Jayden winked back and her sweetheart lips spread into a precious smile that quickly dissipated when Maya nudged her with an elbow.

Maya snarled at me. I laughed before granting Rick one last peck. Just to annoy Maya, I allowed the peck to linger for a few extra seconds. "See you after my yoga class, Babe. Love you."

"Love you, too," Rick said.

I eyed Maya's hefty frame and with a slick, sideways grin added, "You should come to this yoga class with me one of these days. It might help improve your attitude."

Had Maya's glare been a machete, it would have sliced me in half. I waved and traipsed out the door.

CHAPTER 8

 yric

I JUMPED into my car and checked my hair in the mirror. My stylist always made sure I left her chair looking runway-ready. After freshening my lipstick, I dialed Candy through the Bluetooth just before pulling off the curb.

"Hello? Candy speaking." Her tone was professional.

"Hey, girl!"

"What number is this? I didn't know it was you."

"I changed my number," I said, pulling into traffic. A speeding driver obnoxiously honked his horn at me. I waved him off.

"What's up?" Candy's dejected voice seeped through the speakers.

"I just left Shayla's. My hair looks hot, girl." Catching my reflection in the rearview, I twisted my head from left to right, admiring Shayla's work. Not a single hair was out of place. I smiled and then slipped on my sunglasses.

"Yeah," Candy groaned, sounding unenthused.

Before I caught an attitude, I figured I needed to make sure her indifferent tone wasn't directed towards me.

"Are you okay?"

"No," she sucked her teeth. "I'm not."

"You need me to come over there?" I already had my foot hovering over the brake ready to make a U-turn and head toward her apartment on the upper west side of Manhattan.

Candy blew out a long sigh. "That would be nice, but I'm packing. I have to be in Vegas for a video shoot tomorrow." Candy fell silent for a moment. "Let's get together when I get back. I could use a girl's day out."

"Wanna talk about it now?"

Candy's grunt rumbled through the car's interior. "Jeff is divorcing his wife."

"And you're upset about that? He's all yours now!" I said, feeling hopeful.

"Apparently not!"

"What...what happened!" I hated to hear Candy sound so downtrodden.

"He's getting married."

I almost hit the brake as I entered the Westside Highway. "To who?" I nearly caused a crash, but I couldn't believe what my ears had just heard. "Are you serious?"

"As the IRS when they want their money!"

"Aw, Candy. What did he say to you?"

"Nothing!"

"That bastard! So how did you find out?"

"It was in *Hello Fabulous* today."

"You found out through a gossip blog?" I sucked my teeth. "He is so damn trifling," I said, shaking my head.

"They posted pictures of the court documents his wife filed as well as pictures of him and that R&B chick that just got a deal with his label. And get this..." I held my breath as Candy prepared to drop the rest of this bomb on me. "She wore the engagement ring I told him I wanted."

I gasped. It was so much more dramatic than I intended it to be. I didn't want to make Candy feel any worse than she already did. "He's such an asshole! And he has nothing to say about this?"

"I haven't spoken to him. He won't answer my calls."

"If I hadn't just gotten my hair and nails done, I would go over there and kick his ass!"

Candy howled. I knew that would make her feel a little better.

"You ain't messing up your hair and nails for anybody!"

After our laughter died down, I told Candy how sorry I was about what she was going through and broached the topic I had called her for in the first place.

"I saw Cypher last week in L.A."

"No! Did he see you?" Concern was evident in Candy's tone.

"Unfortunately! It was at the after-party Nate's company sponsored.

"He's such a grime ball. Bastard!"

"Did he say anything to you?"

I told Candy the story of our ill-fated encounter. By the time I was done, she was cursing as if she was on the phone with him instead of me.

"Don't let that sleaze bag scare you! I know some dudes from my old block that would be willing to pay him a visit. Who does he think he is?"

"Candy."

"That washed up sociopath! I can't believe him. You don't owe him anything. It took enough for you to get away from him in the first place. He thought he owned you."

"Candy!"

"What does Nate have to say about this? What makes him think Nate would even consider giving him a deal? He ruined his career himself—always putting his big ole foot in his big mouth."

"Candy!" I shouted, finally getting her attention.

"What!"

"Nate doesn't know about all of that."

"We need to go kick his ass!"

This time I laughed, even though fear whirled inside me every time I spoke his name. I looked around as if he might be able to spot me on the parkway as I headed home.

"That's why I changed my number. Hopefully, I won't hear from him anymore—especially since he's in L.A. and I'm here in New Jersey."

"Hold on!" The line muted for a few moments until Candy came back. "That was my driver. The car service is here to take me to the airport. I need to grab my bags. I'll call you when I touch down, okay?"

"Okay. Have a safe flight." I was about to hang up when Candy said, "Don't be scared, Lyric." After a few seconds of grave silence, she said, "Okay?"

"Okay." The silence returned. I wanted to say I wasn't scared, but that would have been a lie. "As long as he stays away from me, I'll be fine," I said and instinctively touched my upper lip. Neither of us spoke for a few moments until I broke the silence. "Go get your flight, girl!"

"Talk to you later," Candy said. Her tone was even more deflated than when we talked about Jeff marrying another woman.

I rode the rest of the way home on autopilot in complete silence. By the time I pulled into my garage, I wondered how I had gotten there. I didn't remember exiting the parkway, stopping at lights, or anything. I only hoped that I hadn't broken any traffic laws along the way.

I was happy to see Nate's SUV in the garage when I pulled

in. I needed to be in his arms right now and couldn't wait to get inside.

When I walked in through the door, Nate's laughter floated through the first floor. I smiled at the sound of it, glad to find him in a good mood. He would be able to help me shake off the tension that had settled in me after my conversation with Candy.

I kicked off my shoes, dropped my purse on the countertop, and tiptoed towards the direction of his voice. He laughed again and I giggled, loving the way his joy sounded. His laughter died down as I approached. I could hear the voice of the person he was talking to so the phone must have been on speaker. I tipped more lightly but stopped suddenly when I recognized the voice.

Vivian! What the hell was he doing cackling on the phone with her?

"You always said there was something wrong with that woman. I can't believe this." That was Nate's voice.

I couldn't make out Vivian's response clearly. Nate had yet to realize I was in the house. I stepped cautiously in my bare feet to make sure he didn't hear me as I drew closer. Stopping outside the entrance to his office, I listened to more of their jolly conversation.

"I couldn't believe it myself. I laugh every time I think about it. Whew!" I could hear Vivian clearly now.

I wondered when they had gotten so chummy. I liked it a lot better when she couldn't stand the sight of him.

"I can imagine."

"So what time should I tell the girls to expect you?"

"Um..." Nate paused. "I guess around six should be good. What do you think? That should give us enough time, right?"

"That will be fine. I'll see you then."

"All right! Talk to you later."

The second Nate ended the call I marched into the room. "You're going to meet up with Vivian."

Nate was startled and then a look of confusion flashed across his face. "Were you eavesdropping on my call?"

"Why? Do you have something to hide?"

Nate's eyes narrowed the way they do when he's exasperated with me. "If I did, I wouldn't have had the phone on speaker." He shook his head and stood with his arms outstretched. "What happened to 'Honey, I'm home?'"

"What happened to the fact that the two of you couldn't stand to be in the same room together, let alone have a cordial conversation on the phone? Now you're all chummy? What's really going on, Nate?"

"Babe!" Nate dropped his arms. It was obvious he wasn't getting a hug from me. "It was a simple phone call."

"Yeah. We started with a simple phone conversation, remember? And that led to a weekly rendezvous across your desk at work."

"Babe. Don't be paranoid. I have to speak to Vivian sometimes. She's the mother of my children."

"You think I need you to remind me of that?" I was trying hard to contain my anger. It pissed me off that Nate didn't see the problem the way I saw it. "You two haven't been this friendly."

"She was just telling me a funny story about one of my old neighbors."

"And where are you going at six? I thought we were going to dinner tonight."

"What?" I couldn't believe he was trying to act as if he didn't know what I was talking about. "We *are* going to dinner."

"You just told Vivian you would be there around six."

Nate dropped his shoulders and huffed. "Six in the morning. I'm picking up Sky and Sydney to take them to the airport. They're going on vacation with some of their girlfriends."

I felt a little stupid, but I refused to let him know. "Well, I don't like all of this."

Nate closed in on the space between us. I folded my arms, but he still wrapped his arms around me. "You have nothing to worry about. That's the past." Nate palmed my butt. "This is the present."

What about our future? It was time for me to keep my eye on Vivian.

CHAPTER 9

erri

I CRAWLED into bed and felt the weight of my tired body seep into the memory foam mattress. Trying my best not to wake Chris, I slowly maneuvered into the most comfortable position I could manage. Still, after working night and day in the grueling, fast-paced, post-production environment, restful sleep was a foreign concept.

Lifting my head just enough to see the green numbers on the alarm clock, I confirmed that it was once again after three in the morning. I could get around four hours of sleep before it was time to head back into the office.

Time went by in what literally felt like the blink of an eye. The prickly hairs of Chris's perfectly trimmed goatee jolted me awake. Disoriented, I looked at him for a few seconds while clearing the haze from my mind. He smiled down at me before planting another big kiss square on my lips.

Covering my mouth, I said, "Babe, I haven't brushed my teeth."

Chris twisted his lips. "So?" He laughed as he straightened to his full length.

"What time is it?" I struggled to push the covers back and lift myself up high enough to see the clock.

"Seven-thirty," Chris responded.

"Oh no!" I jumped from the bed and dashed into the bathroom, taking in Chris's confused expression along the way. "I should be walking out of the door right now!" Snatching my toothbrush out of the holder I ran water over it and squeezed on some Colgate. "Where's Alissa?" I said through the foaming paste.

"Downstairs with your mom. What time do you have to be back?"

"At nine! Oh gosh, I'm going to be late! I must have forgotten to set my alarm."

I pulled the camisole I was wearing over my head and tossed it into the laundry chute, then dashed to the closet in just my undies and pulled out the first maxi dress I touched. Next, I snatched a black blazer off another hanger and tossed the combo on the bed.

Chris grabbed my arm as I rushed past him on the way back to the bathroom.

"Babe! I need to get dressed," I protested.

"Even though we share a bed, I literally haven't seen you awake in days. Can I get a few seconds?"

I sighed and lowered my head. "I miss you," I pouted.

"I miss you too." Chris lowered his eyes to my exposed breast and swiped his thumbs across my nipples. "You don't have to explain. I knew what I signed up for when I married such an ambitious woman. How about we take a mini vacation when you're done with post-production on the show?"

My nipples hardened under his touch and my senses awakened immediately. I had been working so hard I'd forgotten what it felt like to be desired by my husband. I didn't want to shun Chris's show of affection, but I had no time to waste. For a moment I battled with the guilt rising in me, but reality quickly snuffed that out.

"I'd like that." I pecked his lips and ran my finger along his groin. "That way we can make up for lost time, but as for now, I've got to go!" Reluctantly, I pulled away from his grasp and tore through the bedroom towards the shower.

"I'm going to see to it that you do," Chris yelled behind me.

"I'm good for it!" I tossed back in the wind.

"Yes you are," I heard Chris say, and a second later he repeated it.

I showered and dressed in record time and headed downstairs to check in on my mother Mae Kate, and Alisa. Chris was gone.

"Mommy!" Alisa shrieked and jumped down from the stool at the breakfast nook. She wrapped her arms around my neck so tight I thought the hug would put me to sleep.

"Hey, Pumpkin!" I wrapped her arms snugly around Alisa's slim body and rocked with her.

"You're usually gone by the time I get up," Alisa said as I pulled back. Her radiant smile made me miss her more. "And I'm asleep by the time you get in."

"I know. I'm running late this morning." I turned my attention to my mother, who was pouring French vanilla creamer into a thermos.

"Good morning, Mama!" I kissed Mae Kate on her cheek and ran my fingers through her short gray hair.

"Morning, baby!" She handed me the thermos.

I sipped the piping hot coffee and then threw my head back and moaned in response to the strong but pleasant taste. "I swear, Mama, everything you touch tastes amazing. My coffee doesn't come out like this."

"Girl, hush." She waved my praise away, but I didn't miss her proud smile. "I wrapped up a biscuit for you to take with you."

"You made biscuits!" My eyes stretched wide.

"Yep!" Alisa answered for Mae Kate. "I had two with some syrup!"

I laughed. My mouth watered just thinking about how rich and decadent my mother's homemade biscuits tasted.

"Do you have time to sit, drink your coffee, and have one now?" my mother asked sweetly, but raised a brow as she tilted her head towards Alisa.

I got the message. By the time I got home at night, the entire house was in their second or third cycles of sleep. I'd pay for it at the office, but right now I was going to sit and have breakfast with my daughter and mother and try not to think about the 'round-the-clock' mayhem going on at work.

The surprised look and wide smile on Alisa's face when I sat next to her confirmed that I'd made the right decision. My industry didn't consider my family during a crisis, but they were my top priority. What difference would another twenty minutes make?

"Thanks for coming to stay for the week, Ma. I appreciate it, but I told you it wasn't necessary. Camilla always helps me out when my schedule gets crazy like this."

"Humph," Mae Kate simply continued to pack the leftover biscuits in baggies.

I left that alone and turned her attention to Alisa who proceeded to tell me about everything that happened in school during the past week. Alisa spoke excitedly and swiftly. I could hardly keep up with all the drama happening in the last weeks of fifth grade.

Mae Kate looked at her watch. "Okay, baby. Go get your bags. Grandma's got a class to take at the gym as soon as I drop you off."

"Okay, grandma."

Alisa slid off the stool and ran to get her stuff. When I was sure that Alisa was beyond earshot, I turned to my mother. "Camilla and I help each other out all of the time, Ma."

"She's too close to your business. Besides your mama, no other woman should have that kind of access to the home you share with your man!" Mae Kate tossed me a pointed glare.

"Please!" I dismissed that notion. "Camilla doesn't want Chris." I got up from the stool and poured a glass of orange juice. "Did I tell you she's engaged?"

"That's nice." Mae Kate shot off another indifferent reply and continued cleaning up the counter.

"Ma!"

Mae Kate's only response was a tight-lip and a hard stare over the rim of her glasses.

"Why don't you like her?" I cocked my head to the side waiting for her answer.

Mae Kate's hand went to her shapely hip. "I didn't say I didn't like her..." she let that thought hover for a moment before continuing. "I don't trust the situation. Things happen."

I shook my head. Mae Kate was as stubborn as they came. Swallowing the last of my orange juice, I called out to Alisa to say goodbye. Alisa ran back to the kitchen lugging her book bag and violin case behind her. I gave both a snug hug before heading out the door.

As I climbed into my SUV, I chalked my mother's opinions up to her old school upbringing. Mae Kate and her sisters had plenty of outdated beliefs when it came to women and men. Camilla had never given me a reason to believe she was untrustworthy. I also knew that trying to convince my mother otherwise would be a futile effort. As Mae Kate would say, "Some people never forget what good lovers feel like, and every now and then, some folks get..." she would pause, twist her lips and peer over the rim of her glasses before saying, "*nostaaaaalgic*," like she was making the point of all points.

CHAPTER 10

aige

THAT BLASTED scale hadn't moved in two weeks. I felt like throwing it out the bathroom window. I was stuck with eleven pounds to go, but nothing was happening. I'd been in the gym almost every single day and on the days I didn't go to the gym, I went to hot yoga. My ass still hurt from the spin class I took three days ago and now this! Another regretful email from a company thanking me for applying for a position that they weren't hiring me for. On a Saturday, no less. They couldn't wait until Monday? I was trying my best not to let this sour mood spill over into my entire day.

I tossed my cell phone into the passenger seat. At this very moment, I hated the internet and longed for the days where employers actually called you in for an interview and tried to get to know you before rejecting you. Every time I clicked submit on a job application, I felt as if my qualifications were ejected into a digital black hole. Every now and then a response emerged from this cyber abyss with a sorrowful memo like the one I received today. I didn't care if they appreciated my interest in their company. Telling me how impressive my qualifications were and keeping my resume on file didn't make me feel any better. I needed a job.

I sat in the parking lot of the gym for at least another thirty minutes before willing myself inside. I'd gotten to the point where I started to get excited about working out, but now that this fat wouldn't budge, I was getting frustrated.

After a few more minutes, I jumped out the car and charged through the lot into the gym. If I hadn't moved fast, I would have driven back home, and buried my angst in a few bottles of merlot. Instead of starting off with the treadmill or elliptical, I headed straight for the weights. I had too much aggression in me to prance up a stair climber. The problem was that I didn't know how to use that stuff. After 10 minutes, my arms were hurting and I was worn out. Sweat dripped from my brow. I sucked down the last drops of water in my bottle and headed to the fountain to get a refill.

I rounded an abs machine and ran dead into what felt like a damp, rippled wall. A set of strong hands reached out and kept me from falling backward. The water in his opened bottle went airborne and landed on my head and chest. I was drenched. I'm sure he saw steam rise from my shoulders as that water darkened my tank top.

"Oh! I'm so sorry." He dabbed my shoulders with his towel.

"Eww! Stop!" Holding my arms away from my body, I shook the excess water from my hands.

"You're right. That wasn't smart. Let me get you some paper towels. I'm really sorry."

"It wasn't entirely your fault. I wasn't looking."

Up until this point, I still hadn't looked up. I had partially closed my eyes to keep the water in my lashes from dripping in them. When I did open my eyes, I bucked at the chiseled torso visible through his wet t-shirt. Instinctively, my hand went to his twelve-pack. *Damn.* I hadn't seen anything like it up close. I pulled my hand back and apologized. Now, I was a wet idiot. I looked further and was met with rock hard pecks and squared shoulders. Recognition set in when I saw his face.

"Blair?"

"Paige?"

I had literally run into an old flame and he looked so much better than he had when we were in college together.

"I thought you moved to Chicago."

He laughed. "For a short time, but then I received a great offer in New York and moved back for a while. I just bought a condo here in Leonia."

I swallowed. As good as he looked, I didn't want to hear that he lived anywhere near me.

"Oh…well. Nice seeing you."

"You too."

"I'd better go get cleaned up."

"You do that!"

A few moments passed before either of us moved.

"Okay. Bye." I finally said and walked off.

"You look really good," he called after me.

Instead of going to the restroom. I walked straight out of the gym. On the way home I stopped at Wal-Mart to get some things for the house and ended up buying a bicycle. A store clerk loaded it in the car for me.

When I got home, Rick and the girls were hanging out in the family room watching cartoons. I asked him to get the stuff from the car. He came back with his arms loaded and stared at me with one brow raised.

"Who's the bike for?"

"Me," I said, grabbing bags from him as I started to put the food items away.

"Okay," he said slowly.

"Hey! You should get one too. That way we could go out riding as a family."

Rick still held me in his peculiar gaze. "I'll think about that."

"I'm going to take the girls to the park so we can ride. Can you put their bikes in the back of the SUV?"

"Sure."

Poor Rick didn't know what to make of me these days.

"Hey, girls!" I yelled into the family room. Jayden and Scotland came running into the kitchen. "Guess what?"

"What!" They said excitedly.

"Mommy bought a bike!"

"No way!" Jayden said.

"Really? I wanna see." That was Scotland.

"Go outside, Dad's loading it in the SUV along with your bikes. We're going riding in the park."

"Yay!" The girls held their hands and jumped up and down.

"Go get dressed. I'll be ready just as soon as I finish putting this food away."

In no time, the girls were dressed and ready to ride. After a half-hour of rolling over bumps they called pavement, my behind hurt even more. I had to wrap it up and come on home. I was done trying to burn calories for the day.

I came back home and let the girls continue riding up and down the street while I cooked and got myself ready for Tapas with the girls. I couldn't wait to get there and unload the rest of this steam on my chest.

Annoyance was the theme for the day. It took almost an hour for me to find something suitable to wear. Truthfully, I was still rattled about my run in with Blair. With a closet full of clothes, I still seemed to be at a loss for something trendy. When I got my new body, I was getting a new wardrobe. Besides feeling as if everything I owned was drab and outdated, my jeans looked saggy in the behind after losing those nine pounds. After finally settling on a pair with a more reasonable fit, I pulled on a tank top with beading and slipped on a pair of heels.

I'd been playing the role of soccer, PTA, piano and dance mom so long I felt alienated from all things trendy. Sweatpants, mom jeans, comfortable tanks, and flats had replaced cute jeans, form-fitting dresses and stilettos. I almost broke my neck walking to the car. Rick looked at me and shook his head before kissing me goodbye.

Despite my dressing debacle, I managed to arrive at the restaurant first. When Lyric arrived with her Gucci sunglasses, curve-hugging dress and YSL sandals, I wanted to fade into the chair and disappear. She smiled and her hot lavender lips reminded me of the fact that I'd forgotten to put on a lick of make-up. I hugged her and excused myself, running off to the bathroom. Inside, I pulled out my nude Revlon gloss and slid it across my lips several times trying to get a high shine. It wasn't working. I added some eyeliner and a coat of mascara and that was as good as it was going to get for now.

Camilla showed up next and we all prayed that Kerri would be able to make it. Her job had been holding her hostage lately.

"So how are the wedding plans going, Camilla?" I asked.

"Good so far. I can't believe I'm doing this again. Aaron is such a great guy," she gushed.

"Was he married before," Lyric asked.

"Nope!"

"Great! No ex to contend with! No offense to you, Camilla. You're the exception to the rule." Lyric laughed.

The waiter took our order and several varieties of Tapas hit the table before we knew it. After a few drinks, we loosened up even more. I still hoped Kerri would make it.

"Lyric. You always look fabulous. Can you help a sister out?" I hadn't meant for it to sound so desperate, but I needed help.

"Of course! We should go shopping together."

"Let's do that!"

"I'm in for that," Camilla added.

Lyric looked down at her drink and changed the subject. "Maybe you ladies can help me with a few things."

"Like what?" Camilla asked, taking a sip of her fruit infused sangria.

"Nate and his wife have become rather friendly lately and I don't like it at all," Lyric rolled her eyes.

"Oh!" I said, not having any advice for her.

"That's not necessarily a bad thing," Camilla said. "Chris and I are cool."

"But that's different. You and Kerri are cool too and have been from day one. Vivian hates me and I'm not too fond of her ass either." Lyric sucked her teeth this time.

"You feel threatened by their friendship." I stated the obvious.

"No...yes!" Lyric admitted.

"Were they always friendly?"

"Hell no! When she found out about us, she put his ass out. That's how he permanently ended up in my bed. At first, they only communicated through their daughters, but eventually they became more cordial. Now, humph, I came in the other day and they were on the phone cackling and chatting like old friends."

"Is he acting like he's interested in her?" Camilla asked.

"Not really." Lyric shrugged.

Camilla waved her hand and said, "Don't sweat it. You don't want to push him toward her by complaining about it. Just keep your eyes open."

"I will!" Lyric turned to me "So what about this makeover, lady. I'm glad you came to me."

For a second I was offended. Why was she so glad? Did I look that bad?

"I love shopping and even thought about doing image consulting." Lyric sipped her sangria. "You're a great looking woman. Every now and then we have to spruce things up a little. Remind Rick what he's working with."

Realizing my anger was off base, I smiled. Lyric wasn't insulting me. My insecurities were reaching new heights.

"In the bedroom and out!" Lyric added.

"Oh!" I screamed, and everyone laughed.

As the drinks flowed, the conversation got naughtier. The ladies of the PTA didn't talk like this.

"You hold it like this," Lyric said holding her hand like a fist. "And move your hand up and down while you handle your business."

Camilla and I squealed. "I can't believe I'm listening to this!" I said. "Tell me more! Rick is going to wonder where I got all these tips from."

"How do you think I got Nate to marry me? Humph. They say they want virtuous women but when it comes to the bedroom, they want a woman who's willing to get freaky! Woo!" Lyric said.

We slapped high fives around the table and bent over laughing. I was feeling pretty tipsy and decided I needed to slow down so I could still drive myself home.

"It's getting late ladies. I need to head on home," Camilla said, draining the last bit of water in her glass.

"Me too!" I admitted.

"Aww! I was having so much fun. I didn't think you ladies had it in you."

Camilla and I stopped and stared at Lyric.

"Don't think we don't know how to have fun too?" I said.

"No!" Lyric held her hand up in surrender and chuckled. "I didn't mean it like that." We laughed. "I'll make it up to you. Next time, I'll host a girl's night at my house and I'll show you how to clap your booty!"

"What?" Camilla screamed.

"Really!" I asked excitedly.

It was Camilla and Lyric's turn to look at me. "That was a joke, Paige."

"Oh!" I hooted. "Too bad. Maybe we can take pole dancing classes. I heard it's a great upper body workout!"

The three of us couldn't contain ourselves. I waved and laughed all the way to my car. My day ended much better than it had started. Moreover, as funny as the conversation was, it made me think. My sex life was due for an overhaul just like every other part of my life. No better time to start than tonight.

CHAPTER 11

 yric

I STEPPED into my front door and squealed at the site of a small, beautifully wrapped gift box. I smiled wide and shimmied over to the table positioned in the center of our grand foyer. My smile fell flat when I saw that the present wasn't for me.

"To Vivian!" I scoffed. "Nate!" My stilettos clicked against the marble floor as I circled the first floor in search of my husband. "Nate!" I kept screaming while I climbed one of the two stair-cases leading from the foyer to the second floor. I heard the shower water as I burst through the French doors leading to our master suite.

What if he's in there with her? I marched toward the bath-room door and pushed it so hard it slammed against the wall with a loud bang. If Nate was in that shower with Vivian, I was going to snatch her by that boring bob and mop the condensation on the bathroom floor with her. There was no moaning, but Nate was humming one of his favorite jazz tunes. I hated it when he played that old stuff from the likes of Miles Davis and John Coltrane. *Who listened to that crap anyway?* I preferred R&B from Usher or someone like that any day.

"Nate!" I screamed one more time and made myself visible in the entrance to our walk in shower.

"What's up, Babe?" Nate inquired. He was a little too calm for my taste.

"What the hell is this?" I asked, holding the gift dangerously close to the water streaming from the shower.

Jumping out of the shower with soap still clinging to him, Nate snatched the gift from me. "You're going to get the paper wet and I'll have to get it wrapped again!"

My eyes bucked. Did he really just snatch that gift from me to protect it? I watched as Nate wiped his hand across the elongated vanity, checking for wet spots before inspecting the wrapping one last time and gently placing the gift down. Then he turned his wet, naked body around and stepped back under the flow of the shower.

"How was your day, baby?" he asked coolly.

I thought I would burst into a thousand tiny flecks of fire. I slapped the nickel handles down, shutting off the water.

"Why are you buying Vivian jewelry? What's going on between you two? First I come home and you're cackling on the phone with her and now you're buying her gifts! You'd better not be cheating on me with her, Nate. I swear!"

I didn't like the way Nate looked at me. I expected irritation. Instead, what he cast my way looked like pity! I narrowed her eyes at him.

"Babe," Nate turned the water back on to rinse away the rest of the soap. "Stop acting paranoid."

He'd said it! "Paranoid! What am I supposed to think? You wouldn't like it one bit if I snuck around buying gifts for my ex."

"Lyric," he said my name as if it were a command. At least I was finally getting a rise out of him. His nonchalant attitude was getting on my nerves.

"What?" I folded my arms across my breast and shifted my stance.

"First of all, I didn't sneak anything into *my* house." I hated it when he spoke with such claims, reminding me how much I'd actually brought into this union. So what! He shut the water off, snatched a towel off the rack, and dried his face. "If I was hiding it, I wouldn't have left it on the table in the foyer, knowing it could be the first thing you would see if you got in before I left." Nate continued drying off as he spoke. "It's just a little birthday gift for Vivian." He wrapped the towel around him and headed to the bedroom.

I was so close to him I actually stepped on his heels twice while he was walking. He looked back at me both times.

"Why are you buying her gifts at all? You're no longer together." I hated that I sounded as if I was pouting.

Nate turned and I slammed right into him. "Lyric," he grunted. "Babe." His tone was softer. She's the mother of my children. I'm just being cordial. Technically, it's from the girls."

"Bullshit!" After pinning Nate with a narrowed gaze, I sucked my teeth and plopped on the bed. Those girls were grown--a few years younger than me. They could afford to buy their own gifts. "I don't think it's necessary to buy her gifts. She may get the wrong idea and think you want her back."

Nate stood in front of me, looking down with those hooded brown eyes. I turned away. Nate gently turned me back to him by my chin. "The only person worried about me wanting Vivian back is you."

I jerked my head from his hold and cut my eyes. Nate was right, but I refused to confirm his assumption.

Nate leaned in and kissed my forehead. "You have nothing to worry about. Vivian doesn't want me!"

"Maybe you still want her," I rolled my neck. I didn't mean

to. It felt so juvenile, but it reflected how I felt when my doubts about Nate and Vivian's interactions came up. I became that teenage girl all over again--the one who had been cast aside because everyone knew what her mama had done. I wanted to lash out.

"Ha!" Nate laughed at me and made me angrier. My pout grew. He loosened his towel and let it slip to the floor. Taking my chin in his hand once more, he turned my face toward him, smiled, and looked down. I followed his line of sight to his erection. "Does this look like I want anyone but you?"

I tried damned hard not to smile. Nate leaned over and kissed me. At first I refused to give in, but at Nate's persistence, I received his tongue's exploration. He laid me back on the bed, slowly unbuttoning my shirt and then rubbing his thumbs across my pert nipples through the lace of my bra. Nate drew me further away from anger with every caress, every kiss. My body responded despite my attitude.

"All I want is you, Babe," Nate said before slipping his hand under my skirt. He slipped it off me.

Nate stood over me, admiring the expensive silken lace panty and bra set. He ran his hands down my side, following the lines of my curves. He licked his lips and smiled. I wrapped my arms around his neck and initiated a kiss of my own. Liberating my breasts from the confines of my bra, Nate covered them with his mouth and then released them with a pop. I squirmed. He kissed a path down my belly to the moist folds between my legs. Removing my panties, he lapped at my bud until I screamed his name over and over. Before I could recover, he entered me, turning my screams into gasps. He turned me over and entered from behind. I grabbed fists full of silk sheets. I met his steady thrusts, sucking in the length of him with each stroke. He turned me back over so I could face him and then entered me again. I stretched my hips wider, taking as much of him as possible, squeezing him between my walls. Nate's eyes rolled back. Expletives shot from his mouth and he screamed my name. He looked at me, smiled wickedly, and moved in swift circular motions until my body shuddered, sending electrical currents to the edges of my skin. He rode his release with an escalating groan before falling limp over my body. I wrapped my legs and feet around his back and held him tight. Nate was mine.

Several moments passed as we caught our breath. Nate headed back to the shower. I piled my hair atop my head, put on a shower cap, and joined him. We washed each other almost provoking a second round.

Nate stepped out first. When he got to the room, he cursed.

"What's wrong?" I asked from the bathroom while I was drying off. I could hear him rummaging around in the room.

"I'm going to be late."

"Late for what?" I leaned into the room watching him chaotically put on his clothes.

"Vivian's birthday dinner with the girls."

Instantly, I felt my skin heat up. Instead of starting another possible argument, I oiled my body and slipped into a sundress that accentuated all my curves. By the time Nate reached the front door, I was right behind him.

"Where are you going, Babe?" he turned around and asked me.

"With you!" I locked eyes with him as if I dared him to suggest otherwise.

Nate's expression melted into something unreadable. I looked to see which car key he had and then, before another beat passed, I was heading to the passenger side of the sports car closest to the fountain. Halfway to the car, I turned back. Nate was still standing in the doorway.

"Come one. You're going to be late, remember?" Nate closed his eyes and took a breath before calmly making his way to the car. "Don't forget the gift. I'm sure it's beautiful! I can't wait to see what it is."

Nate slid into the car next to me but didn't break his silence.

I purposely ignored him as I flipped the visor down and decorated my lips with a fiery shade of red. I added a light coat of mascara to my expertly applied mink lashes and flicked the visor back in place before sitting back comfortably. When I looked to my left and saw Nate still staring at me with that indecipherable expression, I just smiled sweetly.

Nate simply started the car and pulled out onto the secluded two-lane road. I changed the station from boring jazz to something more hip and sang along with Drake and Nicki Minaj, Kendrick Lamar and The Weekend as we made our way to the restaurant.

As I enjoyed my own little dance party, I imagined the faces of Vivian and his daughters when they laid eyes on me. I looked fabulous! I was almost half Vivian's age. She couldn't compete with my body. It took staunch resistance to keep from laughing aloud.

When we pulled up to the restaurant's lot, Nate turned to me and broke his silence for the first time. His eyes were pleading. "It's Vivian's birthday. The girls asked me to join them for dinner. I need you to be nice."

"Of course!" I said innocently.

I took one last look in the mirror before getting out of the car while Nate handed the keys to the valet. Planting myself right beside Nate, I adjusted my dress, straightened my back and looped my arm in his. As usual, men unsuccessfully tried to keep their eyes off my curves. They couldn't help themselves.

Nate gave the hostess our names and she led us to a table where Vivian, Sydney and Sky were waiting. They stood and looked at each other. I'm sure they wondered why I had come.

"Vivian!" I greeted her with a nod and then turned toward the twins. "Sydney, Sky." I nodded again. "I'm so happy to be able to join you tonight." Those gaped-mouth heifers didn't return a single word.

Vivian's head bobbed between Nate, her daughters, and me as if she were watching a three-way tennis match. Without waiting for Nate, who is always a gentleman, I took the empty seat reserved for him, which was right next to Vivian. The waiter was already bringing another chair.

Vivian looked at her daughters again. They looked at her and in some unspoken agreement, conceded something and slowly returned to their seats. Vivian finally shot Nate a scathing look. I knew they were going to have a serious discussion about this later. All that mattered to me was the fact that they knew that Nate and I were a partnership. That's the statement I was making tonight, and they would just have to get used to it.

"I hope you enjoyed your birthday so far," Nate said, giving her a friendly hug. I felt my insides tighten when his arm went around her.

"Despite, the circumstances," Vivian said, looking me up and down.

"You're looking good." Nate gave her a friendly pat on her back.

"Thanks." Vivian smiled and nodded politely, accepting Nate's praise.

"Yeah." I rolled my eyes hard. "I guess you do look good for your age. What are you now, fifty-six?" I said, knowing she was only forty-five. The look Vivian threw at me would have seared my skin if it had been fire. Truthfully, I was jealous of her ancient ass. Aside from that little bit of gut she tried to hide behind Spanx, she looked amazing! Nathan wasn't blind to it either, I could tell by the way he considered her with such admiration. The rings on my finger said he belonged to me now, but if I was completely honest with myself, I was never too sure about his heart.

CHAPTER 12

 erri

"KERRI!" The girls sang when Lyric's housekeeper, Gilda, led me out onto the upper deck of Lyric's enormous yard.

"Hey, ladies!" I chimed. I was actually happy to be in their company.

"So glad you could make it!" Camilla jumped up and hugged my neck, squeezing me so tight I thought I'd choke. Paige and Lyric lined up behind her.

"Me next!" Paige said, stepping in for a big hug.

Lyric pressed each of her cheeks against mine and handed me a full wine glass. "Hey boo!" she greeted.

Before sitting in one of the four loungers, I walked to the edge of the two-story deck and looked out over her massive backyard. If not for the Japanese garden surrounding a Koi pond with a fountain in the center and the in-ground pool off to the other side, it could be mistaken for a golf course.

"My goodness, Lyric, this is beautiful!" I said, taking in the

Zen-inspired décor on the deck. We sat under a red-stained pergola with silk fabric over the top that flowed down the sides, and a ceramic fountain in the corner caressed our hearing with the soothing sounds of running water.

"Thanks!" She shimmied a little. "It's my own little sanctuary."

"Little!" I said and playfully rolled my eyes. "I know. It's so tiny!" The girls laughed.

"Come on girl, drink up. We missed you at the last gathering so you've got some making up to do," Lyric said.

"I know," I said. "Camilla told me how crazy you guys got— giving fellatio tips!"

Paige and Camilla sunk into their shoulders, and snickered. Lyric twisted her lips proudly.

"How you get 'em, is how you keep 'em," she boasted. "I've got more tips if you want them."

The girls were amused.

"We really did miss you," Paige said after the laughter died down.

"I missed you all too." I told them about spending the past two days soaking up time with Chris and the girls after being imprisoned for weeks by production schedules at work. Besides a few texts here or there, I hadn't spoken to anyone. I took two days this week for the first time in months. The day before, Chris and I spent the time together and yesterday, I kept the girls out of school and hung out with them. Today I was hanging with the big girls.

"Riley couldn't stop talking about how much fun you girls had. By the way, her nails looked really cute," Camilla said.

"Great!" I said, genuinely happy that my stepdaughter had such a great time. I could imagine her droning on and on to Camilla about every detail of our day. "So let's get this party started!" I looked at my glass. "Lyric!" Everyone paused because of the chiding way I said her name. "Why in the world did you fill this wine glass up to the rim?"

"Don't get on my case. I hear it from Nate all the time."

"I'm going to have to teach you some etiquette!" I said.

"Ha!" Lyric laughed, covering her mouth so she wouldn't spray anyone. Paige giggled. Camilla cut her eyes and shook her head. "That and maybe a few other things."

"Meet Kerri, ladies, and please don't be alarmed by her sheer honesty. I must say, Lyric, you're quite honest yourself!" Camilla teased.

"I get in trouble for my 'honesty' sometimes," Lyric said, taking a careful sip from the wine glass she'd just filled to the brim. "No worries with Kerri, though. I pegged her sarcasm on day one," Lyric said and waved the notion away.

"You did? Girl, I thought you missed that." Paige chuckled.

We chatted and laughed some more. The conversation meandered from one topic to another, including the last time they hung out together, shopping, workouts, husbands. and kids.

"Paige, you're looking good there, girl." I assessed her, noticing that she looked slimmer.

"I'm trying! Plus, I went shopping with Ms. Lyric here last week and picked up a few things. Rick looked at me as if he wanted to ask where I hid his wife. I can't tell if he's happy about the changes I've made or not."

"You have to be happy with yourself first before you can be happy for your husband," Camilla said matter-of-factly.

"I'm getting there. It's been a struggle," Paige admitted solemnly.

"Well, you look fabulous!" I said. Paige seemed genuinely pleased that I noticed.

"Thanks, Kerri!"

"Speaking of happy husbands, mine is furious with me," Lyric said, stretching out the word 'furious.'

"What did you do this time?" I teased.

"What do you mean this time?" Lyric sat up from her lounger and placed her free hand on her hips.

"I knew when we met that you were a mess. Go on. Tell us what you did," I said.

"You're the mess," Lyric said, pointing those acrylic tips in my direction. "Anyway," she cut her eyes at me, "I did something yesterday and he's still giving me the cold shoulder. He's never been mad at me this long."

Lyric told us the story of her crashing Vivian's birthday celebration, painting a hilarious picture for us in a way that only she could. Paige's mouth fell open halfway through the story and remained that way until the end. Camilla shook her head repeatedly and I couldn't help but crack up laughing.

"Are you mad? See, like I said, you're a mess. How are all those fellatio tips working for you now?" I teased.

Lyric's laugh was so abrupt she sprayed Paige with half the wine in her mouth before she was able to block it with her hand. Too late, Paige held up her hands to shield her face. Camilla jumped off her lounge chair to avoid being splashed.

"Kerri, you're so wrong," Camilla said.

Lyric ran inside to grab a few paper towels to clean up the mess. Paige went to the bathroom to see how much damage had been done to her yellow sundress.

"So I was wrong?" Lyric asked, directing her question to me.

"Yes, honey. Dead wrong! Besides, you never want the ex to see your insecurities. What you did, simply put them on display. Apologize to hubby and let him know you understand why he was so upset."

"Yeah. You probably should apologize. And going forward, don't give her the satisfaction of witnessing your insecurities," Paige added.

"Plus, they have kids so they have to deal with each other. It's better for you if there's less drama," Camilla chimed in.

"That's for sure!" Paige said, holding her hands up as if she were giving a testimony.

"See, that's why I need you ladies in my life. I don't have any friends who are in successful marriages. My girl Candy would have cheered me on. You're like my..." Lyric put her finger to her lip and thought for a moment. "...marriage mamas."

"Mamas!" The three of us shouted.

"I am not old enough to be your any-kind-of-mama! Big sister, that's another story." I told Lyric.

"Okay! The big sisters I never had. Dang." Lyric threw her hands up.

When the amusement died down, we sat for a few moments in companionable silence, sipping our cocktails, taking in the calming resonances of the fountains and the delicate fragrances emanating from the jasmine and lavender plants nearby. A gentle breeze whispered across our bodies, blowing under my skirt as it passed.

"This is the life," Paige finally said appreciatively.

"I'd love to see the rest of the house, if you don't mind," I said. Paige and Camilla immediately agreed.

Lyric sat up. "I'd be happy to take you on a tour." Placing her drink down, she stood and straightened out her dress. "Follow me."

Lyric took us on an expedition showing us three floors of pure opulence, saving the basement for last, which was divided into four areas, a wine cellar, gym, bar, and what looked like a dance studio.

"Is that what I think it is?" I asked walking towards the stripper's pole in the center of the mirrored studio.

Lyric snickered, "Yep. I had it installed when we moved here just to spice things up."

"Maybe you should apologize to Nate down here." Paige tittered.

"You didn't say anything about this when we teased about

taking a pole dancing class when we were out for Tapas." Camilla smirked.

Lyric flashed an impish smile. "Well you can't tell all your secrets on the first or second date."

"We could do that for Camilla's bachelorette party!" I said. Each of them raised their brows or nodded their head in agreement.

"Oh!" Paige ran for the pole. "Can you teach me how to use it, Lyric? Maybe I can practice on my bed posts. Ha! Rick will really wonder what happened to his wife!"

"Do too much and you'll be asking Lyric for a room to stay in, too. You know men can't take too many changes at once. Next thing you know; he'll wonder if you're getting all these new ideas from another man!" I said and laughed.

"Yep," Camilla agreed.

"That's right," Lyric added.

"You know how they are," I said.

We returned to the deck for more cocktails and conversation. The sun was the first to make its departure. I was next.

"I had a great time, ladies but I need to get going."

"Me too," Camilla and Paige said at the same time.

"I'll walk you ladies out." Lyric rose from her lounge chair and led us to the door.

We hugged as we said our goodbyes.

"Hey, Kerri?" Lyric called me back after we started toward our cars. She met me halfway and then began wringing her hands. She looked to make sure the other ladies were out of earshot. "Um."

I had never been good at shielding my expression from my thoughts. I could feel my brows rise as I wondered what she wanted to say that couldn't be said in front of Paige and Camilla.

"I'm glad you were able to come. I really like you." I looked at her sideways. "Not like that silly!" Lyric said, and with a flick of her wrist dismissed my teasing gesture. "I was just wondering if it was okay to...you know... call you sometimes. I like when we get together like this, but I really don't have mature women to talk to on a regular basis. Sometimes I need a little advice. I never thought I would actually get married, but I did and I really want it to work. I don't have successful couples around me and my friends can't really offer the best advice since they're all single. So...if you don't mind..."

"No problem." I pulled a card from my purse and handed it to her. "You already have my cell number. Call anytime. Work gets a little crazy sometimes so if I don't answer I'll call you back when I get a moment. My schedule is going to get really busy again in a few weeks. When it's like that, I barely get to talk to my own husband, so don't take it personal if it takes some time for me to get back to you, okay?"

"Sure." Lyric's shoulders appeared to settle with ease and she smiled. "I promise I won't be a pest. Thank you." She hugged me again—a warm sisterly hug.

"Okay, honey. Apologize to your hubby tonight. Get him downstairs and put those tips and that pole to good use."

"Ha!" Lyric nodded.

She watched as I walked to my car. Out of all us girls, I wondered what made her pick me?

CHAPTER 13

aige

I FINALLY HAD A JOB INTERVIEW. It was for the perfect consulting position that would give me the chance to put my degrees to work from home. The recruiter advised that I'd only need to come into the office for meetings. I could still drop Scotland off at school every morning and be home to pick her up every day. I'd just have to find a way to keep my inquisitive little lady busy until I was officially off the clock at five. The telephone interview went extremely well and I was expecting to ace the in-person interview.

Despite the fact that my weight still hadn't budged, my suit fit well enough. I could clearly see where I'd lost inches. My hair was another story. It was just there. No shape, no style, nothing! I was tired of ponytails and always looking so undone. At that moment, I decided to take my first check and get my hair and nails done.

Arriving at my interview a half-hour early was supposed to

allow time for me to calm my frazzled nerves before going inside. Neither that nor the large cup of chamomile tea did any good. I could feel the dampness in my armpits and knew my shirt was stained with the evidence of my anxiety. As hot as it was, I refused to take off my suit jacket for fear of exposing my sweaty pits.

I fiddled with my cell phone because I couldn't keep my hands still and the inside of my lip was raw from gnawing on it. I tried doing the deep breathing exercises my yoga instructor showed me, but that did nothing to alleviate my angst. The truth was, I hadn't been on a job interview in six years and the corporate world had changed so much that I wasn't sure how well I'd be able to represent myself. Yes, I'd been the president of the PTA and board member to half the non-profit organizations in northern New Jersey, but it's different when you're getting a salary. *You can do this, Paige!*

"Paige Thompson."

Breathe in. Breathe out!

"Ma'am? Are you Paige Thompson?"

"Y…yes."

"Mrs. Silverstein would like to see you now."

"Oh, wonderful. I gathered my purse and followed the slim, well-dressed brunette through the glass doors separating the reception areas from the offices. I had my iPad. That's what people used to take notes these days, right? I wanted to look like I was with it.

The woman led me through a long corridor that fanned out into a sea of neatly lined cubicles and then continued to a large office on the opposite end. A few heads prairie-dogged above the tops of the cubicles, offering slight smiles, and nods. The closer we got to the office of the vice president, the more aware I became of my heartbeat thumping against my chest cavity.

"Mrs. Silverstein, Ms. Thompson is here."

A tall waif thin woman with a hard jawline stood from

behind a fancy glass desk and walked my way with her hand outstretched. Her fire red hair was short on one side. On the other, the fire swept over her forehead, almost covering her eye.

"Pleasure to meet you, Ms. Thompson," she said shaking my hand with the strength of a man.

'Ouch' would probably have been an inappropriate response, so I settled for, "It's a pleasure to meet you, too. Thank you for considering me for this opportunity."

"Please have a seat," she offered with a smile before rounding her desk to sit down.

The interview moved along well. Before I knew it, we were scheduling my start date. She asked if I could come in during full business hours for training so I could get a feel for the tone of the company. After that, I would only be expected to come into the office for Monday kick-off meetings, which would have me home by the time Scotland got out of school. During my week in the office, I would be set up with a laptop, email, and company phone to use for the duration of my contract. Ms. Silverstein was confident that after the initial six-month consultation period, they'd probably want to sign me on for another six months.

The second I stepped out of the building, I called Rick.

"I got the job!" I screamed when I heard his greeting.

"You did!" I could hear the smile in his voice.

"Yep!"

"I'm so happy for you! Unfortunately, I can't talk right now, but make sure you give me all the details when I get in tonight."

"I will, Babe. Bye."

I felt like skipping, but didn't want to look like a fool hopping through Columbus Circle. Checking Siri for a local Thai restaurant, I found one a few blocks away and treated myself to lunch. As I ate, I imagined what it would be like to get back in the game. Would I make new friends? Would I like my boss? It felt good to be on my way back. My confidence was already beginning to soar.

Instead of rushing home, I spent another hour in the city shopping for a few outfits for work. I still planned to lose the rest of my weight so I didn't get much, but what I had at home was pretty outdated.

By the time I reached Scotland's school, I had figured out the entire game plan for the next half of the year so things would work seamlessly at home. My neighbor could take Scotland to school for me when she dropped her daughter off on Mondays. We were pretty cool and both served on the PTA so I trusted her. I just needed Rick to help out during my week of training. He was the boss and his offices were only fifteen minutes from the house. He could pick Scotland up in the afternoon and let her hang out with him until I got in.

At home, I helped Scotland with her homework and made a nice dinner to celebrate my new beginning. I couldn't wait to share my good news with Rick and tell him all about the interview. When he left work, he texted me and asked me to call the babysitter so he could take me out to dinner. I packed our dinner in containers for the next day, showered, and slipped into one of those cute dresses Lyric picked out for me. Scotland had been dropped off by the time he got home.

I couldn't wait until we got to the restaurant so I started telling him about the job while he was changing out of his work clothes. I was so busy running my mouth that I didn't notice when his expression shifted from excitement to concern. Rick stopped putting his clothes on and slowly sat on the bed.

"What?" I was confused. "You're not happy for me?"

"Babe..." Rick took a breath. "This isn't going to work."

"What do you mean?" My heart started thumping. "What's not going to work?" I started pacing circles on the rug.

"I can't pick up Scotland for a whole week. The company has

a huge job right now and I can't leave her at the office. I'm hardly even in the office these days."

I felt my heart drop into my stomach. "Rick!" my voice cracked. "It's just one week—for training." My chest heaved. The air in the room felt thin.

"There's got to be another option," I said. "I can ask Sheila to pick her up until you get home. You're usually in by five thirty. She'll only be with her for two hours. I'm sure she won't mind."

"Who is Sheila?"

"Leanna's mother. We're on the PTA together. They live a few blocks away."

"I don't know about that, Paige. I don't know this woman."

"Rick!" The pounding in my chest was so strong it could have moved me. "I know her. Scotland plays with Leanna all the time. She's been here several times for play dates. If you don't want Sheila watching her then you have to work with me." I hated the desperate way I sounded. "I'm not scheduled to start until the week after next."

"You also have to be in the city every Monday morning if you take this position. Who's going to take Scotland to school then?"

"You or Sheila can drop her off. I know she wouldn't mind. I've dropped Leanna plenty of times."

Rick stood and walked to the adjoining bathroom. "I don't know about this, Paige." He'd also stopped getting dressed.

"Are you serious?" I couldn't help yelling. Rick's head whipped in my direction. "You can't support me on this for one week?"

Rick's brows knitted. "You said you were going to find a part-time job that didn't interfere with our routine." He came charging from the bathroom with his finger pointed in my direction. "You said you'd make sure you could still be there for our daughter and I accepted that. That's after we agreed that you would stay home until she was ten, she's only six for Christ's sake. You're the one changing the game, not me!"

My eyes stretched so wide I could feel the strain. I couldn't believe he was talking to me this way. Never had I imagined that Rick would refuse to support me on something I really wanted.

My lips tightened into a rigid line. "You don't want me to have a job, do you?"

Rick flipped me a dismissive wave. "Don't be ridiculous! "This is simply not going to work. You'll have to call and let them know you can't accept the position and then find something else."

"I don't want to find something else. I want this opportunity. I need this opportunity."

"What you need to do is stick to the plan we originally set." Rick pulled off his pants and tossed them to the side.

I stood stark still, unable to move. My entire body shook, as if it were about to explode. Hot tears spilled from my eyes. Rick ignored me as he continued undressing. I wanted to choke his ass. I kept my mouth knitted tightly, unsure of what would come out. The words that passed through my mind were sure to cut deep into the fabric of our marriage. Words that once they seeped from my angry tongue, could never be taken back.

The doorbell rang as if someone was being chased. I didn't move. I couldn't move. Rick looked at me, threw his hands up, slipped his pants back on, and headed for the door. When he exited the room, I started breathing again. I unglued my feet from that spot and started pacing again, trying to reel in my breathing.

Maya's loud voice beat the walls, sailing through the house until it reached my ears upstairs. I couldn't hear what she was saying and almost didn't care, but then headed downstairs anyway. They were going back and forth by the time I got down there. When I got to the last step, Maya looked at me, rolled her eyes, and walked out the door. Rick's head volleyed back and forth between her retreating back and me as if he didn't know what hit him. Poor Jayden looked drained as she innocently stood by her dad's side watching her mother leave.

I had my own idea of what was going on, but I wanted to hear what Rick had to say. I shifted my weight to one leg and folded my arms across my chest, waiting for his explanation. Finally, Rick closed the door.

"Go on up to your room, Jayden." He nudged her gently.

Without saying a word, Jayden picked up an overnight back and headed toward the stairs, stopping only to give me a quick hug. I kissed her cheeks and tousled her hair before nudging her toward the stairs.

"Maya needs us to watch Jayden," Rick said without looking at me. "She has an emergency." His hands must have become really interesting to him because he wouldn't take his eyes off them. "She'll be with us until tomorrow night. We'll have to drop her off at school tomorrow."

I felt angry hives rise up my neck and cover my face. As much as I loved my stepdaughter, I wasn't jumping in to save the day for Rick and Maya's sake. I turned on my heels, retrieved my purse from the bedroom, and walked past Rick who was still standing in the foyer when I got back downstairs. I looked at him one last time, narrowing my gaze before I walked through the door.

"You'll have to drop her off at school tomorrow," I said before slamming the door behind me.

"Paige!" Rick opened the door. "Paige!" I didn't stop. "Paige!" His voice was louder, laced with more anger than before. "Paige!" That last one sounded desperate.

I continued down the walk swiftly, jumped in my car, and sped off.

CHAPTER 14

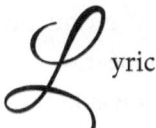 yric

FOLLOWING KERRI'S ADVICE, I finally made it back to Nate's better side. When he invited me to join him on the tail end of his latest business trip to L.A. I was beyond excited. I sent him off to work sated and happy this morning and then went shopping on Rodeo Drive before meeting up with one of the girls I used to model with. We laughed hysterically as she filled me in on all the drama floating through the industry. Of course, I remained part of that talk. People deliberated on how long they thought Nate and I would last. I tried not to let that hurt my feelings.

I headed back to the hotel to drop off my bags and get ready to meet Nate for dinner when he was finished working. A bellman helped me to our suite with all my bags and the new piece of luggage I had to buy in order to get my new items home. Giving him a hefty tip, I closed the door, and kicked off my stilettos, but then he knocked.

"Yes," I said, swinging the door open assuming the bellman had forgotten something. The air in my lungs stopped whirling momentarily when I saw Cypher standing there instead of the bellman.

Quickly, I tried to push the door closed. My efforts failed against his swift, strong hands. Cypher pushed past me and bathed me from head to toe in a glaring sweep. I backed up and reached for my handbag. Cypher blocked my path--his eyes still on me.

I crossed my arms in front of me, refusing to let on how scared I was. "What are you doing here, Cypher?"

He winked and a sick smile spread across his face. "This is my town now."

I rolled my eyes, but the way Cypher impaled me in his scowl made me wish I had the power to simply disappear.

"I don't have time for this. What do you want?" I wanted my cell phone so bad, but I wasn't sure who I would call. I could never explain to Nate why Cypher was in our suite. After the last encounter, he made it clear that he didn't want me near Cypher again.

Cypher licked his lips. "Why you have to be so mean?" He stepped closer, narrowing the space between us. I stepped back into the living area of the suite until my behind was against the couch. Sucking on his bottom lip, Cypher looked me up and down again. "I have to admit you do clean up well. Big man's money has you looking very good. But you always were pretty." He reached out a finger and ran it down the side of my arm. His touch left a repulsive feeling in its wake, like a mass of filthy worms had squirmed under my skin.

I slid away and walked back to the door, opening it wide. "You need to leave."

He walked up on me, leaving only a hairline of space between us. "You're too good for me now, Lyric?"

This time he touched my cheek with the back of his finger,

generating the same icky feeling. I moved away again, holding my body rigid to keep it from shaking. "Get out!"

"I forgot what you feel like." Cypher continued his perverted torture, sliding his finger down my face to the side of my breast, and then resting his hand on my hip.

I pushed him away. "Get off of me! Leave before I call security!"

"Ha!" You're not going to call anyone." His expression turned gravely serious. "I helped you, now it's time for you to help me. If it weren't for me, you never would have met Big Man." Cypher's lip curled into a snarl when he said the term of resentment he attached to Nate, referring to his stature in the industry. "It's time for me to call in my favors."

"I don't owe you anything, Cypher. Now please leave."

The next thing I knew Cypher had pressed his lips against mine. I pushed him off, wiping my mouth with the back of my hand. Before I could protest further, Nate's laugh resonated down the hall. My eyes popped open wide. A brief wave of fear flashed in Cypher's eyes. It wouldn't be good for either of us to be caught in this predicament. I was already on unstable ground with Nate and for Cypher, this would surely lead to a possible arrest. Nate didn't play around with thugs. I pushed the door closed lightly so it wouldn't make noise.

Nate's deep voice, now slightly muffled behind the door, grew louder as he drew closer. I looked left and right. "Get in the bathroom," I said in a hard whisper, pointing to the powder room in the common area. If Nate had to use the bathroom, I could easily direct him to the one in the bedroom.

"What? No!" I'm no punk. I ain't running from no man!"

"You want to end up in jail? You'd better get your ass in the closet!"

Like a toddler, Cypher stomped his feet, looked around, and then apparently came to the conclusion that the nearby bathroom was his best option.

The door lock clicked. I rubbed my hand down the front of my shirt, straightening my clothes. I looked at the bathroom, Cypher was peeking out. I waved my hand angrily. He moved back a little, still peeking, but through a smaller crack. The door to the hotel room opened. I stood at the door ready to greet Nate. He was on the phone and didn't notice me at first. I hoped I didn't look guilty. Unable to look into Nate's face, I wrapped my arms around him and buried my head in his strong chest. Nate hugged me with one hand. The other still held his phone.

"Sure...How about we discuss the rest over dinner? Okay great! See you then." Nate hung up the phone and squeezed me in both hands.

"I missed you!" I held on tighter.

"Aw, baby. I missed you too." Nate kissed me on the top of my head.

I pulled back. "You're here early," I said as I started picking up bags to carry to the bedroom.

"I see you went shopping." Nate chuckled and walked over to the couch, peering into the rest of the bags.

"Are you mad?" Outside I was pouting and couldn't help it. Inside I was shaking. I looked back at the bathroom door. It was slightly ajar. I couldn't see Cypher, but I was sure he could see me. I cut my eyes in his direction.

"Come here," Nate had pushed the bags aside and sat on the couch.

"I," I cleared my throat and looked back once again. "I just got back. I need to take my clothes to the room. Let's go in the bedroom."

"Come here," Nate said again, dismissing my suggestion.

"Nate!" I whined. "Don't we have to get ready for dinner?"

"We have time." Nate stood up and reached for me. He took the bags in my hand and dropped them to the floor. Then, he walked me to the couch. He sat back down and patted his leg, motioning for me to sit on his lap. "That's why I came back early, so we would have some extra time."

"So let's go to the bedroom." I leaned into him, hoping he wouldn't sense how nervous I was.

"I want you right here." Nate twisted my hips so I could face him--straddle him--giving me a clear view of the bathroom. I watched the narrow crack increase an inch. Cypher was definitely watching.

"I'm glad you're here." Nate held my face in his hands. "You're so freaking beautiful!" He pulled his lips to mine. I kept my eyes open as he kissed me and closed them when I saw his flutter back open. I hoped he couldn't taste Cypher on my lips. I got angry about his unwelcomed kiss all over again.

"I'm glad I'm here too." And I was. "I'm glad you're not mad at me anymore."

"You have to trust me, baby."

"I know. I'm sorry. I won't do it again." I tried to lift myself up from his growing erection. "Let's go in the bedroom."

Nate captured my hips and pulled me down on him, grinding his erection into me. "Let's stay right here." He licked his lips, still grinding. "I want you right here, baby."

Before I could continue my protest, Nate kissed me again. This time, he didn't let go. Nate's hands roamed, cupped my breast, found its way to my behind, and squeezed. He pushed himself against me and began unbuttoning my shirt. I looked towards the bathroom, which faced his back.

"Remember what you did to me this morning?" His smile was mischievous. I shook my head. "I want you to do that again." Nate rocked against me and hissed. "I've been thinking about that all day. I ended early so we could do that again before dinner." Nate looked pensive. "And maybe again after dinner. Ha!"

"Okay. Well, let's do it in the room."

"Nope." Nate ground into me again. "I want to do it right here."

By now my shirt was completely open. Nate pulled my breasts out of my bra and buried his face between them before teasing my nipples between his teeth. Against my will, I hissed and my back arched. By far, Nate is the most skilled lover I've ever had. It never took much for him to get my juices flowing. However, the last thing I wanted to do was make love to my husband while Cypher watched. Knowing he was in the bathroom witnessing our escapade made me want to throw up.

"Please, let's go get on the bed." I tried once more, whining this time, hoping to get my way."

"Why?" Nate kept kissing me, not giving me a moment to answer. It gave me time to think of something to say.

"I'd just rather do this in there."

"Okay." Relieved, I sighed. "After this."

Nate took my nipple into his mouth again, flicked his tongue, and sucked while hastily reaching his hand inside my leggings and dipping his fingers into the warm wetness. Another hiss escaped my lips and my head fell back, despite my uninvited audience of one. Instinctively, I swirled my hips, aiding the rhythm Nate created with his fingers. Heat spread through my entire body. Nate strummed faster until his fingers were drenched in the nectar seeping from me.

"Nate!" His name came out as a desperate whisper. I had to try one more time to get him into the room before I completely lost the ability to control my senses.

Nate took that summon as a license to hold me tighter, finger me faster. Urgently, he unzipped his pants, reached in, and pulled out his erection. He squirmed enough to pull his pants past his hips. In a swift movement, he lifted me and pulled my leggings down far enough to enter, filling me to the hilt. I cried out from the sweet pain. Guiding my hips, Nate bounced me on top of him. We collided repeatedly in dizzying ecstasy as he panted my name over and over again. As his release ripped through him, he embraced me tightly. Our hips slammed into each other when his body convulsed, overtaken by his climax. When he was done, he just held me. My eyes peered into the dark crack of the closet door, where I knew a darker set looked back.

When Nate caught his breath, he loosened his grip on me, helped me stand, and stood himself.

He looked at his watch. "Now let's go to the room. We still have a little more time." Stepping out of pants that had now fallen around his ankles, he took my hand and walked to the bedroom, exposed and ready for another round.

When we got inside, I closed the door behind us and prayed that Cypher had enough sense to leave.

CHAPTER 15

erri

I PULLED up in front of Camilla's house, parking a few houses down. It was my job to round up the other woman hiding in their respective cars up and down the block and notify Eve when the limo arrived. Camilla was expecting to have dinner with just her sister Eve and Teresa, her matron of honor, rather than the slew of women waiting for the limo to pull up.

"Come on, girls. Let's go!" I reached behind me and grabbed the bag of goodies for tonight.

Lyric and Paige got out of the car. When the other ladies saw us exiting, they got out of their cars too. Immediately, several pairs of eyes were drawn to Lyric and lingered on the bodacious curves snuggly wrapped in black sequin leggings, a red tank, black leather jacket, and five-inch heels. If she could be accused of tackiness, one might have thought she was tonight's hired entertainment. Fortunately, she was her usual attention-grabbing self, which she always seemed to enjoy. We gathered around and introduced anyone who hadn't met.

"Nice meeting you all," Lyric purred, already a little tipsy from the snifter of cognac she'd had before I picked her up. The other women nodded in agreement and handshakes were exchanged all around. Then we giggled in anticipation of how the night would go.

"Look ladies," I squealed pulling out a sparkling tiara with a veil, a magic wand with a shimmering star at the tip, and a t-shirt that said, "Because I'm the bride, that's why!"

"This is so cute!" Paige said admiring the getup.

"The limo!" One of the other ladies yelled.

Our heads snapped in the direction of the sleek white vehicle coming down the block.

"The champagne!" Lyric trotted on her stilettos, carefully making her way back to the car to retrieve the five bottles of Dom Perignon she'd purchased for tonight.

The rest of us headed for the limo. Once we were all inside and adorned with our "team bride," ribbons, I texted Eve and Teresa to let them know we were ready.

Keeping the dark tinted windows up, we saw Camilla's excited expression when she stepped out of the house and noticed the waiting limo.

Giggles erupted as they approached the car. You would have thought it was a group of teens.

"Shhh! She's going to hear us." I turned back just as Eve reached for the door handle. Silence filled the car. Slowly Eve opened the door and waved her hand for Camilla to climb in.

"Surprise!" We all screamed.

Camilla grabbed her chest and screamed, startled. The interior of the limo erupted with laughter.

"We got you!" I teased.

"You sure did." Camilla dropped her shoulders. "Awe ladies! This is so great. Thank you." She blew kisses to each of us.

"Okay, now move your booty into the car so we can get in too," Teresa teased.

Despite Teresa's urging, Camilla took her time hugging and greeting each of the women inside the limousine.

"You're in for the night of your life, lady. Can you handle it?" Eve asked.

"Bring it on!" Camilla shouted, pumping one fist in the air.

Lyric poured several glasses of champagne and handed them out as I made Camilla change into the t-shirt we bought and then carefully placed the tiara and veil on her head.

"Oh my goodness! I love this shirt!" Camilla tugged on the bottom to get a better view. "This is so cute." She maneuvered her tiara, straightening it on her head. "And this tiara is the bomb! You ladies are so wonderful!"

"Girl, we already know that!" Lyric twisted her lips and sipped her champagne.

Along with everyone else, Camilla laughed and waved Lyric's arrogant silliness away.

"Well, I'm glad you're all here. I can only imagine what's in store for the night and I can't wait. Thanks again everyone."

"You're welcome," some ladies replied.

"No need to thank us, honey!" Teresa said.

"You deserve it!" Eve added.

"The timing couldn't be better either. Aaron has been sick all week and I've been trying to help him get better. That man just refused to go to a doctor. I could really use a night out. Riley's hanging with him tonight." Camilla chuckled.

"How's he doing now?" I asked.

"A little better, I guess."

"He's got that bug that's been going around?" Paige asked.

"I don't know. At first, we thought it was food poisoning. We went out to eat last weekend and later that night he complained of stomach pains. Then he started vomiting. He became nauseous and had a fever so we figured it was a stomach virus. After taking a few over the counter remedies and nothing worked, I told him to go see the doctor. Like most men, he refused." Camilla huffed.

"Did he go to work this week?" Maggie, one of Camilla's bridesmaids asked.

"Yep! All week except today. I told him to stay home, but you all know how macho he is. He was so out of it when he got home yesterday that he finally decided to take a sick day today. The pain did dissipate a little so he said he'll take the weekend to rest and if he's still feeling bad by Monday he'll go see his doctor."

"Well, I hope he's okay," Lyric said.

"He'd better be! We have a wedding to attend next Saturday! I hope I don't have to roll his behind down the aisle. With all the money we spent, we're getting married one way or another, even if he has to say 'I do" in his hospital gown. I'll just pin his boutonniere to that gown and slap a bowtie around his neck." Despite all the laughter, I could see the concern in her eyes.

"The timing couldn't be better. It's obvious you need this little break. Get ready! Woo!" Eve threw her hands in the air. "Driver, turn that up, please." He did and everyone joined in the sing along to the lyrics of Beyoncé's *Love on Top*.

After an amazing seafood dinner at one of Camilla's favorite restaurants in Manhattan, we headed back to a chic Martini Bar in Totowa where we reserved a VIP package for the remainder of the night. I was happy to see Camilla having such a great time. She'd never been a heavy drinker, but she was tipsy tonight. Not too bad, though. I couldn't say the same for Lyric. She, on the other hand, had been slurring and giggling all night. Right now, she was standing near the table, dancing by herself, wiggling that unlawfully large booty to some of Mary J Blige's wailing. She had been swatting men away like flies all night.

When the DJ announced Camilla's name and requested that she come to the DJ booth, she looked at us, smiled, and wagged her finger. "What are you guys up to?" She danced over to the DJ while Eve, Teresa, and I exchanged puzzled looks.

"Did you tell the DJ that it was her bachelorette night?" Eve asked Teresa and me.

"No!" we said in unison.

"I guess someone did," Eve surmised.

"Maybe it was Lyric," I added. "She knows everybody, everywhere! "Lyric!" I shouted over the music and waved her over.

With eyes at half-mast, Lyric sauntered over. "What's up, boo?"

"Did you tell the DJ it was Camilla's bachelorette party?"

"No, but I guess we should have, right?"

"No!" Eve held out her hand. "Camilla is not big on public attention. We were just wondering since the DJ called her name. Maybe the folks here at the bar did since we booked the VIP package using her name."

We all shrugged and went back to chatting, swaying, popping our fingers to the music, and sipping until Camilla raced back looking as pale as if she'd seen the good Lord in the flesh right inside of the Martini Bar.

"We...I mean, I gotta go!" Camilla grabbed her purse and looked around frantically. Her hands trembled as she tried opening the pocketbook to retrieve her cell phone. It tumbled out of her hand and Teresa caught it.

"What's wrong?" Eve stood to her feet knocking into the table. Glasses teetered but didn't fall.

Every one of us abruptly followed suit—the same question expressed in the worried lines of our made up faces.

"It's Aaron!" Tears fell from Camilla's eyes. "He passed out. The ambulance is on its way. Riley said she tried to call us but no one answered so she called the bar directly."

Grabbing her purse, Eve said, "I told her where we would

be." She pulled her cell phone out and thumbed her passcode. "Yes, I have two missed calls."

"Me too." I tossed my phone back in my purse.

Without further inquiry, we all dropped enough money on the table to cover our tabs and headed for the door on Camilla's heels.

"Oh my goodness! The limo!" Camilla said, still shaking.

"I'll call for him to come back now." I dug for my cell phone once again.

"I can't wait for him. I need to get home now. Oh God!" Camilla's breath rushed in short gasps.

"Okay! We can get a taxi," Eve said and ran back inside the bar.

"Let me see where the driver is. Maybe he will get to us before a cab does." My frazzled nerves had ruined my sense of coordination. My hands were shaking so badly I could barely swipe and tap in my password to get to my contacts. Seeing my dilemma, Paige tried to help. She wasn't much better. It literally took the two of us to get the limo driver on the phone. A sense of dread hovered deep in the pit of my core.

"Hello! Hello!" I panicked.

"Magnet Transportation Services. How can I help you?" the driver said calmly. His tone was in such contrast to how I felt at the moment.

"Hi! Uh...this is Kerri Rhodes. I booked the limo for the bachelorette party for tonight. We need you to come back right now. We have an emergency."

"I'm just down the block. Be right there!"

"The limo is coming now." I was so relieved.

"I'll get Eve." Teresa ran back inside the bar.

The rest of the girls surrounded Camilla, held her trembling hands and rubbed her back. She cried uncontrollably, making me feel like this could be worse than she originally let on.

I walked over and stood in front of her. "Honey," I lifted her chin so her eyes could meet mine, "we're right here with you, okay?" She nodded. "What else did Riley say?" Camilla broke down completely, unable to get any words past her quivering lips. I hugged her and held her hand. "It's okay." I felt stupid saying that because I really didn't know if everything was okay, but what else could I say?

Camilla gathered herself enough to speak. "Riley...." her breath hitched "...walked into the kitchen and found him lying on the floor. She sounded so scared, Kerri." Sobs racked her body. "I shouldn't have come out tonight. I should have stayed with him. I should have made him go to the doctor."

"Stop!" Eve put her hand on Camilla's cheek. "You did nothing wrong! This is not your fault. God willing, Aaron will be okay. We just have to get him to the hospital."

Camilla responded with more tears. "I told Riley to dial 911."

The limo arrived and we all piled inside. The driver raced back to the house coming dangerously close to violating several traffic violations along the way. He had hardly brought the car to a full stop when Camilla leapt out. The ambulance had already arrived.

Camilla plowed into the house calling out Aaron's name and we followed behind her. My heart sank at the sight of Aaron's limp body lying on the stretcher. Camilla laid her body over his.

"Baby, can you hear me? Aaron, baby, answer me!" Her desperate pleas crumbled those of us who tried to be her emotional rock. Every eye filled with tears. "Aaron, baby..." Camilla shrieked.

"Ma'am. If you could just answer a few questions for me," one of the EMT's gently grasped her by the arm so the other could continue working on Aaron.

Camilla reached out to Aaron as the EMT led her to the living room. Eve stood by her side and helped the EMT ease Camilla into a nearby chair. He asked a few questions as he returned to Aaron's side to assist the other EMT.

Together, they lifted Aaron onto the stretcher and began wheeling him toward the door. My own breath felt as though it was operating on short supply. I swallowed hard, attempting to push back the rush of emotions that threatened to take me over the edge. Closing my eyes, I took a few deep breaths and counted to ten. Camilla was already a mess. Breaking down wouldn't help her at all.

"Sir. Can you tell us what happened?" I asked as he wheeled Aaron toward the door.

"We're not totally sure. It could be a number of things. We did our best to try to stabilize him for immediate transport to the hospital."

"Okay." I wanted to get angry at him for not having a more detailed answer but, instead, I walked back over to where Camilla was sitting with everyone around her as she tried to catch her breath.

Riley was there now, crying hysterically. I took her in my arms, letting her fall against my chest. "I know, baby." Blinded by my own tears, I laid my head on top of hers and we cried together.

"Now," an EMT returned, capturing our attention. "Would you like to ride in the ambulance, or will you be taking your own car, Ma'am?"

Camilla looked at him but didn't answer. It looked as if his question didn't compute in her brain.

"I'll take her in my car," Eve interjected. "Come on Camilla." She patted her sister's shoulder. Camilla looked beyond us, almost through us into the distance. She gave a faint reply.

"Riley, get in the car with your mom. I'll be right behind you guys," I instructed.

Riley wiped her tears and shook her head. "Yes, Mama K."

We mobilized immediately, filling three cars to carry everyone to the hospital. None of us were willing to leave Camilla's side.

I don't know exactly how fast I drove, but Paige, Lyric, and I beat the ambulance there. We met Camilla, Riley, and the rest of the girls at the emergency room entrance. The EMT's rushed Aaron inside. Doctors met them at the door, promising to let us know something ASAP.

A while later, one of the doctors came out to give Camilla a report. She looked as if she had aged ten years in a few hours. Lines surrounded red swollen eyes. Her cheeks were drawn as if she was malnourished. She stood, greeting the doctor, wringing her hands. The doctor began to speak, but then paused. He looked at us and nodded as if to get Camilla's approval for speaking in our presence. She nodded a silent consent.

He took a deep breath and sighed, pulling his lips together before speaking. We created a chain, holding each other's hands and squeezing tightly at the grave look on the doctor's face.

"It appears that Mr. Washington's appendix ruptured..." The doctor paused and we leaned forward, hanging in the silence, awaiting the next word. "...apparently several days ago."

"What?" Wh..." Camilla's voice shook.

"Can you tell me more about how he was doing before coming here?"

Camilla gave a mousy account of what had transpired with Aaron in the past week. Her voice sounded so weak that the doctor had to lean in to hear her clearly.

He nodded, understanding what Camilla said. "We're going to have to do emergency surgery to try and remove the appendix, however...," he paused again and I wanted to slap the rest of the words right out of his mouth.

"Just tell me, doctor." Camilla was almost indignant, voicing the frustration I felt.

"It doesn't look promising. It appears that infectious matter was released into his system from the rupture and has spread considerably. We won't know exactly how bad it is until the surgeon goes in, but we remain hopeful."

Camilla reached toward the doctor but fell to the floor. Several of us clamored to help her, but the doctor lifted her in his arms and gently sat her down, ordering a nurse to come to her aid.

Camilla spoke, but the only words audible were, "Please help him."

Before leaving, the doctor promised they would do all they could. A while later, the surgeon leading the operation came out, introduced himself, and offered more details on Aaron's prognosis.

"I just don't understand," Camilla said holding her forehead. "Yesterday, he said he was feeling better. He was just tired."

"Appendicitis is painful and if it goes untreated, the appendix can, and often will rupture. When that happens, the patient will initially feel a little relief from the pain, but then the infectious materials, which are poisonous to the body, begin to seep into the abdominal cavity. If that goes untreated the results can be...well...undesirable...fatal even." Camilla wavered on her feet. "But we're not writing him off Ms. Washington. We will certainly do the best we can." Though they weren't married yet, no one bothered to correct the doctor about calling her by Aaron's last name. "I just want you to be fully aware that this is a risky surgery that could go either way. Like I said, we're hoping for the best." The surgeon frowned and tilted his head in a sympathetic manner as he patted Camilla's hand.

"Thank you, doctor." Camilla moaned and sighed. "Is it possible for me to see him now?

"I'm sorry ma'am. He's already inside the OR being prepped. We will send someone out as soon as we have more news." With that, he turned and disappeared behind the double doors leading to the emergency room.

Unable to sit, I walked the length of the waiting room, giving Chris updates. After a while, we collectively decided that some of us would stay at the hospital with Camilla while the others went home to get some rest and return in the morning to give those on first watch a break. Eve, Teresa, Riley, and I stayed, taking turns napping in the uncomfortable plastic chairs. Camilla refused to sleep, so we kept watch over her until the sun began to break through the predawn sky.

Shortly after, the surgeon came out. Camilla stood abruptly, knocking over the full cup of coffee at her feet. The stirring woke Riley and Eve. I was beyond tired and didn't feel sleepy at all anymore. I had spent the past several hours overdosing on bad coffee and periodically talking to Chris who obviously hadn't slept either.

"Doctor! How did it go?" Camilla ran to him frantically. "Is he better?"

The surgeon removed his cap, churning it in his hands along with his face mask. He looked down and back up at Camilla. She followed every gesture, waiting for him to speak, her chest heaving in anticipation—her eyes drooped and her cheeks were drawn from hours of crying. I knew he wasn't going to deliver good news. Tears began to fill Camilla's eyes. He opened his mouth and I could tell he was trying to find the right words. As much death as he must have seen, this part probably didn't get any easier for him. The surgeon parted his lips.

"No!" Camilla shook her head violently before he could speak his first word. She knew. I knew too. "No, please. No!" She continued to plead with him, her first cries breaking her posture. "Please. God. No!" she howled.

"I'm sorry, Mrs. Washington…"

That's all he needed to say. Camilla doubled over. A wail generated from somewhere deep inside of her core and erupted through her lips like a war cry. Her knees gave in and she crumpled to the floor. Instead of trying to pick her up Eve, Teresa, Riley, and I slid down to her and held on to her, swaying with arms wrapped around each other as our bodies rocked from our collective sobs.

No, the doctor needn't say anything. I couldn't bear to hear him say the words anyway. I had already heard them in my head. I couldn't begin to imagine what Camilla felt. The man that she was due to marry in seven days was dead.

CHAPTER 16

 aige

THE BRIGHT MORNING sun invaded my sleep, shining red through my closed lids. I should have pulled the curtains the night before but was too exhausted to get out of bed. Between attending Aaron's services, and Rick and I finally setting aside our issues with one another, the week had been an emotional ride. I couldn't help but wonder what it would be like to be in Camilla's shoes. I felt horrible for her. We stayed by her side as much as possible in the past week, cleaning her up to make a suitable appearance for her fiancé's homegoing services. The normal gleam in her eyes had dulled drastically and her usually supple skin appeared to have lost its natural glow. She had hardly eaten since Aaron passed and it showed. Minimal words had passed her lips. I couldn't remember much more than a cordial 'Thank you' as people offered their condolences. Together, their parents hosted the repast at his mother's church fellowship hall, during which she mostly sat absently staring out the window as if she were expecting Aaron to show up.

Riley took Aaron's death hard as well and it didn't help matters that the burial ended up being on the actual day they were supposed to be wed. Aaron was a wonderful stepfather in the making, having given Riley a commitment ring when he proposed to Camilla, promising to love, cherish, protect, and be the best stepdad he could till death did them part.

I squeezed my eyes shut trying to rid my mind of the languishing images from the past week. There was so much heartbreak—so many tears. The rest of us ladies held tight to our men, valuing every breath they took, not wanting to change places with Camilla no matter how tough things were.

I rolled over and wrapped my arms around Rick, who was still sleeping. Watching his steady breaths, I thanked God for him despite the remnants of tension that still had a foothold in our home since our recent blow-up. After Maya showed up and dropped Jayden on our doorstep like an orphaned child, Rick decided it would make sense to work with me instead of against me. I did take Jayden to school the next day and every day during the two weeks of the month that she normally stays with us and Rick miraculously got over his reluctance to support the job offer. Aaron's death encouraged us to fight to find our happiness again.

The job was working out well so far, but I was going to have to figure out how to tell Rick that my boss wanted me to travel to one of the satellite offices in the midwest in a few weeks. I rolled my eyes just thinking about how that discussion would go. I was still working on making sure Scotland and Jayden could get back and forth to school while I was away, since the trip dates fell on days Jayden would be with us. My last resort was to have my mother come and stay while I was gone.

Rick stirred and pulled my arms around him tighter. I lay

there holding him, not wanting the time to pass, but the thumping of fast approaching feet interrupted the moment. Four hands knocked urgently at our bedroom door. I threw back the covers, climbed out of bed, and grabbed my robe.

The second the lock clicked, Jayden and Scotland rushed into the room and flopped on our bed. I looked at the clock. It was just past seven in the morning.

"What are you two doing up?" I asked, chuckling at their apparent excitement.

The girls rolled Rick's body from side to side as he pretended to still be asleep.

"Daddy's is taking us out! Come on, daddy! Get up." Scotland peeled his eyelids apart with her little fingers.

"You said you were going to take us for pancakes this morning, dad. Stop faking!" Jayden shook him faster.

Rick smiled though his eyes remained closed.

"I saw that!" Jayden said.

Suddenly, Rick grabbed her and tickled her. Jayden screamed and squirmed, kicking her legs wildly.

Scottland giggled and then laid her body next to Rick. "Tickle me too!" Rick obliged and she too squirmed as she laughed uncontrollably.

They turned on Rick and both started tickling him back. This put a smile on my face and I left them to their fun as I went to the bathroom to relieve myself. Through the door, I heard the wild thumping of feet again and knew they were leaving the room. Rick joined me in the bathroom wearing pajama pants and no shirt.

"When I promised to take them out to breakfast, I hadn't anticipated going this early. I wanted to sleep in a little." Rick slid the mirror to the medicine cabinet aside and took out his toothbrush.

"You know how excited they get over that pancake house."

"Yeah!" Rick laid a neat line of toothpaste over the bristles and shoved it in his mouth.

Despite the fact that my gym time had declined considerably since I started working, I was still making the effort to workout at least three times a week. I hadn't lost any more pounds, which was frustrating, but at least I'd lost a few more inches, which made my clothes fit better. I watched Rick's belly jiggle as he brushed vigorously. At first, I wasn't going to mention him joining the gym with me again because he always dismissed the idea with the excuse that he didn't have time. Instead, I asked if he would like to start walking with me in the evenings after work. We could use it as a way to connect and decompress from our hectic days.

Rick hesitated, reaching into the shower to turn on the water before answering. "That may be nice." Non-committal.

"Great, let's start tomorrow?" I said, heading to the linen closet for a towel and washcloth.

"Sure." He still didn't sound convincing. Rick stepped in the shower then peeked his head out from the curtain. "Join me?"

I did, taking in other softening areas of his naked body. Maybe this could be a start to a fit lifestyle for both of us.

In the shower, we kissed and washed one another, giving special attention to sensual areas. If it weren't for the fact that the girls would come bursting back into our room once they were dressed, we could have done a lot more under the spray of that steamy water.

Rick dressed in comfortable sweats and I threw on some workout gear.

"You're not coming to breakfast with us?"

"You go ahead and have fun with the girls. I'm going to take a new class this morning."

"You sure?

"Listen." I tugged at the bit of flesh still hanging in my lower stomach area. "The last thing I need are fluffy stacks of pancakes and gooey syrup."

"Okay," Rick said like it was a warning, certain that I was going to miss a good time.

"I'll be fine. It's good for the girls to have their daddy time."

Jayden and Scotland came barreling back into the room. They didn't seem to mind at all that I wasn't joining them. Hugging me, they simultaneously kissed my cheeks and said their goodbyes. Grabbing Rick by each hand, they practically dragged him down the steps. I headed back to the bathroom to brush my hair back.

My work cell phone rang, but I didn't bother to answer. My boss had a habit of calling anytime she thought of something to say. I wanted to train her not to encroach on my personal time, so I let those calls outside of working hours go straight to voicemail and only replied to emails during business hours. However, I knew that I would be getting an email from her when I didn't answer the call. I continued working on pulling these wiry strands of mine into a ponytail when my phone chimed several times. I'd eventually get to the messages.

"Hey, Babe!" Rick yelled from the bedroom. I hadn't heard him return.

"What's up?"

"Those kids pulled me out of here so fast that I forgot my cell phone and wallet," he chuckled.

I chuckled too, loving the way his girls brought out a less serious, more carefree side of Rick. I heard my phone ring again as I was putting the hair cream I used to tame my hair back into the cabinet.

"That's your work phone, Babe!" Rick called out from the room. "You want it?"

"I'll be out in a minute."

I cleaned loose hairs from the vanity and tossed them into the wastebasket. When I turned, Rick was standing in the doorway with my cell phone in his hand and an accusatory expression on his face.

"You have a message." He held the face of the phone toward me, deepening his expression. I was going to have to change my settings so that details of my messages wouldn't show up on my screen.

"Okay. Why are you looking at me like that?"

"What travel itinerary is your boss talking about?"

At first, I couldn't say anything. My brain didn't operate quickly enough. I vacillated between being upset that he was violating my privacy and being anxious because I wasn't ready to tell him about the trip since I hadn't completely worked out adequate childcare.

"You're reading my messages?" I let the angry side show first.

"Don't sidestep the question. What trip is your boss talking about? We never discussed your traveling. This was supposed to be a job where you worked from home. It wasn't supposed to interfere with our schedule beyond that first week of training."

"Rick!" I said for lack of anything better to say.

He cocked his head to the side, challenging me with a look that warned me not to lie to him as if that had become something he could expect from me.

I huffed but said nothing. Instead, I snatched my phone out of his hand and brushed past him in pursuit of my running shoes and a little distance.

"Paige!" he commanded.

"Can we talk about this later? I don't even know what the email says yet."

Rick threw a serious glare in my direction. Abruptly, he turned to leave. "I told you this wasn't going to work," he shot over his shoulder and kept going. Obviously, he wasn't interested in hearing my response.

I groaned and looked down at my phone, tapped in the passcode, and checked the email. My boss hadn't just sent an email about the trip. She'd sent me a complete travel itinerary and meeting schedule. Flights and hotel accommodations for me and several other co-workers had already been booked. The bit of tension that had dissipated in the past week began to roll back in like fog.

CHAPTER 17

 yric

I COULD HAVE SWORN I heard knocking at my front door. When I pulled back the covers, I heard the bell ring. I wasn't expecting anyone at five past ten in the morning, I was sure it wasn't Candy. After hanging out together the night before, I was certain she was sleeping in just as I was trying to do. I was even more tired since Nate decided to wake me up and have me for breakfast before going to work.

I thought about letting my unannounced visitor stay right there. That's what they get for not calling first. I scooted over and reached for my cell phone on the nightstand to see if I had missed any calls. I had received nine texts—two from Candy and seven from an unknown number with a Los Angeles area code. Intuitively, something churned in the pit of my stomach. I tapped the unknown number just as the knocking turned into banging.

I tiptoed to the window. "Damn it." I couldn't see the door

from up here. I grabbed a robe to sheath my naked body and tiptoed through my own house. I peeked out the front window and Cypher was on my porch. Instantly, I could feel the blood racing through my veins. My hand instinctively flew to my chest. "What the hell?"

I ran back upstairs, threw on a bra, tank top, and a pair of lounge pants. He continued knocking. Checking the texts from the anonymous number, I realized it was Cypher.

I enjoyed the show, but my skills are much better. I used to have you screaming, remember? On a serious note, I need to see you. No more time for games.

My heart rate quickened. I didn't think it was possible. I paced a few moments before going back to read the other messages.

I'm in your hood. Need to talk today.

I just saw your man leave the house.

I'll be back in a minute.

I'm baaaaaaack. Open the door.

Do you hear me knocking?

Don't play with me, Lyric.

The phone dinged again as I held it. My hands started to shake. Cypher wasn't going to leave until I answered that door. It was obvious that he had been watching the house and knew I was home. I just couldn't understand how he found my number and my address. This wasn't good. I closed my eyes and held my breath, then opened my eyes and tapped the phone to retrieve the message that had just come in.

I saw you! Now open the door before I break and enter!

I felt like screaming but headed back downstairs to face Cypher. Meanwhile, I tapped out a code red message to Candy, letting her know what was going on. That was the only person I could share this with, and she'd know what to do. I only hoped she was awake to get it.

"How did you find me and what do you want?" I said as soon

as I snatched the door open, filling the frame with my body. I stood rigid. He wasn't welcome at my home. I could feel the adrenaline coursing through my veins like a stampede of wild stallions. My chest did heave, defying the composed vibe I tried to give off.

"It's about time." Cypher pushed right past me.

Rolling my eyes, I huffed, looked around to make sure no one saw him come in, and slammed the door. I crossed my arms over my breast. I didn't know what else to do with my hands. Nervous energy found its release through my tapping foot. I hoped I came across as impatient and angry as opposed to frightened.

"Cypher." I took a breath, trying to maintain normal breathing rhythms. "How did you get my number and address and why are you here?"

Cypher had ignored me since brushing by me to charge into my house. He looked around in wonder and whistled. "This shit is crazy! Woo! Nate sure knows how to live." Stepping further through the house as if he had been invited, Cypher continued to take in the opulent décor and expensive artwork. "This is just like those big mansions in the movies. How much a house like this cost?" He chuckled. "Gotta be worth about ten mil. You really hit the jackpot this time, baby girl! Whew!" Cypher's laugh made my skin feel as if bugs were crawling all over me. I rubbed my arms.

"What do you want?"

He walked so close to me that I could smell the cognac he'd been drinking. He touched my hand and I snatched it away. "This is a far cry from your..." he pretended to think of the right word." ...humble beginnings with me, huh." He walked away with a sickening laugh. Strolling through the foyer, Cypher stepped into one of the sitting rooms and comfortably parked himself on the couch.

I groaned. "No! You can't do this. You have to go." I marched over to him and pulled his arm.

Cypher pulled me down on top of him. I scampered to my feet. "Cypher! I'm not playing with you!"

"And I'm not playing with you!" The expression on his face turned deathly serious, making my breath catch. I wanted to run but wouldn't make it to the door before he caught me. His penetrating stare lasted for several moments. I challenged him with my own glare as I tried to think of the best way to get out of this situation. He patted the couch beside him. "Now sit down so we can talk. Time is of the essence and I need to make some major moves that I need your help with."

"My help!" I folded my arms defiantly. "I'm not helping you do anything!"

He tittered and slid his lips into a sinister grin. "Cute. I've always loved the feisty side of you. You don't have a choice, baby girl." He patted the couch again. "Now sit!"

I didn't move.

Cypher shrugged his shoulders. "Fair enough." He nodded. "I'm sure you can hear me from there." His eyes washed over my body from my lips to my feet. He smirked. I wrapped my arms around my waist, wishing I had a blanket. "You have always been so damn pretty."

I sucked my teeth and cut my eyes toward the ceiling.

"Okay." Cypher sat up. "I got your number from your phone!"

My face scrunched. How was that possible? "My phone?"

He laughed again. "When your man took your little sexy show to the bedroom at the hotel back in L.A., you left your stuff on the floor by the couch. By the way, your man has nothing on me. Ha!" I cringed but hoped he didn't notice. "Everything I needed was right there in plain view. I simply called my phone from your number and got your address from his wallet. For a rich dude, he doesn't carry a lot of money. Anyway! I snatched up a few dollars and left. It was easy. Now

I'm here. Let's get to more important topics. You're going to help me get this next record deal."

My hand flew in the air. "Oh no, I'm not!"

Cypher stood up and in one leap, we were nose to nose. I flinched, expecting him to grab me.

"Yes. You are," he said with certainty.

"There's nothing I can do to help you get a deal, Cypher. I'm not in the music business. You've burned every bridge you crossed and there's not a record company out there that's willing to touch you. I can't get involved with that!"

A glimpse of hopelessness flashed behind his eyes, but his wicked depths quickly returned. Cypher gnawed his lips, a sign that he was about to lose control. I backed up and looked around for anything solid I could grab to defend myself.

"Cypher," I said smoothly. "I know we have a lot of history, but there's nothing I can do for you."

"Every night, you lay down next to one of the most influential men in the music business. You can help me. You just don't want to."

I shook my head. "Nate and I never discuss business."

"Well, it's time you start," he said sharply. "I need this and you're my last option."

"Why me, Cypher?" I grunted.

"Because you owe me."

"Owe you?" I could feel my face twisting in disbelief. "What do I owe you, Cypher?" Forget being fearful. I was getting mad.

"Bi—" He stopped himself from calling me a female dog. He pressed his lips together for a second before continuing. "If it weren't for me, you would have never met Nate. You wouldn't be in this business. Don't forget, I found you in that club that night. I'm the one who pulled you out of that environment. I took care of you! Cast you in my video. That's how you got discovered."

"Yeah and then you beat the hell out of me that night when

you were drunk and thought I was coming on to that rapper." Tears threatened to spill from my eyes at the memory of me lying on the floor in a bloody heap in the VIP section of the club that night. My dress was torn, hair disheveled. It took half his entourage to get him off me. I'd been afraid of him ever since.

Cypher's face dropped and what looked like genuine concern and possible remorse appeared. "How many times have I told you I was sorry?" His low voice lacked the arrogance he'd come in with. "I don't know what happened to me that night. I said someone put something in my drink."

"Cypher." I gave him a sideways glare.

"I'm serious, Lyric. I've never done anything to you like that again. Did I?"

I inclined my head to the other side and just stared at him again.

"But you were threatening to leave me, then," he said of the time when he ripped my dress off my body.

"You needed help." I contemplated before saying my next words. "And I think you still do."

Cypher stepped closer to me and ran his finger down the side of my arm. "I need you. Things haven't been the same since you've been out of my life. I never met another woman as loyal. I still love you."

I turned away. This man was crazy if he thought I was going to allow him to manipulate me. I knew him way too well. I'd been witness to many of his lies that seemed sincere as they skillfully fell from his lying lips.

"Even after all these years, it hurt like hell to see you with this dude and watch him make love to you."

He touched me again. I jerked away. "It's time for you to leave."

He pulled me by the arm as I tried to walk away. "Not quite yet. I haven't finished."

"We're done here, Cypher."

"No we're not. I haven't told you how you're going to help me and why you won't refuse."

"You're crazy!"

"No, I'm not. You're going to get me a meeting with your husband and the reason you are definitely going to do it is because you certainly don't want him to know all the scandalous details about your past. Now do you?"

"You're blackmailing me!"

"If that's what you want to call it." Cypher shrugged as if what he said was no big deal. "You seem to forget that I have no problem ruining reputations to get what I want. You were party to a few of those situations when we were together. I wonder what Nate would think about that—especially when some of those situations involved talent on his roster back then. Business executives don't take kindly to people interfering with their investments. Ha!" Cypher's laugh made my stomach tighten. "And I'm sure he doesn't know about your humble beginnings as a dancer," Cypher said, using air quotes as he spoke of times I've worked hard to forget about.

"You wouldn't do that!" I narrowed my eyes at him.

"I certainly would. If you don't believe me, check your email." Cypher closed in on me once again. Lifting my chin with his finger, he stared, searching my eyes for a moment. "You thought I was lying when I said I still loved you. After all of this time, you may not believe it, but I actually do. If I could have you today," Cypher sucked in his bottom lip and hissed, "I would, but this isn't about love. This is about business."

Cypher licked my face and headed for the front door. I was stunned and couldn't move. Wiping his moisture from my cheek with the back of my hand, I watched him waltz through my home like his name was on the deed. My cell phone rang. I uprooted my feet from where I stood and searched for my phone. The ringing stopped just as I picked it up. I had missed Candy's call, but it was too late anyway.

CHAPTER 18

erri

"ARE YOU STILL THERE?" Chris asked. His exasperation was evident through the phone.

I pouted, even though he couldn't see me. "Yes. I'm just finishing up a little snack for Camilla and Riley. I'll be home right after." That little snack was pasta with shrimp in vodka sauce and pesto gravy, and a caesar salad—basically, dinner. I wanted to make sure Riley had something substantial to eat since she was essentially here alone. Camilla hadn't quite joined the living yet.

Chris had been so patient these past two weeks since Aaron's death. Camillia's mother occasionally came to New Jersey and her sister, Eve checked in on her around the clock, but Camilla had closed herself off from the world, including Riley. So Riley spent the last few days with Chris and me. When I dropped her off today, Camilla was still in the same position she was in when we left the other day—balled up in bed in a dark room with all the curtains drawn.

With the phone squeezed between my ear and neck, I almost burned my hand removing the garlic bread from the oven. Riley walked into the kitchen and I pointed to the parmesan cheese, gesturing for her to shake some over the salad. She got the message and I went back to Chris in my ear.

"I hate to sound inconsiderate and I think what you're doing is very commendable, but at some point, she has to snap out of it and get on with life. I know this can't be easy, but she can't go on like this." Chris paused for a long while. "And we need you here."

"I know. Ugh!" With spending most of my time between Camilla's and work, I'd neglected my own home. As patient as Chris was, I wasn't surprised by his comment.

"You're about to go into another busy season and I won't see you at all."

And he was right. We were filming the second season of another reality show that my network produced, and although it wasn't as dramatic as the cast from Society Wives, the hours are just as long. Due to a few hiccups with some of our permits, we were a little behind schedule, which meant the post-production would be hectic, leaving little time for my family.

"I'm almost done. I'll call you when I get in the car, okay?"

A long exhale proceeded his unconvinced response. "Okay." Chris hung up the second I said goodbye. I let the phone drop into my hand and checked the consistency of the pasta.

"Riley."

"Yes, Mama K?"

"Get a strainer from the cabinet so I can drain this pasta."

Riley moved swiftly. I drained the pasta, mixed it with the sauce and covered the pot before washing my hands.

"Do me a favor and make sure your mother eats tonight."

"I will." Riley grabbed me around my waist. The move was so

unexpected, I teetered a bit before catching my footing and then hugged her, rubbing her back. When we pulled away, Riley's eyes glistened with tears. "I hate seeing mom hurt this way."

"Me too, sweetheart. All we can do is be there with her until she gets through this."

"I miss him too, Mama K!" Riley buried her head into my chest and sobbed.

I squeezed her in my arms and stayed that way until her whimpering ceased.

"I'm sorry. I'm going to my room to lay down for a while," Riley said. She walked away with slumped shoulders, her head down.

"I'll check on your mom one more time before I leave."

I walked into Camilla's dark bedroom. Aaron's pants were still strewn in the corner as if he'd just dropped them there after a long day's work. Camilla had yet to remove any of his belongings from the house.

"Camilla!" I whispered. She didn't stir. I tiptoed around to her side of the bed where she lay in a fetal position with the covers up to her neck. She was awake. "Camilla."

She looked up at me with eyes so doleful, just looking into them triggered my own tears. I leaned over and kissed her cheek.

"I made dinner. Get up, take a shower, and sit down to the table and have dinner with your daughter tonight. She needs you."

Camilla just nodded her head. I hoped she would do as I suggested.

"I'm heading home now. Eve will come by later tonight, okay?"

Camilla nodded her head again.

After a deep breath and taking a moment to compose myself, I was able to make it to my car without crying. I needed to ride in peace, so I turned off the radio, silenced my phone and headed straight home.

"I thought you said you were going to call when you got in the car," Chris said the moment I walked into the house.

"I know. I just needed some solitude. I'm sorry."

Chris stared at me for a moment and gently pulled me into his arms. "This is wearing you out. I think you need an escape." He kissed my lips before releasing me. "It may benefit Camilla and Riley to see someone that can help them cope with their grief."

"That's not a bad idea." I put my oversized handbag on the counter and sat down. I was tired and all I had done was go to drop off Riley and make their dinner. At two in the afternoon, it already felt like six in the evening. Emotional wear could be so exhausting. I hated to say it, but I needed a nap. Chris had been waiting for me to get home to spend time with him and all I wanted to do was sleep. I felt horrible. "Babe, I think I need a nap."

"Perfect. I think you do too. Go on upstairs. I'll make sure Alisa is situated for the week."

"Okay," I said, a little skeptical. My husband was too eager to jump in and help. He had to be up to something. Right now, it didn't really matter. I just wanted to lie in my bed.

I went into the family room where Alisa was folded on the couch with earbuds stuck in her ears watching some movie on her iPad. She jumped up and ran to me. After a tight squeeze, I released her and her attention went right back to the screen. I couldn't wait to get to my bed. Slipping out of my clothes, I climbed into bed with my underwear on and thought of Camilla as I drifted off to sleep.

"KERRI." Chris's whisper reached into my subconscious. Then I felt him nudge me. "Wake up, Babe."

Disoriented, I looked around, blinking. "What time is it?"

"It's seven."

My eyes grew wide. "P.M.?"

"Yep. Get up. Take a shower, put this on and meet me downstairs in twenty minutes."

"Huh?" I blinked. "What's that?"

"Just do what I said." The mattress shifted when Chris got off the bed. "See you downstairs."

I pulled back the covers and swung my feet over the side of the bed. I sat there for a moment, not believing I'd slept over four hours. I figured I would nap for an hour or two at best.

Doing as Chris had instructed, I showered, put on the short strapless sundress and started down the stairs. Delicious aromas met me at the bottom. In the living room, Chris had set up a bistro table from my garden outside and covered it with white linens. In the center were two candles and a bottle of wine chilling in a stainless steel cooler.

Chris led me to the table.

"You spend so much of your time taking care of others and working, and we can't seem to find the time to go on that trip we've wanted to take, but I want to do something special for you. This is your time."

"Aww!" At first, I held back the tears that filled my eyes at his words, but then let them flow. "Thank you, honey. This is wonderful."

"After dinner I have something else for you."

"Wait!" I looked around, inclining my ear towards the family room, our daughter's favorite place outside of her bedroom. "Where's Alisa?"

"She's with your mom. She's going to take her to school tomorrow. We'll call her in a little while to say goodnight before she goes to bed."

"But she has—"

"Orchestra tomorrow. I know she took her violin with her."

"And—"

"Gym. I know. She had her sneakers with her."

Wow. Chris had thought of everything. I felt incredibly blessed at that moment, but in the next, I thought about what it would be like to lose him. Poor Camilla. I checked my emotions because tonight was about me. I would check on Camilla and Riley later to make sure they ate.

"Looks like everything has been taken care of."

"Yep! Because I'm good like that!"

I shook my head and smiled for the first time today.

Chris served one of my favorite dinners. Sea Bass, garlic mashed potatoes and roasted asparagus, and to my surprise, it was absolutely delicious. He topped it off with a slice of cheesecake. I knew I'd regret it, but I let him feed me the entire decadent dessert, even scraping the remnants from the saucer with the side of the fork. I wondered if he prepared this meal or picked it up from my mother when he dropped Alisa off, but I didn't ask. It didn't matter anyway.

After we finished the first bottle of wine, I felt lighter. Chris led me by the hand to the dimly lit family room where he had a massage table set up in the middle of the room. Beside it was a smaller table with another candle, oils and lotions. Smooth jazz seeped from our home theater speakers and the static image on the flat screen was one of a beautiful seaside paradise.

Sensually, he peeled me out of my clothes and carefully helped me onto the table. I lay face down and he began rubbing vanilla-scented oil into my back. Either the oil was heated or my skin was growing hot because by the time he reached my behind and the back of my legs, I was on fire both inside and out. Chris massaged my feet. The feeling was so euphoric I forgot that I was actually at home.

Chris turned me over and then removed his own clothes. Lovingly, he kissed my lips, massaged my shoulders, moved along to my breasts and kissed each nipple. He continued on to my waist and legs before parting them and sliding his tongue along my heat. The fire that started with the first touch of his hands consumed me completely and had me grasping at Chris with an urgent sense of need. Chris gently put my hands back at my side.

"This is about you, remember?"

Returning to the task at hand, Chris continued lapping at my center until I clawed at him and screamed his name. He feasted on every part of me before leading me up the stairs to our bedroom so we could both get our fill of one another. Between kisses and thrusts, Chris continuously whispered, "I love you." Reaching my fill of both affection and pleasure, my entire body tingled, then spasmed and erupted with a release so deliciously violent that it ripped through me like a tornado. The quivering took several moments before finally releasing its hold on my body. Meanwhile, I watched in delight at the way Chris's peak shot through him in waves, hunching his back repeatedly. Chris rolled and pulled me into his arms. We lay, our drenched bodies touching, our chests heaving until our heartbeats returned to their regular rhythm.

When we reached earth again, instantly, Camilla came to my mind. I wanted to know if she had eaten. Had she gotten out the bed? I know it wasn't fair to Chris, but I could no longer fight the urge to check in on her.

"Let's call Alisa," I said, knowing that once we did that, I would then check in with Camilla, Riley, or Eve without seeming as if I was pushing him aside. I couldn't help but be glad that her fate hadn't found it's way to my house and that made me feel guilty. I never wanted to know what it felt like to lose your companion in such a way. I was so worried about her mental and emotional stability, knowing mine would probably be extremely fragile in the same position.

Chris reached for the phone and dialed Alisa's cell number. While they talked, I texted Riley and Eve to check in on Camilla.

She had taken my suggestion and had dinner with Riley and Eve, but was now back in her darkroom, asleep once again.

I needed to find a more balanced way to be there for my friend without making my family—specifically Chris—feel like they weren't a priority. He'd started to give me sideways leers whenever my phone rang or chirped from endless texts or emails while we were supposed to be spending time together. He just wanted my attention, and rightfully so. He never minded sharing me with family, friends, or my demanding job, but quality time was valuable to him and in all the years that we'd been together, he's always made me feel like I was the most important thing in his life.

When I finally put my phone down, I received a call from Lyric. I decided I'd call her back in the morning until her unanswered call was followed by a series of texts stating that she needed to speak to me right away. Chris cast me one of those sideways glances with one brow higher than the other. I rolled over and wrapped my arms around him, letting him know that nothing mattered more than him right now. Besides, it was late. As soon as he began snoring, I eased out of his arms and checked my messages. What on earth did Lyric need to talk about at this time of the night? Not really feeling like dealing with any more drama, I laid the phone back down, plugged in the charger, and returned to my husband's arms.

CHAPTER 19

 aige

I WAS a career woman when Rick and I met, so the side of him I'd been witnessing lately had me thoroughly confused. Even after my mother agreed to come and stay with the kids while I traveled for work, he continued to give me grief. Here we were arguing again. I was so upset that I'd gone mute and just stared at him.

"What's the real issue here, Rick? Because it has to be more than who watches Scotland." I put down the knife I was using to cut the peppers because my hand was shaking.

"Why should you put your mother out of her way to take care of our kids while you're away? You said you were going to find a job that didn't interfere with you being home with our daughter. Now you're traveling for training and conferences and going into the office more than once a week at times. Maybe this isn't the job for you."

"I can't believe you're saying this." I went back to cutting the peppers for the pasta salad I was making for the dinner party we were supposed to attend later.

"I can't believe you agreed to this. You said you would stay home until Scotland reached middle school." Rick poured juice into a glass, returned the container to the refrigerator with a slam.

"Well, I changed my mind!"

"And that's what I have a problem with. It's not fair and I'm going to have to put my foot down."

I couldn't believe him. "You can't support me in this? I've supported you in every possible way in this marriage!" I realized I was waving the knife and placed it down again. "With the business, with Jayden, hell, you give your ex more support that you give me."

"Don't go bringing Maya into this. She has nothing to do with this."

I slammed my palms against the countertop. "Dammit, she has everything to do with this!"

Rick reared his head back looking confused. "Let's not go there."

"No! We need to go there! Every time she calls or comes to this door, crying another crazy song about needing money for this and that, you reach into our account and give it to her. She can come here unannounced and drop off Jayden anytime she feels the notion, and I'm the one making sure that child is clothed, fed, and in school on time. Not you! You move to the beat of any freaking drum she decides to play, allowing her to manipulate you like a damn puppet, but when I need your support, I catch nothing but attitude. I'm not Maya. I'm not okay with sitting around doing nothing while my ex takes care of my every whim as if he doesn't have a family of his own. You roll over and oblige her like an obedient puppy every time she comes swinging her huge hips in your direction. Now my job wants me to take one trip—one." I held my index finger high in the air. "And I've already taken care of everything to make sure things run smoothly for our child as well as Jayden, and you tell me you're going to put your foot down! I'll tell you what you can do with that foot!" I pushed the cutting board aside, removed my apron, threw it on the countertop and headed out the kitchen. "I can't do this anymore."

"Paige. Paige!" Rick kept calling, but I kept walking.

My body trembled with rage. I fought back the tears because I didn't want him to see me cry.

"Paige!" Rick grabbed my arm and swung me around just before I reached the landing to the stairs.

He looked straight into my eyes. His shoulders slumped. The tears came, wetting my cheeks. I looked away, folding my arms across my chest.

"Babe. I'm sorry. I don't want to argue with you." Rick sounded sincere. Still, I refused to look at him. "I...you're right. You do a lot. You've always been my backbone. We will work on this. I'll work on it—on me! I don't ever want you to think I don't support you and I don't want you to believe that Maya comes first."

"Humph!" I shifted on my feet.

"Just give me some time. It's just that Maya is..."

"Crazy!" Now I looked at him, waiting for him to deny that.

"I wasn't going to say crazy. She's a little difficult and you have to handle her in a certain way."

I glared at him. "You still don't get it. She does these things on purpose. She enjoys manipulating you so she can get just what she wants. The woman doesn't want to see you happy without her. She will do anything to make sure happiness evades you, and you're too stupid to see it. The second you stand your ground, all of that crap will cease."

"But Jayden."

"But Jayden, what? You don't think she sees what's going on? You already have a court-ordered living arrangement. Maya can't stop that. Nothing can stand in your way of being a good father to your daughter, Rick." I dropped my hands to my side, exasperated. "You need to start letting her know where she stands in your life because right now, it appears that she's at the top of the priority chain and everyone else falls somewhere far below her. Open your eyes, Rick. I don't know another wife who would have put up with playing second fiddle to their husband's ex as long as I have, and to be truthful, I'm getting pretty tired of it."

Not wanting to hear a word of one of Rick's weak excuses, I marched up the steps. Rick finally used his head and left me alone for a little while. Eventually, he slowly opened the door a crack and peeked through before venturing all the way into the bedroom.

I heard him taking slow steps and felt the bed shift when he sat. He sighed. I felt his hand touch my shoulder.

"We should be leaving soon."

"I'm not going." I threw off the covers and got out of the bed.

"Babe! Don't do this. What will my family say if you don't show up?"

"That's your problem. I don't care what they say. Take Maya with you." I knew that was a low blow, but the dig escaped my lips before I could pull it back. Rick inhaled sharply.

I headed into the bathroom and closed the door behind me. I was wrong for that and hadn't meant to go there. I walked back into the room. Rick was standing with his hands on his lips. The look on his face showed that his irritation meter was approaching dangerous levels. I could tell he was working hard to bite back a response.

He remained silent for a moment, eyeing me through tight eyes while I put the dress I had taken out to wear to his mother's dinner party back in the closet.

"I want you to come."

"I don't think I should."

"My mother will be upset if you don't show. It wouldn't be fair to her."

I sucked my teeth. He was right. His mother didn't deserve my indignation. I hadn't heard him move, but felt his hands on my shoulder. I turned around slowly.

"You are my top priority and you have my full support. Just give me some time to find a way to work things out and make it right." Rick implored me with his eyes.

Without answering, I took the dress back out of the closet and began to change. While Rick dressed, I went back downstairs to finish the pasta salad. It was one of his mother's favorite dishes. The house remained relatively silent as I wrapped her present and Rick and I prepared to leave. The car ride into Queens was mostly quiet, but Rick held my hand.

I was glad that the girls had spent the night at his sister's house to help get the place ready for their mother's gathering. This way, they didn't have to witness us bickering once again. I hated that this had become such a familiar activity in our home.

The girls came running to the car the second we pulled up in front of Loren's home in Rosedale. Loren ushered us in instantly.

"Come on," she yelled from the front door. "Mom is on her way here. I want everyone to be inside when she gets here."

Rick and I rushed out of the car, handing bags to the girls to bring inside for us. Taking me by the hand, we dashed inside, joining the other family members and friends. Minutes later, Rick's parents pulled up. His mother sauntered through the door like Queen Elizabeth on the arm of the king wearing a beautiful ivory dress with gold embroidery. We burst into the Stevie Wonder version of happy birthday and she danced, lighting up the room with her animated personality.

Scotland, Jayden, and Loren's two boys rushed to Saundra Thompson and lined up waiting to be squeezed in their grandmother's warm, inviting arms and lifted by their burly grandfather. Greeting everyone with hugs and kisses, Saundra made her way through the house, twisting and turning, showing off her beautiful outfit.

"Did you make my salad, honey?" she whispered as she hugged my neck.

"Of course I did."

She clapped her hands. "Yay! Thank you, my love." She moved on to give Rick a tight squeeze while I greeted Rick's father, Roy.

Loren called everyone to stand for grace so that dinner could be served. Then we all filed into a line to fill our plates with all the delectable food she'd spent days preparing. Music played, chatter and laughter ensued as a breeze flowed through the screen of the front door. We continued to eat and talk until we heard a loud voice pierce the excitement.

"Hey! Open the door. My hands are full."

It was as if the music stopped, scratching the record, and everyone paused.

"Well. Y'all just gonna let me stand here? Somebody open the door!" Maya yelled. "At least I didn't come empty-handed."

Loren looked at Rick. I looked at Rick. He shrugged and shook his head. Saundra shook hers as well and snatched in a sharp breath. Maya's nose was pressed against the door. She peered through the screen, looking for someone to let her in.

Jayden came running from the back of the house where the kids were gathered. "Mommy. You didn't say you were coming when you called me earlier."

Maya had done it again. Poor Jayden never knew when she had given her mother too much information.

"Don't worry about that. Just come open the door for me," Maya said, motioning with her head.

Jayden followed her mother's orders and Maya stepped inside holding a large pot.

"Whew. It's about time. What's wrong with you people?" She

waddled over to where Saundra was sitting. "Hi everyone! Happy birthday, Ma!" She gave her a kiss on the cheek. Saundra returned a contrite smile.

Everyone else looked uncomfortable. Maya didn't seem to notice. She stepped over Rick's, cousin's babysitting on the floor. "Loren. I made that rice your mom used to like. Where should I put it?"

Loren sighed. "Bring it in here, Maya."

I narrowed my eyes at Rick who shrugged again and mouthed, "I didn't tell her." I was ready to go. If I didn't respect his family so much, I would have slapped Maya with a few choice words. Instead, I kept my composure and gave Rick a "see what I mean" look. It was time for him to reel that woman in. She had been barging past boundaries for years, but lately, the liberties she was taking were becoming much more audacious.

Low chatter filled the room. Undoubtedly, they were whispering about Maya's unexpected appearance and it made me sick.

I moved next to Rick and whispered, "Are you going to say something to her?"

"I don't want to cause a scene in Loren's house."

I glared at Rick, pressing my lips together. Walking out of the door now would be an indication that Maya had won. I couldn't do that. Besides, I was here for Saundra and I was invited. As much as Maya tried to send messages about how she still belonged to this family, she was the only one who subscribed to her insolence. Showing up uninvited to family affairs didn't help make her point. From the looks on everyone's face and the whispers that floated around the room, it made her look foolish.

Maya was in the kitchen with Loren finding a space for the rice she'd made. Rick's aunt, Glenda, his mother's closest sister, plowed through the door in her usual flamboyant flair carrying a cake box from Saundra's favorite bakery.

"Hey everyone! Sorry I'm late." She blew air kisses around the room and pulled her sister into a tight embrace. "Girl! You don't look a day over fabulous!" She turned around to the rest of us. "Who looks older?" Knowing that she was, laughter erupted, but no one dared answer. She waved off her joke and stopped short, the smile falling off her face.

All eyes followed her line of sight to Maya, who was stepping over the same baby toward Glenda with her arms outstretched.

"Hey, Aunt Glenda!"

Glenda reared her head back and parked her hands on her hips. "Girl! *Who* invited you?"

CHAPTER 20

 yric

I TOLD Candy about Cypher's surprise visit. She suggested we find some brutes willing to rough him up and teach him a lesson. Knowing that wouldn't stop Cypher, I called Kerri to get insight on dealing with an ex that had stalker potential. I figured working in reality television could have given her some insight. Some of the people on the shows she worked on had issues too. I was careful not to give too much information. I wanted to handle this the right way. When she called me back the next day, she jokingly asked if I had any brothers or cousins I could send after him. As an only child whose mother had estranged relationships with family, that wasn't an option. Kerri also strongly recommended I file a police report. That wasn't going to work either. Nate could never know that Cypher had been to our house.

That led me to handle the situation my way—the only way I knew how. It would take a visit to prison. The trip would take hours, so I told Nate that Candy and I had planned a girl's day out starting with spa treatments. I left early the next morning. When I got to the dank facility, I groaned. It had been almost a year since my last visit. A lot had changed since then. A callous officer barked all kinds of instructions to the group of visitors entering with me. Inside, I endured further humiliation as they had me remove my shoes and cardigan. The floor felt like it hadn't been cleaned since the last brick was laid. We were ordered to empty our pockets and turn then inside out and then walk through the metal detectors.

I cringed as they felt and prodded every crevice of my body to make sure I wasn't trying to smuggle anything that the detectors may have missed. Once I finally made it inside, I was led to a small square table that was so low my knees bumped against it. I had to sit sideways. Correction officers were posted along the walls while some patrolled the aisles.

The locks clicked and the steel door rumbled as it rolled open and inmates poured into the large room in search of their visitors. I didn't see her. My hands grew damp. I rubbed them and I continued to watch the prisoners enter. Maybe she didn't feel like seeing anyone today. I wondered if anyone else ever came to see her. That probably wasn't likely. Maybe I should have written her a letter to let her know I was coming. I'm sure she wasn't too happy about the fact that I hadn't come to visit in a long time.

Suddenly there she was. Though hardened, her face was still pretty. Her slick hair was pulled back into a low ponytail that hung to the middle of her back. For a woman in her late forties, she was shapely, even in a drab white t-shirt and gray sweats. She paused when she noticed me, and cut her eyes. For a moment, I thought she would turn around and go back, but she pressed forward, taking her time to get to me.

Justine sat down and several moments trudged by before either of us spoke. She looked me right in my eye. Fortunately, I didn't detect anger, but I did see disappointment. She glanced down at my wedding rings and raised a brow.

"So how's married life."

"Good, I guess."

She didn't respond right away. Instead, we listened to the murmurs of the many voices around us.

"He treats you well?"

"Yes." I lowered my head slightly, suddenly feeling guilty for living so well while she was in here.

"Good." Justine sat back and stretched. "Your wedding was the talk of the jail. They knew you were my daughter. It would have been nice if you visited afterward. What brings you here today?"

"I wanted to see you."

"Hmm."

Justine may not have believed me, but it was true. For some reason, I'd missed her more lately than I had when she first left. "How are you doing?"

"The best I can in this mansion. I never have to cook and I still have three hearty meals a day." Her sarcasm was still intact. She shrugged. "It is what it is."

"Did you get the stuff I sent a few weeks ago?"

"I did. I do appreciate your monthly care packages, but I'd much rather see your face."

Now I felt ashamed. "I'll do better, Mom. I promise. We've been so busy."

"You're working again?"

"No, but I have been traveling with Nate for business." I immediately regretted telling her I wasn't working. She looked even more disappointed.

I knew what she was thinking and she was right. There was no reasonable excuse for me not to visit more often. She'd always been a great mother. I couldn't look at her. She took my hand in hers and I knew I was off the hook.

"I'm sorry." My eyes watered and stung. I blinked back the tears. "My ex is trying to blackmail me."

Calmly she sat back. "Why?" I expected coolness from her. She never riled easily.

"He's a blacklisted artist and he wants me to talk Nate into giving him a deal. He threatened to reveal stuff about my past if I didn't. He emailed pictures to me and threatened to leak them on the internet."

"Who's this? Cypher?" I nodded. "So what! Maybe you'll end up with a reality show. Ha!"

I cast a deadpan look. She dismissed my worry by waving me off. "I could lose Nate," I said.

"Are you scared of this guy or something?"

I didn't answer at first. "A little."

"Where does he live?"

I told her Cypher primarily lived in L.A. but frequented Atlanta and New York. I also gave her all of the details about him recently showing up at my house. We quieted every time one of the offices passed by our table.

"He's desperate and it sounds like he's all talk. Call his bluff!" Justine said.

"I'm not sure about that, mom. I've seen him..." I paused, remembering being party to some of his takedowns. "...do some horrible things to ruin people when he didn't get his way. I don't think calling his bluff would be wise on my part. If you could see all the crap he sent me in that email. Nate doesn't know all this stuff about my past and I'd like to keep it that way."

"Then what are you going to do?"

I threw my hands up. "I don't know. If I go through with this, it can ruin my marriage, and if I don't, it can ruin my marriage."

"What do you want me to do?" Ma asked.

"What can you do?"

"Let me look into it."

"Thanks, Ma!" I felt somewhat hopeful. I may not have been the best daughter, but she was still my protector.

For the rest of our visit, we caught up on what had been happening with us in the past year. I continued to apologize for my lack of visits. She told me they would be moving her to a correction facility closer to home since the end of her sentence was coming up. I couldn't believe that more than a decade had already passed. I promised to be there for her when she was released. After all, she was in there because of me.

CHAPTER 21

erri

"I spoke to Camilla for a little while when I dropped Riley off this evening."

"Yeah?" I picked up my plate and offered to take his and Alisa's. "How did she look?"

"Better." Chris rose and followed me to the sink.

"Mom, dad." Alisa interrupted. "Can I go to my room now?"

"Yep!" Chris answered. Alisa hopped over to us and kissed our cheeks.

Chris began filling the sink with water and squeezed in some dish detergent. I reached for the drying towel hanging on the handle of the oven.

"I hope I haven't been coming across as inconsiderate. I can't imagine how hard this must be for Camilla. I just need you to put yourself first sometimes...and me too. Nevertheless, that's just me being a little selfish. As for you, I hate seeing you run yourself into the ground because you're so busy taking care of everyone else."

"I'll admit I need to work on balance."

"I see how you helping Camilla has affected Riley. This was a huge loss to her as well. Aaron was a good guy. I really liked him and I liked the way he treated Camilla and my daughter."

"You're right." I nudged Chris aside to fill the tea kettle. "Tea?" I asked, raising the kettle a little.

"Sure. I see things are heating up at work."

"Yeah. We just finished post-production for the Society Wives reunion show, which was mayhem. At least all of the civil suits between the women were dropped. Some of them have even become friends. Some are still arch enemies. Those women are something else. I hate to see them going at it."

"What about the one who hit the other one and knocked her out cold?"

"Oh, them! Can you believe they're friends now, teaming up against the others? It's such a circus sometimes. I've pitched some other show ideas. I want to do more than reality, but that's all these networks seem to want. I loved my job. I almost feel stuck."

"That's too bad."

"How's work for you? We've barely talked about your job lately."

"Not much going on. My days are not as adventurous as yours."

The tea kettle whistled and I poured two cups along with a slice of my mother's apple crumb pie. Chris and I sat at the table.

"I'm glad that Camilla finally went back to work. She needed to get out of that dark hole she's been nestled in. Eve paid for a cleaning service to come clean and air out the house.

"Has she done anything with Aaron's belongings yet?"

"Nope."

Chris sighed, taking in a forkful of pie.

"I know. I was thinking about having her over for dinner this weekend. She hasn't ventured out beyond work. It would be nice for her to be surrounded by friends."

"That sounds cool. Will it be just the girls? I can go golfing or something."

"Hmm." I paused for a moment. "It would be nice to have everyone, but would that make Camilla miss Aaron if all of the husbands came?"

"Maybe it should just be the girls."

"Maybe so."

Chris and I sat at the table chatting for a long while after we finished our dessert. Conversation had always come easy for us. When we first started dating, we talked all night and were exhausted at work the next day, but then we'd do it all over again the next night.

"Is there any pie left?" Alisa said, peering at the crumbs on our plate.

"Sure." I got up to get her a piece. "It's almost bedtime, so after you eat this, brush your teeth and get in bed!"

"I will."

I poured Alisa a glass of milk and she joined the conversation. I couldn't remember the last time I was able to share a simple moment like this with my family. I loved every second of it. When the doorbell rang, the three of us just looked at each other.

Chris looked at his watch, then at me. "Were you expecting someone?"

I shook my head, looking just as confused. "I think one of us should answer the door."

We laughed. We'd been enjoying each other's company so much we didn't necessarily welcome the interruption.

"I'll get it." Chris dragged himself from the chair and headed for the door just as the bell rang again.

I stood when I heard Camilla's voice and Riley's quick steps toward the kitchen.

"Hey, Riley! Long time, no see," Alisa teased. It had only been a few hours ago that she and her dad had dropped Riley off at home.

I rounded the table and hugged Camilla as she entered the kitchen. "Hey, hon. What brings you over?"

"I just felt like getting out. I told Riley to jump in the car. We rode around for a while with the windows down so I could get some fresh air and we ended up here."

"Well, come on in. Mom made one of her apple crumb pies this week."

"Oh! I want some!" Riley squealed.

"Me too!" Camilla said, sitting down.

I pulled two saucers from the cabinet, poured one cup of tea and one glass of milk and set them on the table. Chris returned to the kitchen and planted himself in the spare chair.

"How are you doing, Camilla?"

"Okay," she said around a mouth full of pie. Her eyes rolled back and she held her hand to her mouth to keep crumbs from falling. "This is amazing. Your mother's pies are the best."

Riley moaned. "Isn't it!" Taking her last bite, she placed her plate in the sink and ran off in search of Alisa.

"Speaking of your mom, I'd love to speak with her. I need to know how long it took her to get over the loss of your dad. I don't think I'm handling this well at all."

"Oh, Camilla!" I walked to her side of the table and wrapped my arms around her.

Chris took one of her hands in his. Tears began to flow, but she wiped them away.

"I know it won't happen overnight, but I just need to talk to someone. I've never felt so lonely before in my life. Sometimes I wish it would have happened after the wedding because then I would have one more thing to hold onto—his name." Camilla's shoulders shook. "I'm sorry," she said through her sobs.

"No need to apologize. Aaron was a great guy. He's worth every tear you have for him."

"Thanks, Chris."

Camilla exhaled. "I didn't come here to cry. I just needed to be around someone."

"I'm glad you came. Do you want more tea?" I asked, already heading toward the kettle.

Camilla shook her head. "I've had enough. Too much caffeine and I'll be up all night."

"I wish."

"What do you mean by that?" Camilla asked.

"I could drink a cup of coffee and take a nap. I think my system is so used to being in high gear that I'm immune to external stimulants. Caffeine does nothing for me, right Chris?"

"Yep! You should see her when she tries to 'work late.' She'll drink the strongest coffee she can find and still fall asleep across her laptop."

"Ha! Oh! My goodness. That's hilarious." Camilla's smile was like a ray of sun through the clouds after the rain. I longed to see her smile even more.

After a while, Chris left us and headed to the bedroom. I checked in on Alisa and she was already asleep. I sent Riley to her room and promised to make sure she got to school in the morning. I had a feeling Camilla wasn't going home anytime soon.

When I got back to the kitchen, Camilla was sitting right where I had left her.

"Should I go?" she asked, hunching her shoulders sheepishly.

"No. Of course not! I already told Riley to go to bed. She has clothes here. There's no rush. She can grab her books on the way to school tomorrow.

"Got anything stronger?" Camilla held up her teacup and giggled.

"Of course!" I pulled a bottle of cabernet from the wine refrigerator and grabbed two glasses. "You know they say it's good to have a glass before bed."

"I'll take a glass before breakfast these days."

"Camilla!" I scolded and laughed.

We enjoyed our wine in companionable silence. Camilla was the first to speak.

"I realize I'm going through phases."

"How so?"

"When Aaron first died, I was angry. I couldn't believe God allowed that man to come into my life..." she took a moment to catch her breath. "...let him love me the way he did, and then snatch him away just days before we were to get married. I never thought it was possible to feel this much pain and still live." Tears rolled down Camilla's face again. "But then I just wanted to find the darkest corner, roll up into a ball and stay there. Light irritated me because it reminded me of happiness and I was so far from being happy. Then I went from being angry to incredibly sad—the kind of sadness that covers you like a blanket and refuses to let you go. I miss Aaron so much." Camilla paused, hugging herself and shaking her head. Tears dripped down her chin. "I would get up in the middle of the night and put on his clothes or spray them with his cologne and hold them close to me. Now I just...wish I were numb so I couldn't feel anything at all. If it weren't for Riley," Camilla took a sip of her wine and held her glass in the air. "I would drink all day to chase the loneliness away."

Camilla's words broke my heart all over again. I said nothing because I didn't know what to say, so I held her hand and sat there like that for a long while.

"Kerri."

"Yes. Camilla."

"Promise me you'll take care of our Riley." I shook my head vigorously as tears fell from my eyes.

"Of course. She's my daughter too."

"And don't let me become an alcoholic."

The lump in my throat almost choked me.

CHAPTER 22

aige

I HEARD Rick's car pull up into the driveway and groaned. I loved my husband dearly, but had spoken very few words to him since the incident at his sister's house this past weekend. We had argued all the way home, and been short with each other since. I believed he should have pulled Maya aside and said something to her about showing up at family gatherings uninvited. Since it wasn't his house, he felt it wasn't his place. Then I said things to him I probably should have never said, but I was beyond upset. Regardless, telling your husband he is spineless is always out of order.

I stopped turning the chicken when I thought I heard two sets of footsteps entering the house. I turned just in time to see Jayden drop her book bag by the door.

"Hey, sweetie! How did we get so lucky to have you here today?" Jayden fell into my arms and I hugged her tight.

"Mommy didn't come to pick me up today so they called daddy." She stepped over her bag and took off her shoes.

"Oh! Okay," I said, tightening my eyes at Rick, who shrugged. "Well, give mommy a call to make sure she's okay."

"I did. She's not answering." Rick placed the car keys on the hook by the door. "Mommy's probably not feeling well," Rick added. I rolled my eyes and headed back to the kitchen.

"Dinner is ready. Are you hungry?" I tried to maintain some semblance of cheer in my voice for Jayden's sake.

"Starving!"

I shot Rick a tight glare. "I was talking to Jayden."

"Yes, ma'am!" Jayden responded.

"Go wash your hands and get your sister from her room."

"Okay!" Jayden sang down the hall as she ran off.

I tilted my head to the side and snarled at Rick. I was so irritated. The situation with Maya just seemed to be escalating and Rick did nothing about it.

His hands went up, "Look, Paige. I don't want to argue. I don't know what happened with Maya. What did you want me to do? Just leave Jayden at the after school program? Do you have something against my daughter?"

My head whipped around so fast I was afraid I'd caused a case of self-imposed whiplash. My mouth fell open. "Don't you dare make this about Jayden! I love that child as if she was my own, and you know that. This is all about Maya playing games —pulling those puppet strings."

"Well, she's here now. What do you want me to do?"

I threw my hands up in frustration and headed back to the stove.

"You don't get tired of this crap?" I felt him right on my heels. Rick pulled apple juice from the refrigerator and took a long gulp right from the bottle. "Rick!"

"What?" He lifted the empty bottle. "It was at the end. Why waste a glass?"

I took several deep breaths before pulling four plates from the cabinet. "Did you even bother to call her to find out what happened? Is she sick or just MIA?"

"She's not answering."

"Did you stop by to see if she was home?" I asked while spooning rice and veggies onto each plate.

"I came straight here."

I shook my head, rested one hand on the counter and the other on my hip. I needed a moment. "Are the calls going straight to voicemail? Or did the phone ring a few times?"

"It rang. Why? Does it matter?" Rick looked thoroughly confused.

"She's sending you to voicemail, Rick. Stevie Wonder could see that she's playing you for a fool!"

"I don't want to talk about this right now. Okay. I'm done with this whole conversation."

"Oh!" I let out a sinister laugh. Rick glared at me. "You never have a problem being firm with me, do you? Why don't you try that with Maya one of these days?"

Rick had just sat down but then stood abruptly. "Enough, Paige!"

I glared back, tossed the dishtowel I was using to carry the hot pan of cornbread, and stomped out of the kitchen. I felt the urge to scream. If I stayed in that kitchen near Rick another second, I would have done just that.

"Where are you going?" he called after me. "Dammit!"

I marched to my bedroom, threw on some leggings and a tank top, and headed to the gym. I didn't even bother to say goodbye to the girls. I knew they would eat—especially since their plates were half made.

On the way, I decided to ride by Maya's house. I wasn't sure, but with the lights shining through the living room window, it looked like she was home. The new car Rick had purchased for her was sitting in the driveway. My anger blinded me, and then

I realized it was hot tears. This was too much to deal with. Then crazy thoughts began to taunt my mind. Were Maya and Rick sleeping together? What kind of power did she have over him? Would this ever change?

I reached the gym before I knew it. Heading for the treadmill first, I ran for a half-hour then went to the weight benches to release some of the aggression that had taken hold of me. Clearly, I was struggling because I was inexperienced and unable to focus. A shadow emerged and Blair's taunt body and bulging muscles loomed over me. He took hold of my barbell, and with a voice as smooth as silky chocolate said, "Let me help you so you don't hurt yourself."

Immediately I sat up. "I don't need your help."

"Either my help or an ambulance, because the way you're doing that, you're going to hurt yourself."

I wiped sweat from my upper lip with my forearm, not caring if I looked sexy or not. Blair, on the other hand, looked like the poster boy for *Fit and Sexy* magazine.

"Here," he urged. "Lay back. I'm just going to show you the right form, so you don't cause any injuries."

I looked at him for a second, sucked my teeth and laid back. Blair fit my hands around the bar properly and had me adjust my width. Then he spotted me as I did three sets of fifteen reps. I had to admit, it felt different. With arms that now felt like noodles, I sat up.

"Thanks. I'm sorry for being so rude before."

"It's not a problem. I come to the gym when I need to work out some stuff too."

I laughed. "Am I that transparent?"

"That and the fact that you were grunting like you want to hurt somebody!" He looked pensive for a moment. "You know what? I have the perfect workout for times like this. Come on!"

Blair grabbed my hand and dragged me to the opposite side

of the gym. With my hand in his, I felt like I was doing something naughty. A slight pang of guilt flashed through me.

"Here, put these on." I eyed the boxing gloves with one brow raised. "Trust me. You'll love this. It gets the frustration out and it's a damn good workout."

I followed his lead. He put on pads to protect his hands and told me to punch with each hand and then kick. He demonstrated and I mimicked what he'd done.

"Again...again..... again. One more. Yes!" he coached.

It was exhilarating. He showed me another combination with three punches and a knee and a kick.

"Ready?"

I nodded my head vigorously. "Yes!" I was excited.

"Now, before you start, think of what made you upset and really let go."

"Okay!" I bobbed a little and wanted to weave but felt silly. I repeated the combination he showed me ten times.

Blair showed me one more set of moves and by the time I was done with those, I was drenched in sweat. He walked with me to refill my water bottle.

"Oh! My goodness! That was so invigorating!"

"I take it you've never taken kick-boxing before."

"No, I haven't. I only started coming to the gym a few months ago. I decided I needed to get in shape. I was doing well until I stopped losing weight." I took long sips between speaking until all of my water was gone and I had to refill the bottle again.

"Have you been sticking to the same routine?"

"Basically. It worked before."

"It's time for you to change up your routine."

"I'm so new to this. I have no idea what to do." I looked around. "These machines are so intimidating."

"They can be when you're starting out, but I could help you."

I felt a slight tingle in my stomach. That probably wouldn't be the best idea—especially not while I'm at odds with Rick.

"Thanks, but I wouldn't want to impose. I'm sure I could just hire a trainer with the club."

"Have you seen the trainers here? They're all kids. You need someone who knows how to train people in your age range."

I just smiled and looked at my ring finger.

"Oh. You don't have to worry about me."

"Are you saying I'm not attractive?" I teased, twisting my lips then laughing.

"No!" Blair held his hands up in surrender. "It's not like that. You're one fine woman but I respect marriage."

I couldn't believe how my cheeks burned at his compliment. It had been a long time since a man told me I was fine. I wasn't sure how to respond, so I said nothing.

After a few moments of awkward silence, Blair pulled out his card. "I train part-time.

My offer still stands."

"Thanks, Blair." I took the card with every intention of tossing it. "I think I've done enough for one day. I need to get home."

"Yeah. Take care."

I smiled. For some reason, I didn't move right away. "Good night." Finally, I uprooted my feet from the spot they were stuck in and made my way to the door

When I pulled into the driveway at home, Maya was at the front door picking up Jayden. She was talking to Rick. From Rick and Maya's body movements, I could tell they were engaged in a heated exchange.

I stepped between them. "Hey, Babe!" I kissed his lips as if I hadn't just stormed out of the house two hours before. "Maya." I tossed her a curt greeting.

When she didn't respond right away, I planted myself directly in front of her. "Hi, Maya!"

"Hi, Paige! Gosh!"

"That's better!" I walked through the door but didn't go far. I wanted to hear what they were saying.

"Rick. I told you I had an appointment."

"So you don't call or anything? What would have happened if the school couldn't get me on the phone?"

"They got you, right? You're her father. What's wrong with you jumping in when I can't get to her?"

"Ugh! That's not the point. I don't do that to you. I have other obligations."

"Jayden is one of our obligations. What? She's not as important as Paige and your little Scotland?"

"Maya!" There was a warning in his tone.

"I'm ready." Jayden came running from the room with her backpack dangling from one shoulder and her shoes in her hand. "Bye, daddy." Rick leaned over and kissed the top of her head. Jayden ran to me in the living room. "Bye, Paige." We hugged and I could hear Maya suck her teeth through the door.

When Jayden got to the door, Maya snatched her, pulling her outside. "That's not your mother, you know."

"She's my stepmother," Jayden said matter-of-factly."

"Unfortunately!" Maya shot back.

I marched to the door. Rick pushed it shut. His eyes pleaded with me to let it go. I gnawed my bottom lip trying to decide if I should. Cutting my eyes at him, I headed for the shower instead. After checking on Scotland, I climbed into our king-sized bed and drew as close to the edge as possible. I didn't even want Rick to touch me by mistake as we slept. Rick stayed close to the edge on his side as well.

Minutes passed and neither of us had fallen to sleep. We laid there, listening to each other, breathing without speaking.

"I have a question." I finally said. "And I want you to be honest."

"What is it?"

"Are you sleeping with Maya?"

The bed shifted abruptly. Without looking his way, I could feel Rick's eyes boring into me through the darkness.

"I can't believe you asked me that!" Making a fuss of turning his back to me and ruffling the covers, Rick plopped down on his side so hard the mattress bounced and he pulled the duvet up to his chin. Eventually, he fell asleep once his ragged breathing slowed to a steady pace. I lay there wondering if all of that actually meant no.

CHAPTER 23

yric

I WANTED to go outside and flatten Nate's tires, but I had no idea which car he was driving. Since he had been traveling so much lately, I planned a nice evening for just the two of us, but yet again, his ex and the evil twins trumped my plans.

"Why do you have to go?" I couldn't believe I just stomped my foot. Even I had to admit my pouting was getting outlandish, but I think there was something about it that Nate adored even though he looked at me as if I had lost all of my scruples.

"Are you serious, Lyric? She's my daughter. It's her engagement party and her soon-to-be in-laws will be there. Must you ask?"

"Well, why does it have to be at Vivian's house?"

"Why does it matter?" Nate held his forehead.

I didn't care how frustrated he was. I wanted him to stay at home with me.

"Why can't I go with you? I'm her stepmother. They should meet me, too."

Nate cocked his head to the side and looked at me as if my question was the most preposterous thing he'd ever heard.

"I wasn't invited?" I stood with both hands on my hips. They were just jealous of me. All of them! Nate didn't answer. He stepped into his slacks and stuffed his shirt inside. "I guess that means I'm not invited to the wedding, either." I plopped on the bed. "How long are you staying?"

Nate stopped dressing, closed his eyes, and breathed in and out slowly. "For the entire event, why?"

"Why can't you just go for a little while?"

"Lyric, Babe." Nate came to me and held my face in his hands. "I'll be back as soon as possible. We will spend the whole day together tomorrow. We'll shop, eat, and dance, whatever you want to do. Nate gently kissed my lips.

I pushed him away. "Don't patronize me, Nate."

"Oh, we're using big words now." Nate chuckled.

"That's not funny. You act like I'm not smart. I have a degree, just like Vivian."

"Ugh! I wasn't saying that. It was a joke." Nate went back to getting dressed.

That tailored suit fit his broad shoulders and slim waist perfectly. It looked like he was about to hit the runway instead of attending a family gathering. I thought I wouldn't like it when gray hairs began randomly sprouting in his hair and goatee, but those silky strands mingled with jet-black hair against chocolate-colored skin made him look even more handsome.

Now I really didn't want him to leave. Vivian might decide she wanted him back. Now that I had him, I had to keep him.

"Really. Can you just go for a little while?" I sauntered over to him and ran my finger down his lapel and over his groin. He hissed. "I've been waiting to be with you all week." I poked my lips out. Nate smiled. I pressed my body against his. Then I slipped my hands behind his neck and pulled him to me. "Come on." I pleaded with him between kisses.

"As tempting as this is. I have to go."

I covered his lips with mine. Immediately, our tongues danced a wild tango. His arms slid around my waist and I ground my hips against the growing response between his legs.

"See. He doesn't want to go." I palmed his erection, loosened his belt, and unbuttoned his pants.

I kept going because he didn't stop me. Even if I couldn't convince him to stay, I was going to send him over there with me on his mind. I squatted low enough to be eye level with his lower head and took his firm heat into my warm mouth. Nate gasped and then guided my motions with his hands on my head. It didn't take long for him to grunt through his release—it never did. I bet Vivian couldn't accomplish that with her prudish self.

Urgently, Nate scampered toward the bed, his pants at his ankles. He laid me on my back. After a few licks, he entered me, maneuvering his hips like the champion he was. I squeezed my walls, creating suction. A primal sound rumbled from his belly through his throat and erupted out from his mouth. He thrust harder. Together, our bodies tumbled over the edge, filling the room with cries of pleasure. Erotic bliss ripped through me, causing me to thrash under Nate's body. He planted soft pecks across my breasts until euphoria released its hold on me, allowing my body to become still and my breathing to return to normal.

Nate breathed as if he'd just sprinted in a fifty-yard dash. He stretched his hand to help me up. Together we went into our master bathroom to clean ourselves. When he was done, he pulled me to him and kissed me long and hard. A new spark ignited between my thighs.

"I've got to go, Babe. See you later."

I pouted. He frowned and pinched my nose before leaving me right there in the bathroom.

I hated the fact that he was going to be around Vivian without me there. I wasn't buying her friendly charade for a second.

I turned and shot into the bedroom in search of my phone. Just because I wasn't invited or welcome, that didn't mean I couldn't still be there in some way. I dialed Candy. Luckily, she was home and she came right over. I didn't plan to crash the gathering, but I wanted to see how big this shindig was going to be.

We jumped into the SUV and I explained the mission.

"You know you're crazy, right?"

"Whatever, Candy. Don't act like we haven't gone on similar 'missions' for you."

"Ha! Anyway, which way are we going?"

I directed Candy the entire way to Vivian's block. When we reached the house, she slowed down. We passed Vivian's house, crawling along at no more than five miles per hour. When we reached the end of the block, we turned around and rode past again, this time stopping for a few moments to see what was going on. Music floated down the street and luxury cars filled every crevice, including Nate's Ferrari. I couldn't see much of the back yard except for the white tents that had been erected. Helium balloons were placed across the front, letting everyone know exactly where the party was. After spying, but not really being able to see much, Candy and I aborted that useless mission and went out to eat.

After a quick bite, she dropped me off at home and zoomed back to Manhattan. I wanted her to hang out with me at the house, but she had to catch an early flight to Miami the next morning for a video shoot and really needed her rest. I flicked the light on as I walked into the house. It felt eerily large and lonely.

I went to the cellar, picked a random bottle of Moscato, grabbed some crackers and then some cheese from the refrigerator, and filled my glass to the rim. I flopped on the couch in the den and my phone dinged. Candy had texted to let me know she got home safely. While scrolling through my Facebook timeline, I wondered if Vivian or Nate's daughters actively used social media. Searching for their names, I found that they had already posted several pictures of their festivities on Facebook and Instagram. Those fools hadn't even blocked their profiles from people who weren't friends and followers. I was able to see everything they posted.

In several pictures, Sydney was cocooned inside some guy's arms. I assumed that was her fiancé. I continued scrolling, assessing perfectly placed poses and candid shots of people eating, drinking, dancing and laughing. Then one image caused my stomach to tighten, my back to straighten, and my eyes to taper into tight slits. Sydney and Sky flanked Nate in a chair and Vivian sat on his lap with one arm around his neck and the other raised high holding a wine glass. It looked like they were all taking part in a toast. Vivian's head was tossed back in the most carefree manner, and just like everyone else in the picture, her mouth was wide open as if the photographer caught them mid-laugh.

I closed out the app and tossed my phone aside. I finished the bottle I'd opened. All the while, anger simmered as I waited for Nate to walk through the door.

CHAPTER 24

erri

"Did they pick Riley up? Are they on their way? Where's Camilla?"

Chris held his hand up, indicating I should wait as he pressed the phone closer to his ear. I couldn't stand just hearing his side of the conversation. I wished he would have put the phone on speaker. If he had, I wouldn't be so anxious.

"Ok, honey.... Mama K is going over there... as soon as she drops Alisa off at dancing school...she's leaving soon...When? Okay. I'll have her call you when she gets there."

I was standing so close to Chris that when he ended the call and turned, he bumped right into me.

"So, what did Riley say?"

He sighed. "When her friend's mother came to pick her up, Camilla wouldn't get out of the bed. Riley said she thinks she was drunk. There were two bottles of wine on her nightstand when she went into her room that morning."

"Okay!" I whirled around. "Alissa!" I yelled towards the steps. "Come on, honey. We've got to get going." I turned back toward Chris. "I need to stop by the grocery store. I'll pick up a few things for Camilla's house and go there after I drop off Alisa.

"This is a lot for Riley to deal with. Camilla needs to see someone. If something isn't done soon, Riley is going to have to see a therapist too." Chris pressed his lips together.

"I know. I'm glad she's spending the weekend away with her friend, but I don't think taking Riley away from her mother will help either one of them. I'm really concerned. I thought that when she started talking more that things were getting better. Now she just goes to work, comes home, and drinks." I sat at the kitchen table and looked at my watch. "Alissa!"

"Coming, mommy!" I heard her in the distance.

"Something has to be done," Chris said. "I'm concerned for Camilla too, but I can't help but think about what Riley might be witnessing over there. I don't want my daughter to have to deal with that."

I walked over to where he was standing and placed my hands on his chest. "Babe. Riley is stronger than you think."

Alisa finally came barreling down the steps with her dance bag stuffed and tights hanging out. I waved her over, opened the bag, and pushed the tights inside.

"I'll call you when I get there, okay?" This situation was wearing the entire family down.

Chris walked us to the door. Alisa waved goodbye until we pulled down the block and couldn't see him anymore. After dropping her off, I was headed to the grocery store when a call from work came in.

"Kerri! Sorry to bother you on your day off, but we need you, now!" My director's frantic words toppled out her mouth before I could say hello.

"What's going on?" I pulled over so I could focus.

"We arrived at our location but have been fighting with the

folks here all morning. They're saying they never signed anything for us to use the studio for today's filming. If we don't get this footage today, it's going to throw us way off schedule."

"Are you kidding me? Who did you speak to?"

"I don't know their names, but they want the boss, and they're not budging. That's the only reason I called. Otherwise, I never would have bothered you."

"Midtown, right?"

"Yes!"

I pulled out, made a U-turn, and headed for the George Washington Bridge. "I'm on my way. Do you have the contracts and permits on you?"

"I'm sure they are here somewhere."

"Have them out by the time I get there." I ended that call and dialed Rick to explain what was going on and then asked him to go check on Camilla for me.

"Babe. Can't you just go when you leave the studio?" he asked.

"I have no idea how long I will be there. This could take hours. You know that. And, from the way Riley sounded, someone needs to get there ASAP."

After a while, Rick sighed and finally responded. "Alright." It was obvious Rick wasn't happy. He didn't take well to sentimental situations. His patience ran low.

"Thanks, Babe. I'm headed to the bridge. I'll see you later."

When I arrived at the studio, my entire crew was on the sidewalk. I pulled my car up and jumped out. "Did you guys ever make it inside?"

"Nope!" That was my cameraman, James.

"Here's the paperwork." The production assistant handed me two folders. The permits are in the one on top."

I rummaged through the documents in search of the name of the person who signed the contract. I pulled out the signature page and headed inside. A slight guy with a slick smile met me at the door.

"I'm going to tell you like I told them. There won't be any shooting happening here today. We have something else going on and don't have the space." He folded his arms and firmly planted his feet shoulder-width apart, punctuating his statement. "Unless of course," he rubbed his fingers together, "the price is right."

"Okay." I nodded.

He smiled at first, assuming I would be willing to put some money in his hands until he read my expression more closely.

"Then I hope you don't mind the crowd that's about to appear outside in the next thirty minutes."

The man twisted his lips. "Crowd? What crowd?"

"Of news vans and reporters." I opened the folder and looked at the signature before continuing. "Tony will be surprised to see his studio on TV when we announce we are suing him for breach of contract, and for letting the world know how you tried to bribe me."

"Hey!" He pointed a finger at me. "You can't prove that!"

"Wanna call my bluff? You see, I work in reality TV. No publicity is bad publicity for me, but you, Tony, and this place..." I didn't bother finishing my sentence. He got the picture.

I held up my phone so he could see I was on video chat. I made sure to run the camera past him so they could see his face. "And now everyone knows what the guy who tried to bribe the network looks like. Natalie!" I called out to the production assistant. "Get Tony on the phone."

"Wait!" My slick friend said.

"How long will all of this take?"

"All day and then some now that you've managed to delay us a few hours."

"Give me a moment." He ran off behind a closed door.

The muffled sounds of several voices and chairs scraping the floor could be heard through the walls. This guy was obviously getting some push back from whoever was on the other side of that door. I turned the face of the phone toward the room so my crew could hear and see. Moments later, he came back with a different attitude.

"Just give us a few minutes to clear things out here and you can bring your crew in."

"Okay!"

"Hey!" he said. I turned back to him. "Tony doesn't have to know about any of this, okay?"

"As long as you cooperate, no one has to know anything." I went back outside where the crew was gathered and let them know everything was fine.

"Where's the talent?" I asked.

"In the trailers."

"Okay." I ran down to where the trailers were parked and checked in on our stars. None of this mattered to them because they were still being paid.

It took a while, but eventually, we saw several men, looking as slick as the one who tried to bribe us, along with a few girls who looked half their age exit from the side of the building and get into several black cars. There was obviously more going on at Tony's studios than he knew about. I didn't ask any questions because I didn't want to know.

Once our crew was able to get inside and set up, I headed back home. This hiccup had taken much less time than I anticipated. As close as I lived to Manhattan, traveling between there and home was always an unpredictable hike. Traffic at the bridge was backed up due to an accident. I called Chris to see if he'd made it to Camilla's but didn't get an answer. I hoped he did.

Stopping for a few staples for both homes, I raced over to Camilla's without being pulled over for any of the many traffic violations I committed. Somewhere along the way I stopped counting the number of stop signs I blew.

I felt a sense of relief when I pulled up to Camilla's house and saw Chris's car outside. Grabbing the lighter bags, I jogged up the walkway. I'd send Chris out to get the heavier bags. It was difficult to knock with my purse and those grocery bags in my hand, but I managed. Obviously, I didn't tap loudly enough. Remembering what Riley had said, there was a good chance that Camilla was still in her bed and her room was all the way in the back of the house.

"Duh!" I said to myself aloud. I put the bags down and dug in the purse for the key I'd had since the day after Aaron passed. Eve made a set for both of us since we were the ones checking on Camilla during the time she refused to leave the solitude of her bedroom. I slipped the key in the lock, pushed the door open and grabbed the groceries. I wobbled inside and kicked the door closed with the back of my foot.

"Hey! I'm—" the words were cut off at the sight of Camilla on top of my husband on the couch in the living room saying, 'please' in a way that sounded like a desperate cry. Her lips moved sloppily over his mouth.

At first, they didn't notice I was standing there, unable to speak. The only movement came from my blinking eyes. The bags I was holding hit the floor with a loud thump and Chris' head snapped in my direction. His hands were pinned between them, but with a quick swift shove, he knocked Camilla off him and jumped to his feet. Camilla sat on the floor holding her head.

"Babe, this isn't what you think." His shirt was disheveled and his hands stretched out toward me.

My mouth was finally able to move, but words still refused to come. My chest heaved like an asthmatic. I found my voice and screamed, "What the—"

"Babe!" Chris sounded distraught.

Rage propelled my feet into motion and I charged Chris, knocking him onto the couch. Camilla was still on the floor in some kind of stupor. I dragged her to her feet, made her face me and her eyes grew wide.

"Kerri! Oh my goodness, Kerri." She looked at Chris and then back at me. "What happened?"

I lunged at her and pushed her hard. I was amazed at my own strength. She landed on top of Chris. I wanted to pummel them both. Instead, I headed for the door. The walk seemed so long. Stepping over the groceries, I picked up my bag and kept moving. I was floating. I didn't feel my feet touch the ground. I made it to my car, ignoring them as they called out my name. I heard Camilla's sobs and Chris' pleas and curses but refused to acknowledge either one of them. I found myself inside the car behind the wheel, but didn't remember actually climbing in. I blinked back tears, started the car and took off. I didn't know where I was going but kept driving anyway. All I heard was my mother's words repeating in my head, "Some people never forget what good lovers feel like and every now and then, some folks get...*nostaaaaalgic*." Had their friendship all these years been a sham?

CHAPTER 25

 aige

"Ugh!" I still hadn't lost any more weight. I stepped off the scale and kicked it, injuring my big toe. *Bad idea*, I thought as I hopped around on one foot, holding the other in my hand. The toe trumped as if it had its own heartbeat.

Everything was frustrating me—Rick, Maya, and the extra pounds that clung to me like a gang of leeches. I pulled on some leggings and a tank and was happy to notice that at least they fit a little looser. I never understood how my body could lose inches and my weight continued to be unaffected.

"Scotland!" Grabbing sneakers, I headed for her room. "Let's go, girl. You're going to make me miss my spin class and you're going to be late for your violin lesson."

"I'm coming, mommy!" I walked in to find Scotland leaping around her room, trying to pull on a pair of jeans.

"Scottie, are those jeans too tight?"

"No!" she claimed, still yanking them on. "See?" she said,

panting once she finally got them up. "They're super skinnies. Auntie bought them for me. They're not tight."

I pulled on the waist and the fit was snug, but she was right, they weren't tight. I gave her a sideways glance.

"Well, I don't know how much longer you're going to be able to wear those. Let's go."

Scotland grabbed her instrument and trotted down the steps. Rick was tinkering with his tools inside the garage when we got into the car.

"See you later." There wasn't much enthusiasm in my salutation.

"See you later." He gave me a quick peck and swallowed Scotland in a bear hug, spun her around, and kissed her cheek.

"Bye, daddy."

I hated it when Rick and I were like this. It had been happening more frequently lately, but I was going to stand my ground. Something needed to be done about this Maya situation and if Rick wasn't going to initiate some changes, then I needed to. Prior to our latest fallout, I'd always taken the high road, never wanting to aggravate him further since Maya was already such a nuisance. Unfortunately, my passive approach hadn't gotten me anywhere besides being angry and tired. Absolutely nothing changed between Rick and Maya. In fact, she became bolder.

He was so angry with me when I asked if he was sleeping with Maya that he hadn't said a single word to me the following day. When I asked again the following night, he yelled, 'No!' Our communication continued to be strained. We had tried talking things out in a civil manner this morning and ended up arguing again. Rick took to cleaning out the garage to put distance between us. At this point, we were both tired of quarreling, but couldn't find our way out of the cloud of tension that engulfed us.

I hoped that by the time I worked off my anger in spin class, maybe Rick and I could try to engage each other in civil conversation again later on.

The ten-minute ride to Scotland's music class took a half-hour due to an accident. I arrived at my spin class too late so I hit the stair climber before the weight machines. I smelled Blair's masculine scent before I saw him and wondered why I anticipated seeing him.

"Hey!"

"Hey!" I said, putting the barbell down.

"How have you been?" Blair rested his arm against the machine next to him and I couldn't help but notice how toned he was.

His smooth brown skin dipped and curved with every bulging muscle, like chocolate poured over an ice cream sundae. I thought about Rick's soft arms and abs and got annoyed all over again about how he kept turning me down every time I invited him to join me at the gym.

"Still not losing weight, so I guess I need to step things up a little." I didn't want to tell him I was mad at my husband again.

"Still nothing?"

"Nope."

"You're probably losing inches," Blair said, assessing me from head to toe. Usually, I would squirm under that kind of scrutiny, but I was surprised to find that I welcomed it. "Plus, you've been doing more weights, and muscle is heavier than fat, so don't get discouraged."

"I'm trying not to."

Blair parked himself on the bench next to where I stood. "Talk to me. What's your diet like and what have you been doing in the gym?"

Frustrated, I flopped down next to him and shared what I remembered from this past week. I told Blair everything I ate and all the classes I had been taking.

"Do more weights. Limit your cardio to no more than a half-hour and do more strength training. It seems that your body is accustomed to what you've been doing and it's not as effective. You should be eating protein after every workout and make sure you have some kind of veggies with every meal."

I nodded my head, listening intently. Blair was actually telling me things I hadn't heard before. Every time I shared my weight loss struggles with someone, they'd offer all kinds of solutions and swore they would make the difference. All of them failed.

"Okay! More protein, veggies, fewer carbs, keep up the strength training, and switch up my routine frequently. I'll try it out."

"I'll help if you let me." Blair read the skeptic look on my face and held his hands up innocently. "To get you started on the right track."

I huffed, and after a few moments of wondering if I wanted to be that close to him, I finally said yes and shook his hands.

"I'll show you a few different exercises and help you with a meal plan. Follow that and you should start seeing results again."

Rick led me to the mats near the rear of the gym and we did some work with a kettlebell. Then we hit some of the other machines I was always too intimidated to use and he showed me what to do with them. By the time he was done, I'd worked muscles I didn't know I had and my skin tingled from him touching my arms and legs to make sure I was positioned right.

"I have to admit," I started between breaths. "That was the best workout I've had in weeks."

"Now, let's get some protein in you."

We headed to the gym's juice bar and Blair ordered me a tasty veggie protein shake. As we sat, Blair wrote down a few meal options for me to consider during the week. I planned to follow his instructions exactly, hoping I would begin to see results once again.

"You know, sometimes I don't understand you women."

"Why?"

"If you ask me, I'd say you look damn good. I don't see where you need to lose weight. I can understand toning, but I love a woman with a little substance."

"Yeah! Lean substance!"

When Blair leaned back and laughed, I found myself noticing his dimples, strong jaw and perfect teeth.

Blair caught me staring and pinned me with a penetrating gaze. I noticed the gold flecks in his pretty brown eyes and the sexy way he held his lips together.

"Sometimes, I wonder what could have happened had we not gone off to different colleges."

My smile was my response. I didn't want to open my mouth and say something that could lead me down a path that a mad wife would later regret. My mind almost ran down memory lane, recalling the few dates we went on before ending up in different cities.

"I've often wondered if you were the one that got away. I mean, it's too late now." Blair paused. I didn't know if he was looking for me to give him some indication that there was still a chance. I lowered my head and slurped the remnants of my protein shake, making a loud gurgling noise. "But I have thought of you several times over the years. Imagine my surprise when I came to the gym and saw you."

"Yeah! Heh. I can only imagine. I can't believe you're single."

"I haven't found the right one. That could be my fault since I keep comparing them to you."

I refused to look at him. I stood, shook my empty cup and tossed it in the garbage and then grabbed my bag.

"Thank you so much, Blair. I'm going to put all of the information you gave me to the test. I hope to see some results."

"Paige." His voice was low. He reached out for me. Fortunately, my arm was just out of his reach. I turned to him and he said nothing.

A hint of longing sparkled in his eyes. At least, that's what I thought I noticed. As he sat there, lapping at me with those hooded orbs, I took notice of how he glistened and how his tank top clung to him, outlining his taut chest. I knew then that I couldn't have him 'help' me anymore. Especially when Rick and I were skating on such transparent ice. I could almost see straight to our marital doom. Despite how upset I was, I didn't want to cheat on my husband.

"Bye, Blair."

"Bye, Paige." I felt his eyes on me as I left.

CHAPTER 26

yric

"WHERE ARE YOU GOING NOW?"

"Lyric! You have to stop this. It's...ridiculous!"

I narrowed my eyes at Nate. "There was nothing ridiculous about wanting to know my husband's whereabouts."

"You already know where I'm going. Why are you acting like this?"

I was breathing so hard, my chest hurt. "Because I don't..." I clamped my mouth shut.

Nate dropped his shoulders, hung his head sideways and cast me a pitiful gaze. "You don't trust me? Is that what you were going to say?"

I refused to answer.

"What have I ever done to you to lose your trust?" Nate shook his head. His expression became strained as if his feelings were truly hurt.

I folded my arms across my heaving breast. It was Vivian I

didn't trust. She was too friendly lately and I think it's more than just being happy about their daughter getting married.

Nate shook his head and walked around the kitchen's center island to where I stood.

"Babe." He placed his hands on my waist.

I twisted out of his reach, averting my eyes. "I wasn't going to say I didn't trust you, Nate." I folded my arms.

He threw his hands up. "Then what's the problem? Help me understand. I haven't hidden anything from you. Vivian and I are paying for the wedding. Sydney wants to show us the venue to get our feedback. This evening is the only time that worked for everyone this entire week."

"Why can't I come?" Nate gave me a side-eye. Ever since he claimed that I acted out at Vivian's birthday dinner, he'd kept me away from her and the girls. "They don't like me, do they?"

Nate dropped his head back. "Lyric!" he pleaded with me in that one word. I know he didn't want to admit it. They couldn't stand me. I guess I could understand, but when were they going to get used to the fact that I was his wife now? They had to accept that someday. "So, I'm not invited to the wedding either?" I was pouting again.

Nate looked as if he didn't know what to say. "Babe."

I stared at him. "They despise me. Go ahead and say it."

Nate sighed. "I don't think they hate you."

"I don't care." I threw my hands up this time. "Go to your family," I said that word as if it tasted bad. "I'm just your wife."

"Lyric. Don't do this." Nate took a step toward me and stopped.

What could he really do? What could possibly change? Vivian and her tribe would never accept me or respect the fact that I was now Nate's wife. I hated feeling like they had all the advantages. They called, he came, leaving me behind all the time. As much as I was against it initially, I now realize it's time to make a family of my own if I am to hold onto my husband. I needed a reason to keep Nate home with me.

When Nate and I got married, I assumed that his kids wouldn't be a problem because they were grown. I was wrong.

Nate's phone rang and before he could snatch it from the counter, I saw Vivian's name pop up. I sucked my teeth. Nate answered, turning away from me and walking out of the room. I followed him.

"I'm coming...so I'll meet you there...text me the address...I told you I'll be there!" Nate raised his voice and I smiled a little.

It made me feel better when he spoke to her in irritated tones. Nate ended the call and snapped the phone onto his belt clip. He turned and bumped right into me, shaking his head.

"I'll be right back." Nate gave me a distant peck and left. I waited for him to walk out of the front door before I let the tears fall.

Taking to the stairs, I ran to my room and laid across my bed, crying and wondering what pictures the girls would put on Instagram and Facebook to torture me this time. I couldn't control the fact that every time they did something as a family, I took it as a personal dig as if they were purposely trying to throw their ties in my face. Sometimes I even regretted falling in love with Nate. When we first got together, he made me feel like the world revolved around me. He was captivated by me and by the attention I lavished on him. I remember walking into his office and he would practically salivate. He'd tell his secretary to hold calls or push back meetings, putting the world on hold for a little time with his kitty. He called me that because he loved the way I purred when we made love. Sometimes we did it right across his desk at work. Nate gave me everything I ever wanted. I felt powerful then. When I called, he came.

The day he trudged through my door looking dejected and telling me that she asked for a divorce was the happiest day of my life. I nursed him back to happy with some great loving and tricks that had him howling my name. I tried my best to remind him that he didn't need Vivian in the first place, and I waited patiently for that divorce to become final.

When I told him I was pregnant and suggested we should get married, I didn't expect much, but when he showed up a week later with a five-karat ring, I felt like Cinderella. Since money wasn't a hindrance, I planned our wedding in two short months. I pinched myself through every detail of planning. I was getting married—and not just to anyone or some mangy rapper. I'd caught the largest fish in the music industry's sea. The week after the wedding, I faked a miscarriage and blamed it on the stress from all the planning and travel.

I'd wake up some days with Nate's toned body sleeping next to me and shake my head. It seemed surreal. I had to marry him before he faded like a dream or a figment of my overzealous imagination. I couldn't imagine being anyone's wife, let alone Nate Delaney's.

My wedding was the most extravagant affair I'd ever attended in my entire life. I was sure to invite all the right people. They may not have been real friends, but the buzz they created still lingers. I felt like royalty. When we went house hunting, or should I say mansion hunting, I felt like we were shopping for our very own castle.

Now I feel like number three or four on his list of priorities. My reality as a wife isn't the magical fairytale I imagined. However, I loved Nate and intended to do everything in my power to make this work. I jumped off the bed, grabbed my purse, pulled out my birth control pills and tossed them in the garbage. The first pregnancy may have been a sham, but this time it will be real.

CHAPTER 27

erri

I WASN'T sure how long I'd been sitting in front of my house when I saw Chris peek through the blinds. I acted like I didn't see him and waited some more. We both waited. I guess it was to see who would make the first move. Would I get out of the car? Or would he be a gentleman, come to the door, and usher me in?

I didn't even know if I wanted to be ushered in. I wasn't sure if I was ready to see him. More than a week had passed and I still hadn't spoken to him, but I did listen to the long dejected messages he left me several times a day—every single day. Messages that said he missed me, that pleaded with me to come home so we could talk—so he could explain. Chris begged me to call him back, stop by, tell him where I was. Never once did he say he was sorry. That's why I hadn't called him back yet.

I spoke to my Alisa constantly and we texted like teens. I

didn't miss a beat in her life. She thought mommy was on a business trip. I told her I would be back this weekend, thinking it would give me enough time to get myself together so I could come back home and, at least, try to figure out what my next move would be. I had to go in the house. Alisa was waiting for me, but Chris kept peeking through the window.

I let my head fall back against the headrest. It felt like there was a hand inside my chest, squeezing my heart. This pain hurt physically. I would have gone straight to the emergency room if I didn't already know for sure that the pain was caused by my heartbreaking. That's why the blood flowed so savagely, so undirected through my veins. My heart no longer worked properly.

Water pooled in the wells of my eyes but didn't fall. I didn't want to cry. Didn't feel like doing that anymore. I couldn't even believe I had more tears to release after all the crying I'd done the past week. Who knew that it was humanly possible to shed so many tears? I should be dehydrated by now.

Chris was my hurdle, peeking out of the window, standing in the way of me getting to my daughter. I pulled out my cell phone to text her, thinking I could just have her come outside and meet me. There was no way to avoid the inevitable, though, so I tossed the phone onto the passenger seat.

Finally, I shut the engine off and opened the door. I put one leg out and stayed that way for a while. I willed the other leg past the door frame, but it stayed there for a long time too. Taking a deep breath, I hauled my body out of the car and slowly closed the door. Another breath and I started taking steps toward the front door of the home that I thought was perfect until a week ago.

"One foot in front of the other, Kerri." Had anyone heard me whispering to myself they would have thought I needed to be institutionalized. "Keep walking." Had I not talked myself through it, I would have gotten back in that car and drove to the hotel I'd been staying in. "Your baby's in there and she's expecting you." Another breath and then another. They helped me make it to the door.

With a few more feet to go, the door creaked open. Chris stood in the center of the frame, looking as if he hadn't slept in days. Gone was the handsome glow I'd always adored. Unshaven and gaunt, he stared at me through eyes that looked like a road map of red lines. I was happy to know that at least he was suffering too. That didn't make me forgive him, but it did remind me that I loved him more than I knew was even possible —even in that moment.

I stopped walking, leaving a foot of space between us. My chest felt like someone was sitting on it. Resentment dried my tears, for now. Despite him standing before me, all I could see was a distorted image of him and Camilla on that couch, but this time, they were bathed in a red hot glow. I wanted to leap the rest of the way and beat that miserable expression off his face. He didn't deserve to be distraught. I was the one betrayed.

"Are you coming in?" Chris spoke so softly. I almost didn't hear him.

I stood for another moment before walking past him, knocking against his shoulder.

Stepping into my own house felt unfamiliar. "Where's Alisa?"

"She's at Zoie's house. I let her go hang out there for a while."

I turned to leave and Chris blocked the exit. I folded my arms and avoided his imploring eyes.

"She knew I was coming."

"So did I. I told her she could go down the street and play for a while. I figured that would give us time to talk."

"What is there to talk about?"

"Kerri!"

I closed my eyes, hoping to hold back the tears. I didn't want to cry in front of Chris. I jerked away when I felt his hand on my arm.

"Don't. Touch me."

Chris took a step back and held up his hands. "Then, can you please sit?"

I did as he asked. It didn't make sense to prolong this. Stepping into the living room, I looked around. My absence was blatant. Dust bunnies settled underneath the furniture and in the corners. The curtains were drawn, leaving the room dim and gloomy. I wondered what else had been left unattended in the few days I'd been gone. The laundry was probably piled up too. I sat on the nearest chair.

Chris shoved his hands in his jean pockets and paced. I watched him move for a while. Finally, he grunted and turned toward me.

"It's not what you think, Kerri."

I sucked my teeth and stood.

"No!" Chris reached for my arms. I twisted out of his reach. "Don't go. Please. Sit down."

Glaring at him, I slowly returned to the chair.

"I didn't do anything to Camilla. When I got there, she was drunk. Riley was right to be worried. The entire house reeked of liquor. It was coming out of her pores. I was trying to get her to eat something. She fought me every step of the way. I got angry and poured the bottle of liquor she'd been drinking down the sink. She clawed at me, trying to grab the bottle from my hands." Chris pointed to the faded scratches running up and down his forearm. "That's when I grabbed her, hauled her to the couch. She was literally kicking and screaming. I forced her down and she started crying. I never saw Camilla act this way— ever. I sat down next to her and tried to calm her down. She started mumbling about how she didn't want to live without Aaron. She told me I was lucky to still have someone to love me."

Chris stopped talking, dropped his head and closed his eyes. I wanted to hear the rest, but remained quiet.

"Then she…she pounced on me, saying something about how she was so lonely it was killing her." Chris held his hand out as if he was reenacting the scene. "I was trying to get her off me without pushing her too hard. She kept calling Aaron's name, pressing herself against me. Then she tried to kiss me. I think she really thought I was Aaron in that moment—or wanted me to be. That's when you walked in." Chris sighed as if getting this out removed imaginary weights from his shoulders.

"Camilla was hallucinating? That's your excuse? I know what I saw Chris!" Anger spiked my adrenaline. I was on my feet, arms flailing as I cursed him over and over. "I know what I saw. She was on top of you with her shirt halfway over her head."

"Baby. I swear I was trying to stop her."

"Bull—!" I stomped.

"You can ask her. She apologized after she realized what she had done."

"I'm not asking her anything!" I headed for Alisa's room. "Where's my damn daughter?" I couldn't believe my own mouth, yet I couldn't stop myself from cursing. Anger had spiked my tongue, too.

I looked around Alisa's room before marching to my own. I couldn't accept the story that Chris had just told me and I didn't want to hear any more. Already, I had too many questions I wasn't prepared to consider the answers to. Chris was a burly man. How could Camilla overpower him enough to pin his back to the couch? All I could think about was what my mother said about old lovers. Camilla wanted to feel Chris again. I wasn't going to be stupid enough to believe she was hallucinating and that Chris was completely innocent.

I snatched another overnight bag from my closet and started yanking clothes from hangers. I didn't care how wrinkled they got as I stuffed them inside. Chris ran in and tried to wrestle the clothes from my hands.

"Kerri! Stop it. We have to work through this." He stood between the closet and me.

"Get out of my way." I tried to push him, but he didn't budge.

"Kerri!"

"Leave me alone!" I screamed. My hands shook. "Just get out of my way." My voice cracked.

"Kerri!" The desperate way Chris yelled my name made me pause. "Don't do this, please. I didn't do anything. Camilla needs help."

My eyes squeezed into slips. I glared at him. "Oh! Now you're defending her."

Without bothering to get more clothes, I grabbed the half-filled bag off the bed and marched downstairs.

"Kerri!"

"Tell Alisa, I'll be here to get her tomorrow," I yelled from the landing.

"Come on now, Kerri!"

By the time I got to my car, I was out of breath. Chris was steps behind me. I kept moving as if it didn't tear at my heart every time he yelled my name. I swung the car door open and tossed the bag into the passenger seat. I climbed in and Chris was at my door, holding it open.

"Stop this. What about our family? What about Alisa?" This time, Chris's voice wavered. I couldn't let his emotions send mine reeling. I had to get away—fast.

"Don't bring Alisa into this. You and Camilla are the problems. You caused this."

"What about Riley?"

I stopped breathing for a moment. Alisa would be just fine. Riley, I wasn't so sure. That poor girl was dealing with so much. I snapped out of the moment I was having and pulled on my car door.

"You should have thought about Riley then."

Chris had maneuvered his body between the car door and me. I couldn't close it. He was still rambling about me coming back inside so we can work this thing out. Refusing to hear him, I stuck the key in the ignition and lurched forward, clearing enough space to close the door. I sped off, looking at him through the rearview mirror.

CHAPTER 28

 aige

"PAIGE, I don't want to argue anymore."

I looked at up my husband and the serious expression on his face. I was so caught up in what I was reading I hadn't even heard him walk into the room. I set the magazine aside and sat up.

"I don't want to argue anymore, either." I meant that. I was tired of it. The more we quarreled, the more I thought about Blair. Spending time with him in my head had become my escape. I hadn't been to the gym since the last time I saw him there. With my emotions so frazzled, I didn't trust myself around him. "So, where do we go from here?" I truly hoped Rick had an answer.

"Maybe we need some time away—shake things up a little. I don't know. I just feel like we need to reconnect. Just me and you."

"I think that's a great idea." Pushing the covers back, I got up and walked over to Rick. He put his arms around me and held me as if he never meant to let me go again. "We still have to deal with the issue of Maya. That way we can really move on. Don't worry. I'll put on my big girl panties and promise not to get mad."

"I will too. I mean, I'll put on my big dude drawers—I don't wear girly panties."

Rick and I laughed together for the first time in weeks. It felt like we'd already made a little progress.

Rick stared at me for a few moments. "What?" I asked.

"I'm sorry about all the grief I've been giving you about the trip for your job. Do what you have to do. I'm sure everything will work out. It always does." Rick paused. "I love you and I don't think I've told you enough lately."

That was it. I melted in my husband's arms. Rick held my face in his hands and kissed me. It had been so long since I felt my husband's lips.

"When do you want to go on our little trip? We need this so bad."

"What do you have planned for this weekend?"

"Rick!" I pulled back and looked in his face. He was serious. "I don't have anything, but I thought you were doing inspections this weekend."

"That kind of work can wait. Right now I need to work on my marriage. This is more important."

Rick captured my lips right in the midst of my smile. This time, his kiss weakened my knees.

"So, what do you have in mind?"

"Can you call your mom and see if she's available to watch Scotland? We can drop her off along the way."

"On the way to where?"

"I don't know yet. Just call and see if it's okay to drop her off in about two hours. Tell her we will pick her up tomorrow night."

I literally giggled! Something I hadn't done in years. Rick was reminding me why I loved him so much. Rick's hand slid from my lower back to my bottom. He squeezed my cheeks and kissed me so long he left me panting.

"Call your mom and get Scotland together and I'll work out the details for our little spontaneous excursion."

I skipped to Scotland's room and peeked in. She was still curled into a tight ball in the center of her bed. The way she slept always made me laugh. I decided to give her a few more minutes before waking her. Saturday was her only day to sleep a little later. She'd have to miss her activities for the day, but her attendance was so great one day wouldn't hurt.

Back in our bedroom, Rick was studying the screen on his laptop, checking a travel site for last-minute deals. I grabbed my cell and called my mom. She was excited to have Scotland for the weekend and told me to bring clothes for her to wear to church Sunday.

"Got it!" Rick's outburst startled me as I rummaged through my closet for something to wear.

"Got what?"

"I know what we're going to do. Pack a bathing suit."

Excited didn't properly describe what I was feeling. It seemed the rip in our marital fabric was already repairing itself. I couldn't wait to get my husband alone later that evening and started working on a few plans to show him how much I appreciated him. This weekend was going to be magical.

Within two hours we had packed and dropped off Scotland. She whined all the way to my mother's house about why she couldn't go with us. But, by the time my mother rambled through the list of all the things they were going to do together, she'd forgotten about being upset.

The nearly two-hour ride to our destination flew by, reminding me of when we first got together. We blasted the radio and sang along with our favorite artists, laughing and joking all the way there. We arrived in the Pocono Mountains around noon. Rick had booked a room with one of those heart-shaped tubs.

The plan was to drop off our bags and head out for some fun. The thick, sexual tension in the elevator was like foreplay. We made it inside the room just before our loins exploded on us. Rick grabbed me, pulled me in tightly against the length of his full-blown erection, covered my mouth with his and kicked the door closed with his foot.

We tore off each other's clothes and tossed them, leaving a trail of scattered garments across the floor. By the time we reached the bed, we were in our natural glory.

"I love you, baby," Rick said breathlessly. His chest heaved.

"I. Love. You. Too." I kissed him between each word.

Sweat covered his chest with a light sheen and made it difficult for me to hold his back. My internal temperature gauge felt close to a thousand degrees. I wanted my husband so badly it blinded me. I felt giddy. When Rick took my nipples between his teeth, a spark shot through me and hit every nerve ending in my body. He descended from my nipples to my navel and on to the warmth waiting on him between my legs.

When Rick's tongue touched my bud, I screamed. I did not know if the folks in the next room could hear me or not, but I didn't care.

"That's right, baby," Rick hissed.

With my eyes squeezed tight, I saw nothing. I could only feel the incredible sensations that raced through me at Rick's skilled command. Then I felt nothing. When I opened my eyes, Rick was over me, staring.

"Paige."

"Yes. What?"

Rick's expression was serious. It scared me.

"I'm sorry, baby. I'm so sorry. I love you."

"I'm sorry too."

Overcome with emotion, I cried. Rick kissed them away, reminding me between each kiss that he loved me and never meant to hurt me. The delicate state of our emotions changed the way we made love. Gropes became tender caresses. Hard, hungry kisses became gentle yet passionate explorations. We held onto one another as if letting go could cost us our lives.

Rick stared into my eyes as he entered me, fitting perfectly. The passion behind the long, deliberate, deep strokes became ultra-sensitive. We refused to take our eyes off each other. Every touch was magnified, seeping deep into our souls until tears glistened and fell from both of our eyes.

"I love you," Rick repeated over and over. We wept. I reaffirmed those words back to him as we rode a beautiful wave of deep love.

The smooth, steady rhythm of our lovemaking broke. Rick's eyes rolled back. We collided with each other faster and faster until decadent pleasure ripped through us. My nails dug into Rick's skin. He grunted. I howled. Together we bucked until we exploded. Rick collapsed on top of me and I wrapped my arm around him, caressing his back. He continued declaring his love for me with sweet whispers in my ear.

Despite our robust plans to shop, zip line, horseback ride, and swim in the resort's grand pool, we never left the room. Instead, we indulged in one another's lost files, becoming reacquainted in the most intimate ways possible. From the afternoon into the night, we snacked, watched TV, held each other, and made love.

We spent the next morning in bed and finally left the room to have a decent meal and take in some local excursions before heading back home. The only thing we'd left undone was talk about our problems.

CHAPTER 29

 yric

"YOU SENT GOONS AFTER ME!" Cypher pushed his way into my house seconds after Nate's departure.

"What?"

"Don't play games with me, Lyric! You know what the hell I'm talking about."

"Cypher!" Lyric remembered her mother's comment about seeing what she could do.

"You threatened me!" Cypher came so close to me I could feel the heat of his breath against my face. His pointed finger was dangerously close to my eye. I blinked, already feeling the potential sting and dry pain after his possible poke. Cypher growled. I mean, he actually growled! I flinched before I could try to mask my fear.

"That wasn't a threat. I promise you if you don't do your part, I'll ruin you."

"Cypher, calm down!"

Stepping back, he paced circles in my foyer like a lion preparing to antagonize prey. I finally closed the door. I didn't want to be behind closed doors with Cypher, but couldn't risk anyone seeing him in my house.

At first, I stood there watching him pace, wondering how to get out of this situation. If the air was flammable, Cypher's breathing would have set my entire first floor on fire. He looked crazed. His chest heaved, his tight jaw twitched, and his eyes held contempt.

"Cypher!" Hands behind his back, he glared at me.

"I'm running out of time. Handle your business tonight or the same thing that happened to the goons you sent will happen to you."

Cypher marched out of my house.

I couldn't move. What had happened? I needed to speak to my mother and the only way to do that was to go and see her.

I canceled all my plans for the day and headed to visit Justine. She could tell me what happened. I drove the few hours it took to get to the prison and when I arrived, they advised that my mother had been transferred. I almost broke down right in front of the officer who delivered that blow of a message. He gave me the new facility, which was actually closer to home but was still a few hours from where I was.

Why hadn't my mother told me she was being moved so soon? Now I was annoyed and scared. Either way, I needed to get to her today even though it would make me late for my dinner plans with Nate. He was pacifying me for all of the time he'd been spending with his family.

As I drove, the vicious look Cypher laid on me with his finger pointed in my face kept appearing in front of me. Now that my mother's plan had made him angrier, I was losing hope. Cypher knew that I had something to do with what happened. He knew where Nate and I lived. There was no hiding. I knew what he was capable of from my days with him in the past. I was going to have to help him whether I liked it or not.

Being alone never bothered me before. Heck! I was an only child who'd secretly lived by myself from fifteen until eighteen so that I wouldn't be forced into the foster care system after my mother was sentenced. I did whatever I had to do to survive without fear. Yet, Cypher's visit rattled me so much that riding alone in the car made me feel vulnerable. I kept looking in my rearview mirror, worried that he'd show up behind me. I flinched every time a car sped past me. I called Candy just to keep my mind off my own paranoia.

"Hey, Girl!" I tried to sound cheerful as if the blood wasn't pumping through my veins at warp speed.

"Hey!" Candy sang.

"What are you so happy about?" I asked, hoping to absorb some of her glee.

"I just booked a shoot with Jase!" Candy squealed and giggled.

"Oh. My. Goodness! Are you kidding me?" Jase was Candy's favorite R&B singer. She'd pined over him for years. "Video or photo!"

"Both! First, I was called for the album cover, and then he had them call me back for his new video! Ah!"

Candy's great news calmed my nerves. "And you didn't call me?"

"It literally just happened. The second I got off the phone, you called. I am so excited. I can't believe he actually asked for me."

"Wow, Candy. That's huge. Maybe he likes you. Oh!"

"Ha! Girl! Don't get me started. I'm waiting for my new boo to come and get me right now."

"Wait a minute! New boo? What about...never mind."

"Exactly! Never mind. I'm done with rappers, by the way."

"Is it someone I know?" Despite my excitement, I looked at

my navigation screen, which said I had another hour and ten minutes to go. I sighed. I tried to keep the merriment in my voice for Candy's sake. I certainly didn't want her to think I was raining on her happiness parade.

"Probably. He's more of a 'behind-the-scenes' kind of guy. It's Jason Whitman."

I gasped. "Of course, I know him. He's been in the industry for years. Isn't he in his thirties or forties?"

"Yep! The men our age don't know how to treat women. You should know that better than any of us."

Candy's comment brought Cypher and Nate to mind. "You can say that again."

"When you first started messing around with Nate, I thought you were crazy because he was so much older than us. Now I understand. Jason treats me like no man has ever treated me before. I think this might be the one, Lyric. I can see this becoming something big. Maybe you'll get to be my matron of honor soon."

"Really!" I put my hand over my mouth to stifle my laugh. We both giggled. I was happy for her but sad for myself. With what I had to do, I wasn't sure how it would affect my relationship with Nate.

I chatted with Candy for the rest of the ride, counting down the miles and minutes until I reached the prison. Inside, I had to endure the same humiliation I experienced at the previous facility. Being searched, yelled at by officers warning visitors not to try to bring in any contraband.

I sat in the massive room and twirled my thumbs as I waited for my mother. Since it was a weekday this time, there weren't as many visitors. The day was half over and I needed to get back home before Nate started asking questions. I was at least two hours away from home and it was already four in the afternoon. I tried not to fidget but failed. My mother would notice for sure.

"What's wrong with you?"

My mother startled me. I was so caught up in my thoughts and fidgeting that I hadn't seen her come in. She swung one leg over the bench and sat at the small table.

"It didn't work. Whatever you did, it didn't work. Cypher came to my house this morning and threatened to do to me whatever he thought I tried to do to him. What happened, Ma?"

Justine shook her head and sighed. "I asked a friend for help. I just found out things didn't go the way they planned. One of his boys is in the hospital...critical condition...broken ribs...and a busted eye that he may never see out of again."

"Oh!" I held my heart when it jumped into a frantic rhythm. I could hardly breathe. "My goodness." I wiped tears with my trembling hands.

"Stop crying."

I couldn't. There was nothing I could do to stop the tears from flowing. "If I don't help him get a deal, he's going to hurt me."

"No, he won't." My mother waved away my concern as if I'd just told her that a boy was bullying me in grade school.

"Ma! This is serious." Instinctively, I stood. One of the officers started in my direction. His serious expression and no-nonsense walk made me sit back down. He retreated back to his post near the corner of the room. "What am I going to do?"

"Stop worrying. They're..." Mom looked left and then right, gauging how close the guards were. "...going after him again."

"But in the meantime, he knows where I live. He said he's running out of time. I need to do something, Ma!"

Justine threw her head back and grunted. "Just let me think. I'll see what I can do."

I stood again. "Forget it, Ma! I'm just going to have to do what I can."

"You can't give in!" My mother was on her feet too. Guards moved closer but stopped a short distance away. "That will mean he wins. You give a man like that a win and he'll always come after you."

"I don't have a choice. I need to go. Bye, Ma!"

"Lyric! Let me handle this."

I kept walking. "You've done enough. Thanks, but I'll take it from here."

"Don't let him scare you, Lyric!" Her words hit my back. I stood without turning as I waited for the guard to open the imposing steel door.

I held my tears until I reached my car. Behind the wheel, I let them go. My phone dinged several times, in different tones, indicating I had several types of alerts. One was an email from Cypher with no subject line. Pictures were attached. I had to wait until my hands stopped shaking before I could tap on the icon to download the images. Two of them depicted a badly beaten man lying in a hospital bed. Another email consisted of pictures of me entering a hotel with a brown envelope. I remembered that day. Cypher asked me to deliver something to his 'friend'—a new artist with Nate's company that was rising fast. The public loved him. Hours later, the news reported that he'd been arrested and charged with murder. A murder Cypher probably committed himself.

In the body of the email, Cypher said, "Get it done." The last thing he sent was a text with a picture of me bent over near a pole from my 'dancer' days. *There's more where that came from.*

I wailed, not caring if anyone heard me. Cypher had left me no choice. I had to help him. What else was there for me to do?

CHAPTER 30

erri

I WAS HEADING toward the bathroom when I heard a knock on my hotel room door. I hadn't called room service, nor was I scheduled to check out, and I sure wasn't expecting any visitors. I couldn't imagine who it was.

"Mama K!"

I turned around, wondering if I'd heard correctly. It sounded like Riley. The knock became more insistent. I looked through the peephole and Riley was standing there. I swung the door open, pulling her into my arms. That's when I saw her. Camilla was standing off to the side, looking as if Riley had just dragged her off the street. My heart plunged at seeing only remnants of the Camilla I knew. Her dry hair hung lifelessly, without shape or style. Bright eyes that used to sparkle now looked like someone had turned off the lights behind her irises. Her cheeks were drawn and her skin clung to her high cheekbones. Even in the oversized, dingy sweatshirt and leggings that were once a deep ebony, I could tell she'd lost a considerable amount of weight. Camilla wrung her ashen hands and had yet to look me in the eyes. She kept her focus on the carpet.

"Can we come in?" Riley's sweet voice seeped into my cognizance.

"Uh…sure." I couldn't refuse my stepdaughter.

Riley touched my arms lovingly as she walked through the door. Camilla squeezed past, trying not to touch me. Taking the chair near the window, Camilla sat and stared outside. Riley flopped on the bed. I couldn't sit, so I paced. Camilla still wouldn't look at me. Despite being outraged at what she'd done, my heart went out to her. She looked awful.

"How did you find me?" I asked when I was able to form words.

"Dad."

That was all Riley said. I wondered if Chris had sent them.

"Does Alisa know I'm here?" I held my breath waiting for her reply.

"I don't think so."

I exhaled. Finally, I sat on the bed next to Riley. Camilla still didn't speak. Looking out of the window was safer.

Riley put her arm around me and buried her head in my chest.

"I'm sorry for all of this, Mama K."

"Oh, baby! You have nothing to be sorry for."

"I'm just sorry about everything. Losing Aaron, and now whatever happened between you, mommy and daddy. It's tearing our family apart."

Apparently, Riley hadn't been told the whole story and if her mom and dad hadn't said anything, I wasn't going to be the one to tell her.

"What could be so bad that it had to break our whole family apart?"

I pulled back and searched Riley's face. Tears stained her

cheeks. I swallowed the raw emotions rising in my throat. "Honey, is that why you're here?"

"Yes! Since all of the adults in my life are acting like children, I figured maybe I needed to act like the adult and figure out how to get you guys to act like a family again."

I truly wished I could explain to Riley all that happened, but I was afraid she'd end up feeling worse. With no idea how to get past this, I didn't have any answers for her. Instead, I just held Riley in my arms, wishing life had never brought us down this road.

Riley's body shook gently and I knew she was crying again. I wished Alisa was here too, so I could hold her in my arms. I felt like a horrible mother. Selfishly, I had deserted her while I pouted in a hotel that was miles away from home. Chris was a wonderful father, and I knew he would take great care of her, but I was her mother. I was supposed to be by her side no matter what. Here I was comforting Riley through this, and she wasn't even my biological child. I had to go home.

Interrupting my self-scolding, Riley looked up at me. "Mom needs you. She needs help. I can't do this alone." Her sad eyes pleaded with me to return to the role of being the caretaker of the family. Everyone listened to me and often held off on decisions until I provided my input. "This can't be fixed without you, Mama K."

With those simple words, Riley reached inside my chest and tugged on my heart. Hearing sniffles, I turned to the window and saw Camilla's shoulders shaking softly. Her head was buried in her hands. I wasn't ready to comfort her, so I pulled Riley closer to me.

"It will work out, honey."

Riley's response was more tears. "So you're coming home?"

I couldn't look in her face and tell her no. Her brown eyes reminded me of her little sister. Both had inherited them from their father. I was still confused, hurt, and mad as hell, but I knew I had to do something.

"Yes, sweetie."

"Good." Riley pulled back. "That's a start." She stood and headed for the door.

I walked with Riley. Together we turned and looked back at Camilla, who had yet to move. Sensing that we were waiting on her, she kept her face toward the window and wiped the remnants of her tears. I refused to feel sorry for her. When Camilla stood, she kept her eyes on the floor and walked past Riley and me out the door.

Riley lifted to her toes and hugged my neck as if she were afraid of never seeing me again.

"I love you, Mama K."

I squeezed Riley tighter, cocooning her between my arms. "I love you too, Riley!" She held on for a while before letting go.

Camilla watched us hug. I sensed it. As I released Riley, my eyes connected with Camilla's for the first time since they'd arrived. I locked in, my eyes boring into hers. I couldn't look away. I wanted to find out something from those eyes. Receive some kind of confirmation that there was possibly some validity to Chris's version of the story, or was there something else— something that I may have missed all these years. I focused harder as if I could see more that way. All that stared back at me in those sunken, red eyes where light used to shine was pain--too much pain. I wasn't sure if it masked the truth, or if that was the truth. Camilla blinked, releasing the hold, and slowly lowered her head.

"Come on, Ma." Riley gently placed her hand in the small of Camilla's back. The roles had reversed. Riley was the adult now, Camilla was the distraught child. Camilla obliged by turning and walking away. I watched them until they turned into the elevator bank.

I stayed at the door a while longer, listening to the elevator ding and the doors open and close. Stepping back in the room, I closed the door and leaned against it before sliding to the floor, in tears once more. The visit rattled me and left me with more questions. How could I leave my children alone in this mess? They needed me.

When I was able to reign in my emotions, I packed my bags and headed back home. I wasn't going to make up with my husband. Not now, without knowing what Camilla's actions meant today. I wasn't any closer to the truth. If anything, I was more confused. My heart hurt for my girls, for me, and for Camilla, even though I didn't want to feel sorry for her. If I hurried, I could spend a little quality time with Alisa before sending her off to bed. It was Sunday. Perhaps we could take in dinner and a movie or go and get our nails done and talk about what I'd missed in the week that I was gone on my fake business trip. I owed her that much. I just didn't know what I would do once she went to sleep and left Chris and me to face one another.

CHAPTER 31

 aige

I THOUGHT things would change after Rick and I spent such a lovely weekend together, but I was wrong. So wrong! The week was going wonderfully until Maya showed up unexpectedly and took Jayden with her just as we were going to leave for a family dinner to celebrate Rick's birthday the other night. That put a damper on our outing because Rick really wanted to enjoy this with his entire family. Poor Jayden cried the entire time it took Maya to drag her to the car.

And now this—I pulled into the parking lot at my husband's office, prepared to take him for a nice lunch to make up for the horrible situation from the other night. Immediately, I spotted Maya's car. What was she doing here? I contained my annoyance as I greeted the receptionist and made my way up to Rick's office. I noticed how the employees eyed me worriedly as I headed upstairs instead of getting on the elevator. The moment I hit the landing, I could hear Maya's mouth.

I walked right up to Rick's office and opened the door. Maya's head whipped in my direction. She scowled. Rick's expression was one of pure exasperation.

"Hey, honey." Ignoring Maya's scowl, I walked over to my husband, gently kissed his lips and smiled as I wiped the remnants of my pink lipstick away. "Hey Maya," I said and watched her roll her eyes and suck her teeth while I took a seat in one of the large comfy chairs.

Maya folded her arms and huffed. "She needs to leave. This conversation is private!"

"Excuse me!" I raised up from the chair.

Instantly, Rick was by my side. A gentle touch on my shoulder let me know that Rick intended to take care of this one.

"Maya! Anything that has to do with Jayden is also Paige's business. She's her stepmother and has been instrumental in raising her for years now."

"She's nothing to my daughter. In fact, she's the reason I'm here in the first place. You know what?" Now Maya's buxom breasts were heaving up and down. "Forget it. Jayden won't be back. If you want to see her again, contact the lawyer."

Maya stormed out. The room seemed to shake with every angry thump of her feet as she marched out. Rick went after her. I stayed put.

I don't know why Rick was so nervous. She'd hurled that threat at him so many times before. When Rick finally returned to the office, a vein was visibly throbbing on the side of his neck. Tightly knit lips held back words he dared not say in any professional atmosphere. He slammed his office door hard behind him. Pictures and awards shifted on the walls.

"Babe!" I stood. "Calm down."

Rick paced up and down the carpet in his office,, murmuring in anger under his breath.

"Hey!" I touched Rick's shoulder this time. He fired a heated glare at me as if I had done something wrong. I pulled away as if his shoulder had scorched my fingers. I knew just how Maya could get inside you so deep it would make you mad at the world. "Let's go to lunch. That will make you feel better."

"Lunch!" he spat. "Maya just told me she is trying to take Jayden away from me. Lunch is going to do nothing to make me feel better!"

"Okay. Okay, but you do need to calm down. Let's go for a drive or a walk or something so you can get some air."

"I don't need air."

"Honey! Maya has threatened you with this before but never made good on any of those threats. She's just calling your bluff. Next thing you know, she's going to call you and ask for more money. Don't you see? It's part of her game."

"This is no game, Paige!"

"Fine, but stop yelling at me. I'm not the one who upset you. I'm just trying to help."

"Really?" Rick twisted his lips, cocked his head sideways and peered at me questionably.

"What, Rick?" *He can't be serious.* "The culprit just stormed out of your office. Don't take your anger out on me."

Rick took slow steps toward me. His eyes bore into me with every step. "What did you say to Jayden the other night?"

"What are you talking about?" I was baffled. "Where is this coming from?"

"Maya told me you said something to Jayden and that's why she came and got her the other night. Jayden feels as if you don't like her."

"Are you kidding me?" I was on my feet immediately. I would never have imagined Rick saying the words that were now coming out of his mouth. "And you believed that?"

"You treat Jayden differently than you treat Scotland."

From the inflection in Rick's voice, I couldn't tell if that was a statement or a question. The feeling of hot anger that I contained as I entered the building burst through my exterior. I was so full of rage that I felt my eyes could pop right out of their sockets.

"Are you asking me or telling me that, Rick?" The words slid harshly through my gritted teeth. Before he could respond, I exploded. "How dare you question me about how I treat Jayden. I have never..." my hands shook, "...ever..." my voice wavered, "...treated Jayden any different than I have Scotland. I have loved that little girl from the day she came into my life, despite her toxic, manipulative mother. I've had your back in this from the day you asked me for my hand in marriage. Maya started her antics way before that, and I still stayed by your side and now you're questioning me? How. Dare. You." I pointed my finger in his face.

Tears fell furiously. My heart physically broke. I could feel it in my chest. Gasping for air, I continued. "I have put up with everything that woman dished out and now you come questioning me?" I poked my own chest.

Rick's expression fell, but I couldn't stop.

"She has tried everything, and now that nothing has worked, she's trying to attack our marriage head on and you're allowing her to do it. You're allowing her to make you question me—my loyalty—my actions—my mothering!" I looked around for my purse and snatched it from the chair I was sitting in. I headed for the door. Rick stood in the middle of the floor blinking. My voice elevated to a high-pitched screech. "I thought you knew me better than that! Better yet, I thought I knew you! Maybe if I start acting like her I could get some respect around here!" Rick balked at that. I turned on my heels and left.

I was hurt when Rick didn't come running down the corridor after me the way he had with Maya. That was the sign I needed. I cried all the way to the car, wishing I had somewhere else to go besides home. When I got in the car, I just sat there bawling, hoping no one would notice. My marriage was slipping through my hands to someplace off in the distance, Maya, the wicked witch, was rubbing her clammy hands together, snickering. I even tried to think back to anything I said or did that could have possibly alienated Jayden, but came up with nothing. I shook my head. Those fools had me second-guessing myself. I treated her better than her own mother did.

I started the car and drove out of the lot. I had no idea where I was heading, but I knew that the last place I wanted to go was home. I ended up at the restaurant I had visited with Lyric and Kerri. Pulling over to the valet, I stopped and handed him the keys and went inside. I had no appetite, so why was I here? Mindlessly, I followed the hostess to a seat near the rear. It was perfect. I wouldn't have to see folks or be seen if I didn't want to. Shortly after, a petite waitress placed a basket of bread in front of me and I ordered a bottle of wine. No food. She left me alone. I appreciated her and decided to leave her a huge tip. I sat for a long while nibbling on bread so I wouldn't get sick from all the wine I was drinking.

Eventually, I called both Kerri and Lyric to see if either were available to meet with me. It was a Friday, so I assumed Kerri would probably be at work, but I tried anyway. As far as I knew, Lyric didn't work, but she didn't answer her phone. I put my cell phone down on the table and it buzzed. When I picked it up, I saw Blair's name. I hesitated but answered anyway—with counterfeit cheerfulness.

"What's wrong?"

I guess I didn't fool him. Instead of answering, I started crying.

"Where are you?" he asked, sounding genuinely concerned.

I told him.

CHAPTER 32

 yric

I ALMOST HATED that Nate was so wonderful lately. After his outing visiting reception halls with the evil twins and Vivian, he'd been extra nice. He wasn't upset when I got back late from visiting my mother and we had to cancel our dinner plans. In the past week alone, we'd gone out to some of my favorite restaurants. He took a day off and we hung out, shopped, and enjoyed each other's company. That day was therapeutic. I'd been pouring out the love lately, too. Fixing dinner—yes I cooked—and making sure he was comfortable when he came home from work. One night I cooked in lingerie. After we ate, we enjoyed each other for dessert.

Everything was great until I received a text from Cypher. The beauty of the past few days evaporated in a rush with one swipe on my cell phone. I hated feeling scared. When my mother left me alone at fifteen after being sentenced to fifteen years by that ornery judge, I had to learn to fend for myself.

There was no support system for me to fall back on. No grand-mother, aunties, uncles, no one. My mother proceeded to raise me from jail through letters, visits, and phone calls, teaching me how to watch my back and helping me become fearless. She taught me how to survive. As an overdeveloped teen, I looked much older than my age, so I lied on applications and worked to feed myself. I kept going to school and eventually graduated in the top ten percentile of my class. I had no friends because we didn't want anyone in our business.

Justine was strict, even from behind bars, but she knew that even conventional mothering couldn't save me from the streets without daily supervision. I struggled to pay rent on time so our landlord wouldn't come snooping around and find out I was living alone. Finally, a girl I worked with who always looked so well-put-together told me how much money she made as a dancer at the strip club. Life got better financially after I started dancing, but worse in other ways. I had to constantly fight off men and watch my back as I left the club at night to make sure none of them followed me home.

Mom told me to apply for college, guiding me through the entire process. She said with good grades and little income, I'd be eligible for grants and scholarships. She never knew that I danced to survive and eventually cover leftover tuition costs and books. One of the strippers introduced me to a more upscale club. She told me I was too pretty to work at the rinky-dink place I was dancing at. The owner at the other club hired me on sight but treated me horribly when I refused to sleep with him. He treated me even worse when I refused to sleep with some of his famous customers at their request. Again, the money got better, but life got harder. Despite my boss's ill-treat-ment, I made more money in that first month than I had ever seen in my entire life. Then one night, Cypher walked in.

I cringed even now at the reminder of how that bastard slithered into my life veiled as a savior. As an older, wiser woman, I never would have fallen into his snare. But as a naive and desperate young adult living on her own and trying her damnedest to survive in the pits of the hideous underbelly of New York City Streets, Cypher seemed like a knight rescuing me from a dungeon full of flesh-eating dragons.

I shook my head. I didn't want to think about the past anymore. I was a different woman now—a wife. My past wasn't pretty, but it was behind me. Well, it was until Cypher showed up. Now I had to figure out the best way to approach Nate about getting Cypher a deal. For a moment, I actually wondered how bad it would be if I had enough nerve to tell Cypher no. He had a few pictures of my stripping days and images of people he'd hurt. I'd survived his beatings before. Then I thought about the one picture of me going into the hotel room of that singer Jay Collins from Karma Records right before he was charged with murder. Another time, he made me deliver a package to someone else who ended up dead the same day. He wasn't as famous as Jay, so that incident didn't make the news. I never knew what was inside those packages, and I had no idea Cypher had taken pictures of me delivering them. What else had he done without my knowledge? Could I be framed for that guy's murder? My stomach lurched and I felt nauseous.

What would Nate think of me? What if I lost this life with Nate? The one thing mom wasn't able to teach me was how to make my money last. I made it and spent it. With Nate, I never had to worry about anything.

Another text came in from Cypher as if he was listening to my thoughts.

Time's up. You have 24 hours. I want a meeting with Nate by Friday.

I had to do this tonight. Cypher wanted to meet in three days. He was looking for progress, and so far, I had made none. Avoiding his calls didn't help since he wasn't too shy to show up at my door. I dreaded the day he knocked on the door when

Nate was home. I was a ball of frazzled nerves the other day when Nate took off. I kept looking outside to make sure I didn't see Cypher cruising by or sitting across from the house spying on us. I hoped my jitteriness wasn't noticeable, but then Nate asked why I was so tense. I gave him some bogus response that I can't recall now, but it seemed to work.

Still, I didn't want to be party to Cypher's grimy undertakings. I couldn't think of any feasible way to get out of this situation. My phone dinged again. As if I needed any more encouragement, Cypher sent me a picture of a slain body. I could see death in the mangled man's eyes even through the image. The next image he sent was the screenshot of a map and the destination was the new prison where my mom had recently been transferred. I knew now that I had no choice. I hated Cypher and wished someone would kill him.

Nate called my name and I jumped up from the couch, backed out of my text messages, and shoved the phone in my bra. I'd been so engrossed in my fear and thoughts that I hadn't heard him pull up. I missed the keys turning in the locks and obviously hadn't heard the door open as my husband walked in.

"Where are you, Babe?"

"In...I'm in here." I pushed the lump that lodged itself in my throat down with a gulp of cognac and hid the bottle. Wine wasn't going to cut it this evening.

"Hey!" Nate stepped into our family room swinging his briefcase and then hugged me tight with his free hand. A wide smile spread across his lips as he dined on me visually from head to toe, admiring the skimpy piece of lingerie I wore. His smile grew wider than I thought possible when his gaze landed on my white stilettos. "A little appetizer before heading out to dinner?" he teased.

"Uh. No. We're having dinner here." Taking Nate by the hand, I led him to the steps. "Now go upstairs and freshen up so you can get ready for the main course."

Nate raised his brows. "I like how this is going." With a quick peck, Nate turned and headed upstairs. "I'll be right back."

While Nate was upstairs, I calmed myself. I still couldn't get the image of the dead man out of my mind but worked through it. I was still unsure of how to broach the subject. I heated the food delivered earlier that day and made plates for Nate and I. One of Nate's favorite vintages from his collection in the cellar sat in the crystal wine cooler. Once everything was set, I lit candles and turned off the lights. The warm glow of the evening sun gave the room a beautiful, soft radiance. When I heard Nate coming back down the stairs, I sat on my side and crossed my legs over the edge of the table.

Nate followed the soft sounds of the R&B soul music wafting from the speakers in the dining room and stopped short at the entrance. He smiled again and longing flashed in his eyes. I loved it when my husband looked at me that way. Before taking his seat at the other end of the table, Nate stepped over to me and graced my lips with a soft, yet deeply sensual kiss.

After a quick grace, we dug in, moaning our delight. The food was delicious.

"How's work?"

Nate talked about the industry with that usual gleam in his eye. He updated me on the latest deals, rising stars and the ugliest scandals. The conversation turned to those who were no longer around and our speculation of why their spotlight faded. I thought about bringing up Cypher then but I was nervous.

"I want to work again."

Nate stopped eating and put his fork down. At first I thought he was going to object. "Really." That's all he said, then started eating again.

"Are you against it?" I pushed my fork around my plate and barely ate. My appetite was non-existent.

"Well." Nate leaned his head to one side and then the other.

"It depends on what kind of work. You don't need to go back to doing videos. You're above that now."

"I could still model."

"Baby. You don't have an average model's body!"

I threw my napkin at Nate and he ducked despite that fact that it hadn't even reached the center of the table. "Shush!"

"Supermodels don't have your type of body." He chuckled. "Seriously. They'd book you for shoots with magazines like Big Booty Judy not Essence or Elle." We both laughed at his silliness. "Regular magazines wouldn't know what to do with curves like yours."

"You're insane! There's no magazine called Big Booty Judy." Then I huffed. "You're right. Maybe I could get into acting. Oh! I could open a school for models."

"Those aren't bad ideas. I could help you get started either way."

"It would be easy for me to get back into videos, but I would be very selective in what type of jobs I take. I would avoid rap videos where all they want is for you to put on a tiny bathing suit. I would take roles that would let me show off my acting skills or something like that."

"That may be possible. Let me see what's coming up for some of our artists. Maybe I could get you placed in some of those videos. No rap, like you said, maybe something with one of our R&B or jazz artists."

"Great!" Nate continued his meal. My food remained untouched, but I was on my third glass of wine. "Speaking of R&B." The liquid inside my stomach swirled, making a gurgling sound. "You know Cypher X has some new stuff out. He's been shopping labels."

Nate put his glass down and looked at me. I couldn't read his expression, but it didn't seem pleasant. I wasn't sure if I should continue or not, but I knew I had to press on.

"He was a chart-topper until he stepped off the scene. Maybe your company should consider signing him." Nate placed his glass on the table and rested his chin on his folded hands. I cleared my throat and moved my fork around my pasta. I couldn't take the penetrating gaze he directed my way. "What do you think?"

Silence.

Nate said nothing. Absolutely nothing! The entire feel of the room shifted. Gone was the airy, pleasant, somewhat sexually charged vibe that we'd enjoyed since our meal began. It was as if something had sucked that nice vibe right out the room with a powerful vacuum. My stomach churned.

"What?" I finally asked innocently, shrugging my shoulders when I couldn't take his overbearing silence anymore.

"Why are you asking about Cypher X?" His expression was serious.

"No special reason." I poured another glass of wine and took a long sip. "I just heard he's got new stuff out and figured since he did well before, why not have him rake in some cash under your company."

Nate continued to stare at me. His glare was suspicious.

"So what is it to you?"

"Nothing. I was just making a suggestion. I still have many friends in the industry. I know when things are happening, and I know he's been shopping labels."

"Cypher's not shopping anything. No one in this industry will touch him, so don't concern yourself with him. Do we have dessert?" Nate picked up his fork and ate the remnants of his meal, dismissing the conversation.

I knew Nate. Continuing this discussion would only upset him, but I had no choice.

"Well, you've never been one to follow what everyone else did. That's why you're so successful. Just because the other folks in the industry don't want to work with him doesn't mean you shouldn't at least hear his music. This could be—"

"Lyric!" I jumped, startled by the harsh way he yelled my name. "I'm done with that conversation."

Nate's jaw was tight—a clear sign he'd had enough. I pressed on anyway.

"Could you just...have a meeting with him?" I couldn't look at Nate as I asked. I kept my eyes on the scattered, uneaten food on my plate.

"What are you? His manager? Why..." I looked up when Nate paused. I knew his mind was conjuring all kinds of scenarios. "You've been talking to him?"

"I..."

"Answer me, Lyric!"

"I saw him." I was annoyed at how sheepish I sounded.

"When. Lyric?"

"Um...at um...the..." I tried to think of a time that I could admit. "When we were in L.A., remember?" I tried to make it sound like it was no big deal, but that obviously wasn't my best answer. I'd been by Nate's side for most of that night. When would I have had time to chat with Cypher besides when I went to the bathroom? That certainly would not have been enough time to engage in a casual conversation about his career goals.

Nate squeezed his eyes tighter. "That was months ago. Don't bullshit me, Lyric. You've been in contact with him, haven't you?" My mouth opened and my lips moved, but nothing came out. Nate was on his feet and in my face in less than a split second. "You stay away from him, Lyric, and don't bring his name up in my presence again. Do you hear me? I'm warning you!"

"Nate!" I was shocked at how wicked he looked as he threatened me. "You're jealous! As much time as you spend with Vivian, you—"

"Don't go there! This has nothing to do with Vivian and it's certainly not the same." I sucked my teeth. Nate leaned in closer. "Don't think I don't know you have a history with Cypher." I looked at him, trying to mask my surprise with a look of annoyance. Nate nodded. "Yeah. There's not much that happens in this business that I don't know about. I advise you to keep his name out of your mouth and out of my house."

Without another word, Nate tossed the napkin he'd been holding onto the table and marched out of the dining room.

Glued to my seat in disbelief, I sat at the table by myself for a long while. The night had been ruined, but this wasn't anything compared to what would happen when Cypher found out that the meeting he was asking for between him and Nate would never happen.

CHAPTER 33

erri

I THOUGHT COMING BACK HOME WOULD BE the right thing to do, but all Chris and I have shown Alisa is how to be mad at one another. Our conflict dimmed the light of joy in areas that were usually impenetrable by issues in the past. Even Alisa mopped around, not really understanding why. Laughter had become foreign. We used to sit down to dinner as a family. Now we avoided one another's presence—or I avoid Chris's. He tried to talk to me, but being back at home didn't mean I was ready to take him on. I was doing this for Alisa.

When I went to work, I left Chris and Alisa at the table, silent, save the crunching of her cereal. I had to get on her twice for being sassy. At work, my staff avoided me, only coming into my office for absolute necessities. I preferred it that way since I was incapable of being my usual upbeat self. This way, I had less apologizing to do for my irritable disposition. Once I got my head all the way into work, I was able to function better. It took a few days, but I finally started to loosen up. I even laughed at one of my co-worker's horrible jokes. I went back to my office to figure out what I wanted for lunch and panicked when I saw I had missed three calls from my daughter's school. Without hesitating, I called back, tapping my thumb on my leg as I waited for someone to answer.

"Hello! This is Kerri Rhodes, mother of Alisa Rhodes. Is everything all right?"

"One moment, please, Mrs. Rhodes." I tapped again until someone came back to the phone. "Please hold for Mr. Winters."

"Good afternoon, Mrs. Rhodes."

"Is everything all right with Alisa?" Forget the formalities. I needed to know if everything was okay with my daughter. I never get calls from the school. "Is she sick? Hurt?"

"No, Mrs. Rhodes. Alisa seems to have gotten herself into a...altercation."

"Excuse me?"

"Yes. Ma'am. I was just as surprised. We will need one of you to come pick her up. She's being expelled."

"Expelled!" I jumped up from my chair.

"Yes. Ma'am. We can give you more information when you arrive."

"I'm coming from Manhattan. I'll be there as soon as I can. Thank you for calling Mr. Winters."

I put the phone down without ending the call and dialed for my assistant on my office phone. "Get me a car." That's all I said. A few minutes later, my assistant came into my office to let me know the car would be arriving in ten minutes.

"Is everything all right, Mrs. Kerri?" No matter how many times I asked, she wouldn't stop calling me Mrs. Kerri. Coming from a young, well-mannered recent graduate raised in the south, I understood it as a show of respect.

"Something happened with Alisa at school. I have to get there ASAP."

"I knew something was wrong by the sound of your voice. That country culture slipped past her tongue again.

"Thank you and sorry if I snapped at you."

"No worries, Ms. Kerri. Just let me know that your daughter is fine."

"Will do," I promised.

Minutes later she came back to let me know my car had arrived. Usually, I hated the reckless way these services drove, but today, I couldn't get to my daughter's school fast enough. From the back seat, I encouraged him to switch lanes to get around slower cars. I cursed incompetent drivers as if I were at the wheel. When the driver shook his head at me, I wasn't sure if it was because he thought I was funny, or if I had annoyed him. I didn't care.

The moment we reached the school, I snatched the invoice from him, scribbled my name, tossed him a cash tip and jumped out of the car. I quickly ran up the cement steps leading to Alisa's grade school and whipped out my license to gain entry past the odd-shaped school safety guard.

"Mrs. Rhodes!"

What does she want? I whirled around to see her holding my license between her fingers. I marched back in my loud heels, took my license from her hands, and headed back in the direction I'd just come from.

"Mrs. Rhodes." This time, she sang my name.

Clearly annoyed, I turned and shot her a hard glare. "What?"

She raised both brows and smiled. "The main office is that way." She pointed in the opposite direction.

"I knew that." I huffed, turned and marched in the other direction. I could hear her snickering all the way to the office.

Just as I stepped in, Mr. Winters approached me.

"Impeccable timing! Please join us."

His cheerfulness irritated me. My daughter's permanent record had been marred and he was acting as I'd come for a

PTA meeting. Without bothering to use the good manners my mother had instilled in me, I followed the wave of his hand through the door without responding.

Inside, I grunted when my eyes landed on Chris seated next to Alisa, but I hadn't intended for it to be so audible. I looked back toward the door. Mr. Winters had yet to enter but stood near the entrance speaking to his secretary. I sat down on the opposite side of Alisa, not wanting to sit next to Chris. Inclining my head to look at the scratch across her forehead, she cast her gaze downward, avoiding eye contact with me. Alisa fidgeted with her thumb, looking on as if it were the most interesting activity in the world. Looking back one more time to make sure the principal wouldn't hear me, I leaned toward Chris and whispered. "What are you doing here?"

He looked at me incredulously. "The school called me."

"They called me too. Why did they have to call both of us?"

"They said they got your voicemail when they called so I just came."

"Well, when I called back, why didn't they tell me you were coming?"

"I don't know. Why don't you ask them?" Chris was becoming annoyed.

"Mr. and Mrs. Rhodes," Mr. Winters said with a clap. "Thank you for coming on such short notice. "Can my secretary get you something to drink? Coffee, tea, or water?"

"No, thank you. Can you pl—"

"I'll take water, please," Chris said politely and pinned me with a chastising glare.

I sat back and exhaled. I wasn't fazed by my behavior at all. I knew I'd left my manners back at the office. "What happened with our daughter?"

Mr. Winters took a deep breath and let it out slowly as he rounded his desk and sat. "I was asking the same question, Mrs. Rhodes. This is not something I'd ever expect from Alisa."

"Well?" I wished he'd get to the point. Chris pinned me with another glare.

"It appears that Alisa has been having a bad week and today during lunch this apparent bad mood the teachers have been witnessing appears to have gotten the best of her. She claims that one of the other students was bothering her..."

Claims! What did he mean by 'claims'? Is this man calling my baby a liar?"

"Before we knew it there was a huge commotion. Alisa picked up a chair and tossed it at the young man, causing him to fall backward. Then she hit him. That's when the teachers broke it up. The young man was banged up, but not hurt too badly. He just has a few scratches and a bruise on his arm from the fall. It appears that Alisa may have gotten that scratch on her forehead from the young man flailing to protect himself.

Mentally, I applauded Alisa for taking up for herself, but Chris must have obviously heard something different because when I looked at him, his mouth was wide open. He turned his shocked expression in Alisa's direction. She sunk further into her shoulders as if she were trying to disappear in the chair.

"Is this true, Alisa?"

"Yes." Her voice was so mousy; we could barely hear her response.

"Answer me, Alisa!" Chris's voice boomed. Alisa flinched and nodded.

That's when I knew Alisa had done just what the principal said. Alisa was silent. I felt like this wasn't my child. If I properly assessed the Rhodes in the past weeks, I could say that I felt like this entire family wasn't mine. I looked at Chris. Fury danced in his narrowed eyes and called out the small veins that usually wiggled through the whites of his eyes when he was upset. He stared at Alisa so intently that I had to turn away.

Mr. Winters allowed our family to have that moment. Remaining quiet for some time, he continued after a while. He directed his next statement toward me since Chris's eyes were still on Alisa.

"I'm sure you'll agree that this is not Alisa's usual behavior. So that begs a question." Mr. Winters paused, shifting his gaze back and forth between Chris and me. "Is there something going on at home?"

Chris and I looked at each other, but neither of us answered. Finally, Chris cleared his throat. "My wife and I have been at odds lately. I hadn't realized it was affecting Alisa."

"The children are usually the silent victims, and like Alisa, they take it all in until someone pushes their buttons and then they act out their aggression. I think that's what happened today. Sometimes it's even worse. Alisa has always been a great student—diligent, hardworking, involved—a fine example. When the teachers mentioned that she seemed withdrawn, we began watching her to see if it was just a bad day or something bigger. Today's outburst showed us there is something bigger going on."

I lowered my head. Did I cause this? Mr. Winters continued, and I just wished he would stop. I was ashamed enough.

"Normally..." He stood and paced behind his desk. Both Chris and I watched him walk circles. "...this kind of behavior is punishable by expulsion. I was quite surprised when I found out that Alisa was at the center of this situation. Instead, I decided to just offer a one-day suspension during which Alisa will need to write an essay expressing alternative methods for dealing with her anger and aggression." He directed his next statement toward Alisa. "This is not the example we want our fifth graders to set for the younger students." Alisa drew into her shoulders.

Chris jumped to his feet, clasped Mr. Winters's outstretched hand between both of his, and shook vigorously. "Thank you, Mr. Winters." He turned towards me. "My wife and I will talk to Alisa about this and make sure she gets the essay done." Chris turned his attention to Alisa. "Say thank you to Mr. Winters. He's giving you a huge break.

"Thank you, Mr. Winters," Alisa said with her head still down.

"When I see you again, Alisa, I hope to see that young lady I know so well, the one who is bright, cheerful and hardworking. Okay?"

As we exited, Mr. Winters advised that the school had resources if we were interested in utilizing them. Chris politely declined. I walked right out the door. We didn't need counseling. I just needed to know the real reason why Camilla was climbing all over my husband. My mother's words rang in my ears again.

I sent the company car back and rode home with Chris and Alisa. Not a single word was exchanged until we made it inside. Alisa went straight to her room and I let her. Normally, I would have given her a lengthy lecture, but what would I say when I'd been a walking ball of anger and aggression myself?

I busied myself making dinner for the family for the first time in two weeks. Chris moved around from the bedroom to the garage. I wasn't sure what he was doing. Alisa stayed in her room. When I finished, I carried a tray with a plate and cup of juice up to Alisa's room. She'd been lying down and rose as the door creaked.

Again, Alisa averted her eyes. I put the tray down on her nightstand, kicked my slippers off, and sat up with my feet on the bed. Holding my arm out, I summoned Alisa with a tilt of my head. Sheepishly, she crawled over to me and placed her head in the crook of my arm.

"Talk to me."

"I don't know what happened." She paused. I wanted to nudge her to keep going yet remained quiet. "He called me a name because I wouldn't share my snack with him. Then he said my parents didn't love me anyway since I never get to have

Oreos as a snack, so he didn't want my stupid snack. I just got so mad at him. I told him to shut up, but he kept bothering me—talking about my yucky snacks, and that's when I threw the chair at him. I didn't mean for it to turn out like this."

Rubbing her arm, I shook my head. "Sometimes we do things we regret later."

"You and daddy love me, right?"

Whipping my head toward my daughter, I grabbed her shoulders. "Alisa! Of course, we love you!"

"Then why did you leave?"

"Baby!" I hated keeping up the lie. "That was for work."

"You don't have to lie to me, Mom." I wanted to swat her mouth for being sassy, but she obviously knew the truth. "Riley told me that something bad happened. She said you and Auntie Camilla were mad at each other. Will I get to see my sister again?"

Alisa was ripping my heart out right through my esophagus. "Of course you will!" I didn't want to talk anymore. "Don't worry about that. Eat your dinner. Tomorrow, I'll stay home from work and edit that essay you're going to write for Mr. Winters."

"You're not mad at me, mommy?"

"I'm disappointed." Alisa sighed—clearly relieved. "But no matter how mad or disappointed I may get with you, I'll never stop loving you." I kissed Alisa's nose. "Now eat!"

"Okay." She smiled, despite the sadness that still flickered in her eyes.

I'd lost my appetite, so instead of returning to the kitchen to make my plate, I showered and changed into pajamas. Before retreating, I checked in on Alisa to make sure she had eaten. She was watching TV. Chris was still making his presence scarce. I contemplated whether or not I should go back to the guest room where I'd been sleeping, or actually sleep in my own bedroom tonight.

I didn't want Chris to think it was some kind of truce, and I was still angry with him for sending Riley and Camilla to my hotel room. Yet, my own words haunted me. As mad as I was, I loved Chris. And, like Alisa, would any level of anger or disappointment change that? I wasn't sure if I was ready to leave my husband, but I didn't know if I should stay, either. I just knew I had to do something before I caused my daughter any more pain. Living in this flux affected both home and work. It was like a bottleneck in my mind.

The evening gave way to the night and I was still sitting at the edge of the bed in my guest room. The thud of Chris's footsteps thumped, along with my heart. I wondered if he was expecting me to go into our bedroom. The soft thud drew closer to the door and stopped. I closed my eyes. I wanted him to come in, and then again I didn't. I could see the shadow of his feet at the bottom of the door. I didn't move. Maybe he would think I was asleep and go away. A few more beats passed and the knob turned. The dim lighting in the hallway filtered into the room through the crack. Chris pushed the door open a little more. And then a little more.

He peeked first and then walked in. I kept my eyes closed.

"It's time to talk," Chris said.

CHAPTER 34

 aige

I LOOKED at the text Blair just sent and dropped my head. Guilt shrouded me like a cloak. All we had done when he met me at the restaurant the other night was talk, but there was also undeniable chemistry encapsulating the air. The next morning, we worked out together. At times, Blair was so close to me I could feel the hairs on his arm. I felt shock waves ripple through me every time we touched. I had opened a door that I wasn't sure how to close. I wasn't even sure I wanted it closed.

"Ugh." I looked at the text again, which just read *"breakfast?"* Working from home afforded me flexibility, so Rick knew nothing of my recent visits with Blair. I was careful to never mention Blair's name in Rick's presence.

I moved my thumb over the screen to type a response. Before I could hit send, Rick's number flashed up on my phone. I took a breath before answering.

"Hi," I said.

"Hi."

Neither of us said anything else for a moment. Silence joined the conversation like a third party, saying much about how strained communication between us had become.

"What's up?"

Rick cleared his throat. "Are we still doing Jayden's party this weekend?"

I scrunched my face and looked at the phone. "Why wouldn't we, Rick?" I huffed, loud enough for him to hear it clearly through the phone.

"I was just asking," he said defensively. His voice was stronger now.

"We have been working on this party for months. We shouldn't cancel just because her parents are acting like fools."

Rick chuckled. "We have been a little out of sorts, huh?"

I didn't laugh. "I was referring to you and Maya," I snapped.

"Let's not go there. I didn't call for that," Rick snapped back.

"Well, what did you call for?" Now I was pacing my home office.

"I'm not going to argue with you right now. I'll just send a text with a few things I'd like you to pick up before Saturday." Click.

My mouth fell open when I realized Rick had hung up on me. When the call screen disappeared, the message screen reappeared with Blair's message. I tapped, *name the place.*

Rick suggested IHOP, but I recommended that we go to a small diner in the next town. I didn't want to run the risk of seeing anyone from my neighborhood. My stomach fluttered all the way there. I even talked myself out of going through a few red lights, but when they turned, the angry side of me pressed the gas and kept going.

I looked around before pulling into the parking lot. When I

got out, I hung my head and scurried inside the diner. I was probably very conspicuous in my attempts to be inconspicuous. It felt like someone was watching me.

Blair was already inside when I arrived. He stood, placed his large hand on the small of my back, leaned over, and kissed me softly on my cheek. A nervous surge ran through me. I looked around again. No one was paying attention. The hostess grabbed two menus, offered a polite greeting, and then instructed us to follow her. Blair took me by the hand to lead the way. I should have pulled away, but didn't. I continued to look around with my head slightly down.

The hostess waved her hand, inviting us to sit. I slid all the way in the booth and sat with my back to the window.

"Are you okay?" Blair asked, looking genuinely concerned.

For a moment, I just looked at him. I wanted to ask what he thought. Married women shouldn't be sneaking around with ex-boyfriends. "I'm fine." I didn't mean to be short. I had made the choice to meet him. At any point, I could have told him no, but I didn't.

I was cautious, leaving the proverbial door open. My marriage was hanging on by a dry-rotted thread. My life had become tiresome with Maya's unrelenting interference and I wasn't sure how much more I could take. My husband never had my back and I'd never gained the upper hand. Hearing that I had possibly made Jayden feel unwanted was by far the most upsetting. I hadn't even had the chance to talk to Jayden to verify that she'd said anything to Maya, but just the thought that I'd done anything to that wonderful girl to make her think I didn't love her had already wounded my heart.

I didn't really want to leave my husband but didn't see much recourse unless things changed. So far, in all these years, they hadn't. Now that I had a job, I felt more secure about the possibility of leaving.

"Paige!"

"Huh?" I shook my head.

"Did you hear a word I said?" Blair asked.

"Oh. Sorry, Ri…" I cleared my throat. "Um. Blair." I'd be a fool if I thought he didn't realize that I almost called him Rick. "I'm sorry."

Blair smiled knowingly. "It's okay. You're dealing with a lot right now." He handed me the menu. "What do you want to order?"

"Pancakes?"

"You sure about that? "You've been working so hard."

I didn't need him telling me what to eat. Rick never did that. "Yes, I'm sure."

"Okay!" he drew that word out long enough to equal the space of a full sentence.

I sucked my teeth and felt Blair's hand over mine. The skin where he touched tingled. I looked up into eyes that smiled soothingly, yet held both concern and lust in them. Blair licked his lips and I looked away.

"I didn't mean to upset you."

"I'm not upset. I'm just fine."

My phone chirped. Rick sent the list of things he wanted me to pick up for Jayden's party. With his work schedule, he wouldn't be able to do it. I shut the phone off and stuffed it in my purse.

"So." I tried to dial up a better mood. "How are things going with work? Are you off today or 'working from home' like me?" I needed to talk about something that would take my mind off Rick and make me feel a tad more comfortable—if that were possible.

Blair's eyes brightened up. "It's cool! Right now, I'm house hunting. This looks like it's going to be a permanent move, so I'd like to get rooted in my new city."

"Oh!" This wasn't going to be good for me. "That's great!" I feigned excitement, hoping my reaction went over well enough for him to buy it.

"Where are you looking, specifically?"

"I'm open. I've even considered Manhattan since the office will be right across the bridge. I've always wanted to live in the city."

"Cool!"

We continued our conversation, but I was unable to give Blair all of my focus. Scanning the diner for familiar faces, feeling uncomfortable and thinking about Rick made it hard for me to sit still. He noticed but obviously gave me a pass.

After paying the bill, Blair grabbed my hand again. We walked out of there like a normal couple. He didn't even seem to mind the sweat pooling in my palm by the time we made it to my car.

"Well! I guess I'll see you later." I reached for my car door and Blair stopped me.

His touch had energy. I kept my head lowered. Blair lifted my chin and before I could protest, he kissed me. His warm minty tongue swirled over my motionless one. I just stood there, eyes opened, not moving. Blair moved closer, placed his hand on my back, and pressed his body against mine. I stayed put, peering past him to see if anyone was watching. He pulled me in tighter. I could feel his taut torso against my soft breast and then a moan escaped from his throat. I kissed him back. Our tongues dueled at first but quickly found a rhythm. My eyes closed and I melted against him.

My eyes popped open. What was I doing? This wasn't supposed to happen. I ripped myself from his lure and stumbled backward.

Shaking my head, I fumbled with my keys. "No!"

Blair sighed. "I'm sorry if you weren't ready for that."

"Bye, Blair."

I jumped into my car, jammed the keys into the ignition, started it and stepped on the gas. I could see Blair standing in the same spot as I peeled out of the lot. I kept going, blowing traffic signs, laws, and a couple of lights. When I finally came to a stop, I banged my hands against the steering wheel. That's when the tears came. I didn't want Blair to kiss me, but he did. I didn't want to like it—but I did.

CHAPTER 35

yric

"Get up!"

"Huh? What!" My heart pounded in my chest. Nate had scared the sleep out of me. I peeled open my eyes to see my husband standing over me, looking like a god draped in all white with a buttoned-down shirt and slacks. "What's going on?"

"It's our anniversary and we've got a long day ahead of us, so get up and get ready." With that, Nate walked right out of the room.

Now fully awake, I threw back the covers and jumped up. What was more surprising was that it was a Monday and my husband never took off from work. I figured we would celebrate over the past weekend and now I see why we didn't. I was glad he wasn't mad enough to let this day go by without acknowledging it. My cheeks hurt from smiling so hard. The past few days had been rough. Nate hadn't been very talkative since the other night when I brought up Cypher. And, since the meeting on Friday never happened, I'd been on edge all weekend waiting for Cypher to emerge from the shadows. Nate would never have to worry about me saying that monster's name in his house ever again. I knew Cypher would be angry. The fact that I tried wouldn't matter to him. He was going to show up soon enough. I had to worry about that later. Today was my one-year anniversary, and I couldn't wait to see what Nate had in store.

Slipping my feet into a fresh pair of fluffy white slippers, I shuffled to the window. My bedroom overlooked our expansive yard and the brook behind it. On a warm, sunny day like this one, it resembled a postcard taken from one of those national parks. I opened the window and stuck my hand out. The warm air was still and I could already tell it was going to be a little humid. I thought back to the year before and my grand wedding, and giggled. I was so proud to be a bride.

Inside my dressing room, a white flowing maxi dress was laid across the leather bench. Next to it was an overnight bag and a garment bag with a note that read, *No need to pack. Put on this dress. Don't take too long. No questions allowed!"*

I pressed my hands against my heart and laughed. It was like I was already intoxicated. Of course, champagne was going to be a huge part of our day. It was necessary, both for the sake of our celebration, and to keep my nerves intact. Quickly, I dressed, did my hair and simply applied liner, mascara, and a pink gloss to make my lips pop. When I reached the bottom of the stairs, Nate handed me a mimosa.

Weaving his arm in mine, we brought the glasses to our lips. Nate leaned in and kissed me before taking a sip. "Congratulations, baby. I know this year hasn't been easy."

"I love you, Nate!"

He licked my lips and kissed me again, this time leaving me breathless before we sipped our mimosas together.

"Let's get going!" Nate slapped me on my behind, drained the remnants of the champagne flute and headed to the kitchen. "The driver will be here in five minutes."

Following him, I asked, "What are we doing first?"

"Uh! No questions, remember."

I groaned. "Okay!"

In exactly five minutes, our driver arrived. Nate brought down all the bags.

Twenty minutes later, we were having breakfast at an exclusive rooftop restaurant that normally didn't open until five in the afternoon. Of course, I wasn't surprised. With Nate's money, anything was possible. After breakfast, our driver took us to SoHo. Nate blindfolded me before I got out of the car. I wanted to ask questions but kept them behind my grinning lips. Gently he held my hand, guiding me out of the car. We walked a few feet and before taking my blindfold off, he kissed me again.

"Are you ready?"

"Yes!" I hopped up and down. "What is it, Nate?"

Nate removed the material. I looked around, trying to figure out the big surprise. I saw dense traffic along Broadway, scores of people walking and talking on wide sidewalks, and heard the usual swift rhythm of lower Manhattan, heels against the concrete, conversations meshing together into one upbeat city song. There was nothing out of the ordinary. Nothing surprising. I looked at Nate and inclined my head sideways.

"Nate!" I droned. Slowly he turned me around and I screamed.

On a storefront, right on Broadway in the center of the fashion capital, was a huge, beautiful display window with bold white lettering that said, "The Delaney Agency", and below that read, "Modeling School," and in the lower right, Proprietor: Lyric Delaney. The right side of the window featured a silhouette of a model, which looked a lot like me.

I squealed so loud that several people stopped in the midst of their morning rush to look at us. "Oh! My goodness! Is that me?" Nate nodded and caught me in his arms when I jumped and wrapped my arms and legs around him, not caring that I had on a dress. I painted his face with pink lip prints. "Thank you, baby!" I slid from his grasp and kissed his lips passionately. "I can't believe this. I covered my mouth to stifle my scream so that I wouldn't look completely crazy to the people on the street. I mentioned this dream to Nate once, and now I had my very own modeling school!

"Let's go inside."

Inside was as impressive as the outside. There was a reception area in my favorite colors. Yellow, purple, black, and silver furniture and accents popped against stark white walls. Normally, I would have never put those colors together in one room, but it looked absolutely stunning. Surely, Nate had hired a designer to make this work. There was space behind a purple partition for my new receptionist, and a large flat-screen TV hanging on an unobstructed wall to the right. There were two studios with gorgeous hi-gloss wood floors and one office with my name etched on a silver placard on the door.

Instead of walking, I bounced through the entire tour—unable to contain my excitement.

"I could hire Candy to help me out when she's not traveling. It will be convenient for her since she's right here in the city. I'll do a model search. Oh! I'll need to run some ads to get people interested. Wait! I have to have a launch event and invite all the media. This is going to be amazing, Babe!" My mouth was moving too fast for my words to form properly.

I knew I was babbling, but I couldn't help it. Besides my wedding last year, I couldn't remember being happier. Nate had made me the happiest woman alive for the second time in my life. As the wife of music mogul Nate Delaney, neither of us wanted me to go back to modeling in videos. It seemed beneath me even though I missed being in the industry. This...this was a venture worthy of a mogul's wife.

I spun around in the center of one of the studios, visions of wall-to-wall models flipping through my mind. Nate stood by the door in all his refined handsomeness, with his hands stuffed in his pockets, smiling. I walked over to him. No! Scratch that! I sauntered over to him with a slow runway gait, gently put my arms around my magnificent man, and gave him a kiss that let him know just how much I appreciate him. His hand caressed my backside before roaming up my back. He held me tight again, making me a happy woman. I promised myself I'd never worry about Vivian again.

Nate pulled back and looked me in my eyes as he dug in his pocket. He jingled keys in my face. I snatched them from his hands. Giggling all over again, I planted several kisses all over his face. As I wiped the lipstick stains from his cheeks, Nate peeked at his watch and grabbed my hand.

"We've got to go!" Nate led me back to the front of the school, allowing me to lock the doors before dragging me back to the car.

We drove through heavy midday traffic. Even though I grew up in New York City, being with Nate had shown me a version of the city I'd never known before. I'd gone from the suburbs to the projects to penthouses and mansions. Even now, as I looked out of the window with a new sense of wonder, I saw a different city. Despite the lush perspective I'd become accustomed to, I knew and understood the unforgiving harshness that belied the infamous landscape. I'd live in it long enough to never want to return. I shivered.

"You're cold. Want me to tell him to turn down the A.C.?"

"I snuggled closer to Nate. No, Babe, I'm good." That shiver had nothing to do with the cool air inside the car.

We arrived at the West Side heliport. The driver helped us out and grabbed our bags. I wanted to ask Nate where we were going but didn't want to ruin the surprise. Nate told me to stay by the car while he went to talk to a man who looked like the pilot.

"This is why I packed for you." He chuckled. "You would have made the bags too heavy. Let's go." Grabbing my hand, Nate led me to the helicopter.

I swatted his arm even though he was right. Within the hour, the landscape under us changed from tall buildings to shorter buildings, open fields, parks, quaint suburban neighborhoods, and sprawling estates. The ocean seemed vast and mysterious. I'd never paid much attention before. The helicopter ride offered a more intimate view than airplanes did. Our final destination was in the Hamptons.

Another driver met us there and took us straight to a studio where Nate and I changed clothes and enjoyed a sexy photoshoot both inside and outside with a lush garden as a beautiful backdrop. Then we headed to the beach and took a few shots there. Nate watched with a wicked smile as the photographer took various shots of me on the beach, first wearing a long flowing dress that fluttered in the wind, and then some in bikinis covered in bling. Nate joined me for some pictures in both outfits.

After that, we had a romantic seaside dinner under the setting sun before heading to a huge waterfront home with incredible views of the ocean. My heels echoed as I walked into the expansive foyer. Our home in New Jersey was beautiful, but this place was...majestic. It had an old-world European feel with ornate chandeliers and sculptures and columns. Royalty must have lived there at some point.

"Oh my goodness, Nate! This place is unbelievable. I feel like it's a castle."

"Fit for a princess," Nate said, hugging me from behind.

"Whose place is this?"

"Mine."

I turned around. "Yours? You never told me you had a place in The Hamptons."

"It was being rented until last month. I thought it would be the perfect setting for our first anniversary."

I wasn't sure how happy I was about him keeping this place a secret, but I did appreciate the surprise.

"Go take a look out back."

The backyard was massive with a pool house the size of my grandmother's old three-bedroom home. I remembered visiting as a child before she passed. There was a U-shaped pool, water fountains, a koi pond and the landscaping was immaculate.

"Nate!" I was astonished as I stepped out onto the deck. "This is...incredible!" I said, holding the railing as I looked out over the entire yard. Immediately, I regretted signing that prenuptial agreement and then shook that thought right out of my head. In fact, I had expected that, and had even suggested terms that didn't seem like a big deal to Nate, but would help me walk away with a nice package if we were to ever break up.

"How come you never told me about this place?"

Nate shrugged as if it was no big deal. "It has always been rented. I hardly ever come here." He walked up behind me and pressed his front against my back. "But now that they're gone, I'm thinking about using it more." He kissed the back of my neck. No better time than the present." He turned me around and covered my lips.

This day was more than I had ever imagined. I wasn't sure what Nate was thinking, but my mind was certainly on the fact that all these events were the perfect lead-in to a night of baby-making love—a night where I was sure to get pregnant since I had stopped taking my birth control pills. No need to worry about a prenuptial agreement when you have a child.

CHAPTER 36

erri

I STILL HADN'T SPOKEN to Chris. When he came in the room the other night demanding that we talk, I just wasn't ready. Now a few more days had passed and he was getting irritated—as if he had the right. Chris's patience had become as thin as a veil. During the first few days after I returned, his actions and words were cautious as if to maintain an emotional balance. I was the volcano ready to erupt at the slightest nudging. We were as polite as two strangers. His niceties had turned into aggravated sighs, sideway glares and accusatory head nods. Slowly, he convinced himself that I was being ridiculous. That was my summation.

Like most nights, I cooked, checked Alisa's homework and made sure she made it to bed before retreating to the guest room. Conversations between Chris and I were minimal and cordial. We performed in front of Alisa, but she was too smart to be fooled, regardless of how hard we tried. The eye rolls and twisted lips at our unsuccessful attempts of acting like a happy couple showed me that she wasn't sold on our antics.

Tossing my clothes, I went into the adjoining bathroom to take a shower. I waited, letting the water get good and hot before stepping in. I wanted to feel my worries wash down the drain along with the scalding water. I wasn't able to cleanse myself from the doubt that clogged my brain in this situation, nor the guilt that I felt for leaving my daughter behind to fend for herself.

The curtain was snatched back and I screamed, startled by the sudden action. Instantly, my hand covered my heart and I squeezed my thighs together as if I were being exposed to a stranger.

"Chris!" Chris stood right outside the shower with his head cocked to the side a bit and his arms crossed over his chest.

"This has gone far enough! We need to talk tonight."

"Seriously? Can I get out of the shower?"

"Your choice. I'm not going to bed until we talk." Chris slapped the lid down on the toilet and sat. "I'll be right here."

I narrowed my eyes at him and pulled the curtains closed. Quickly finishing my shower, I wrapped myself in a towel and stepped out much sooner than I intended. My time had run out. I had to jump this hurdle tonight.

I walked into the room. Chris followed closely behind. He tried not to watch as I lotioned my body and slipped on a nightgown. However, he hadn't taken his eyes off me from the moment I left the bathroom.

Chris plopped on the bed and patted the space beside him. I hesitated a beat, but trudged over and sat down anyway.

"How do we fix us?" he asked.

"You tell me. I didn't break us." I refused to make eye contact. Instead, I found interest in the smoothness of my manicure.

Chris took my hands in his and lifted my chin, forcing me to look at him. "I didn't break us either. I love you Kerri but I can't go on like this. I told you the truth and I don't know what else to say. So, I need you to tell me what has to happen for us to fix this."

Why was he putting this on me? The tears started right after my lip trembled. "I don't know if it can be fixed. I don't know if I want to fix it."

"What?" Chris's voice was hardly a whisper. "Kerri! You don't mean that! We can get Camilla over here so she can explain what happened."

My head whipped in his direction. "Don't you dare." I finally looked directly at him.

"Then tell me what to do! I'm trying here." Chris was on his feet. "I. Have. Never. Cheated on you! I don't have anything going on with Camilla. I didn't come on to her that day. Dammit, I haven't even tried to help her because I don't want you thinking there's something going on!" Chris dropped to the floor in front of me and once again lifted my chin to meet me eye-to-eye. "I need you to believe me."

The only thing I could do was shake my head. I kept shaking it, wishing this would all go away. "I don't trust you. How can we go on if I don't trust you?"

"I didn't do anything to betray your trust, but if I have to earn it all over again, I'll do whatever it takes. You'll learn to trust me again."

I covered my ears, yet Chris kept talking, recounting the same scenario all over again. He moved my hands. Hearing him tell the story, made me relive it. The images played before me like a silent movie. I wanted to believe him but didn't want to play the fool. I'd been lied to before, coaxed into believing untruths that ended in heartbreak. Fortunately, I wasn't married with kids then. I didn't want to fall for a trick and find out later that I'd been hoodwinked. I didn't want to find out some time in the future that Camilla and Chris had never stopped loving each other and that I'd been duped into believing they simply got along great all those years. How could I protect my heart from that?

Those very thoughts spilled out of my mouth. By the time I was done. Chris stood before me, looking shocked.

"You think I've been messing around with Camilla behind your back all these years?" The pain of that reality took his breath. "All this time?" Despair was etched in his face. "What have I done to make you think this? How long have you felt this way?"

Chris hadn't done anything to make me question his loyalty —until now. I looked away.

"Tell me, Kerri." Chris sat on the edge of the bed, his eyes darting as he tried to put it all together. "Have you ever trusted me?"

Until now, I had trusted him wholeheartedly. Seeing Camilla laying on top of him on that couch, for that instant, put everything into question.

"Yes." My response was more of a whisper.

Chris exhaled, seemingly relieved by my answer. "So when did you stop trusting me."

"When I saw Camilla on top of you!"

Chris walked out of the room, leaving me to wallow in my confusion. I paced for a while, then listened to his footsteps as he went down the stairs. When I heard his car, I ran to the window, hoping he wasn't going to do what I thought he might.

I reset the blinds and slipped into bed. Unable to sleep, I laid awake, trying to determine if I should believe Chris, if what I'd seen made sense based on what he'd told me. After a while, I heard footsteps again. This time, a lighter set accompanied Chris's heavy thud. Together they made their way down the hall to the door of the guest room where I laid. The doorknob turned. I shut my eyes and tried to steady my breath. Chris flipped on the light and by the time I turned to glare at him, he was at my bedside, nudging my arm.

"Get up, Kerri!"

Annoyed, I sat up, my lips pursed and eyes narrowed at Chris before moving to Camilla. She was standing between us and the door, looking like a child ready for a scolding.

"It wasn't his fault," she said. Her head remained down.

"Are you serious, Chris? You brought her here to plead your case?"

Chris looked at Camilla, urging her to continue. She looked up at him, and then me, and then took a breath. Shame filled her eyes and her posture.

"It was my fault, Kerri. *All* mine. I'm working on myself now...finally. Please don't make Chris suffer for my mistake. He loves you."

Throwing the covers back, I jumped out of bed. Chris blocked the path between Camilla and me.

She took a step back. "I didn't mean to hurt you, Kerri. I'd never do anything like that intentionally."

Chris held my arms. What was I supposed to do now? I yanked myself from Chris's grip and slowly made my way over to Camilla until I was a hair's width away from her face. "Then, why?"

Camilla closed her eyes when I spoke. I waited for her answer.

"I can't explain why. I'm not sure if I know."

I sucked my teeth. I was disgusted by her ambiguous response and by the fact that Chris had even brought her to the house. I left both of them standing in the middle of the room. I was pulling out of the driveway, still in my pajamas, before they made it to the door. I needed to process what they had just said and I needed to do it in the fresh air, far away from that distress in Chris's eyes and the anguish in Camilla's. I needed to come to terms with this without them staring me down through all that misery. I had to figure out what my decision would be, knowing that whatever the outcome, things would never be the same.

CHAPTER 37

 aige

For the past week, I had poured all of my time and energy into making this day a hit for Jayden. Planning her party and spending two days traveling for work proved to be great distractions from my broken life. Despite Maya's empty threat of not letting Rick see Jayden, Maya had her stay with us all week. That gave Jayden and I time to talk about what I might have said to make Jayden feel like I didn't like her. When I asked her about it she looked confused. Just as I suspected, Maya had lied to Rick in another attempt to stir the pot.

Jayden enjoyed every exhausting minute of last-minute planning. My mother also stayed over. According to her, everything ran smoothly. The girls really enjoyed her company.

Jayden thanked me for everything I was doing to make her birthday special and acknowledged that Maya would never have gone through the same trouble. I locked myself in my bathroom and cried. That made me work even harder.

Rick and I still weren't back to normal but he did acknowledge that he appreciated all that I was putting into making Jayden's party a success. However, he wouldn't admit that things went well in my absence. My mother had even made him breakfast before he left for work both days. She said that he devoured it.

Soon the house would be filled with preteens in tiaras, hot pink robes, and boas for Jayden's birthday. I hired a company that did mobile spa parties. My added touches included champagne flutes filled with fruit-infused apple juice and flavored teas, finger sandwiches, gourmet chocolates, cupcakes, and a mini fashion show. I planned to tire them out, making the sleepover effortless—hopefully. Rick insisted on sparking up the grill, despite the fact that the girls told him that burgers and franks weren't appropriate meal choices for divas and models.

Jayden bounced down the steps all decked out in her pink and white dress. Her excitement sizzled, keeping her from being able to stay still.

"What time does the bus come, Paige?"

"It's a mobile spa, honey. Not a bus."

Jayden giggled. "Well, what time does the *mobile spa* come?" she said with a horrible, but funny, British accent. Scotland cackled at her side, wearing the same colors, always wanting to be like her big sister.

I looked at my watch. "You ladies still have an hour. Are the gift bags all ready?"

"Yep!" both yelled.

"Okay, bring them down here."

The girls sprinted up the steps to get the huge pink and silver glitter bags that I'd purchased with Jayden's name on them. Earlier, they'd filled them with all the goodies I'd been stacking up in recent weeks—animal print pencils, nail art stickers and polish, lip glosses, colorful diaries with locks and keys, and loot bags full of candy. The two of them ran down the steps sounding more like an army than two girls.

"Place the bags neatly in the living room. We'll give those out after the fashion show."

Jayden squealed, spun on her heels, and headed to the living room with Scotland at her heels, mimicking every movement. I put the final touches on their playful canapés and got dressed. The girls fell into fits of laughter when I descended the steps in my white outfit, a tiara on top of my head, and a hot pink boa around my neck.

Ten girls and a few of our friends arrived before the mobile spa. Kerri and Chris arrived with Alisa. Lyric and Nate came with jewelry for Jayden and a dollhouse for Scotland that was almost the size of my garage! Rick's mother and Loren pulled up shortly after.

When the mobile spa pulled up in front of the house, I was sure that every neighbor within a half-mile radius could hear the frenzy. The adults headed to the backyard for cocktails while the girls were being indulged—all except Lyric.

For two hours they were pampered, manicured, pedicured and made up while sipping on their fancy drinks, and dancing to the music playing from the unit's speakers. A few of them exited the mobile unit looking as if a make-up bag had blown up on their faces. I laughed so hard my side hurt. Lyric sipped right along with them, offering up beauty and modeling tips for later. They loved her.

Kerri and I made sure the runway was ready for their fashion show while the girls barreled through the house to get ready.

"We're ready," Jayden yelled from their bedroom window.

"Then come on down!" I waved. Rick laughed and shook his head as he flipped burgers, ribs, chicken, and the steaks he'd added to the menu.

Lyric went inside to work with the girls. They lined up

behind her strutting out the back door runway-ready. Their cute little colorful lips were twisted just as confidently as Lyrics and had the adults roaring with laughter. Just as I got ready to announce our first model, Maya walked into the yard.

"Mommy!" Jayden yelled and ran to her. "You didn't tell me you were coming!"

My chest felt tight. I clamped my lips shut. I didn't want to act a fool in front of our guests and the girls. My eyes shot to Rick and he shrugged his shoulders. He was just as baffled as I was. I didn't miss the shocked expressions plastered on Lyric and Kerri's faces. Rick's sister and mother looked at each other and shook their heads before looking at Rick, admonishing him to handle this with their expressions. Rick nodded back.

Jayden grabbed Maya by the hand. "You're just in time for the fashion show."

"I am!" Maya looked at Rick and me as if she dared us to make her leave. She then looked around the yard taking in the decorations with a twisted lip.

I looked at Rick and he held his hand up, a plea for me to keep cool.

"Yes! Come sit." Jayden dragged her to a seat next to Kerri. "We're about to start!" When Maya was seated, Jayden ran back to where the girls were waiting to start the show.

"Hi," Maya said with an attitude and a cold shoulder. Lyric looked at her as if she was diseased. I couldn't help the chuckle that escaped my lips. Kerri replied cordially.

I swallowed all the foul words I wanted to express and pulled the microphone closer to my mouth. After a deep breath, I delivered a poised description of each model's attire. Then the girls took to the microphone for Karaoke. Thankfully, they were having so much fun they seemed oblivious to the sharp change in the atmosphere.

"What's to eat?" Maya jumped up and headed toward Rick at the grill.

I was on her heels. "That's for our invited guests." Maya parked her hands on her fat hip and turned slowly. Undeterred, I met her at the grill. I didn't want to cause a scene, but I couldn't let this go unaddressed. "And I don't remember you being invited!"

Maya huffed. "I need an invite to my own daughter's party?"

"Yes!"

"Maya!" Rick finally interjected. "Come inside." Maya snarled but stepped inside behind Rick. I marched behind them, leaving the guests outside.

"Why are you here?" I could feel my pressure rising.

"For Jayden!"

My finger was an inch from her nose. "I'm tired of you and your bul—"

"Maya!" Rick yelled, grabbing our attention before I could finish my expletive. He stood beside me, rubbing my back. "You should have called."

I looked from Rick to Maya. "That's all you're going to say?"

"Paige. We have guests. I don't want a scene."

I stomped out, leaving both of them standing there. Rick's mother met me at the door. She must have noticed the flash of fire in my eyes. She took me by the hand and pulled me into the formal dining room, out of earshot.

"Relax, baby. There are ways to handle this. You're the queen of this castle. Don't let her think she has won by letting her get you all ruffled." My breathing had become erratic. Ms. Thompson handled me delicately, softly touching my shoulder. "I can see how much work you put into this party for Jayden. Go and enjoy your guests." She took my hand and led me past Maya and Rick still quarreling in the kitchen.

When I got outside, she locked the door behind me. Through the glass, I watched as she approached Rick and Maya. Whatever she said, they offered no response. Ms. Thompson waltzed back outside with an unruffled smile. Rick returned to the grill and Maya sat her worrisome behind down and shut up for a little while.

The atmosphere at the party turned from festive to tense. No one engaged Maya in conversation except Jayden when she wasn't playing with her friends. Even Rick's sister Loren kept her distance. Maya seemed unaffected, as long as she had food on her plate.

The girls changed into their bathing suits and Maya went and sat by the pool as they frolicked.

"Give that back!" Maya yelled. Each of the adults turned around to see why she was yelling. Maya stood over the edge of the pool. "You heard me. Give it back!"

Jayden's guests all froze, afraid of being yelled at, too.

"Mom!" Jayden said. "It's okay. We're just playing."

Before I knew it, I was at the edge of the pool beside Maya. Rick, Loren, Kerri, Lyric, and Mrs. Thompson were right behind me.

"What's going on?" Maya glared at me and rolled her eyes. "Jayden, what happened?" Jayden just blinked at me. "Answer me, Jayden." My tone was firm. Jayden put her head down.

"Jayden!" I said in a softer tone. "Tell me what's going on, sweetie."

"Scotland took the noodle from me and mommy yelled at her. I was trying to tell her that we were all just playing a game."

"You yelled at my child?" I took a step toward Maya and Rick grabbed my arm.

"She was being mean!"

"No, she wasn't!" Jayden spoke up and Maya shot her a glare so hard Jayden literally moved back.

"Shut your mouth. Are you taking up for her? How many times do I have to tell you that she's not your mother? Get out of the pool and get your stuff." Maya marched to the side of the pool where Jayden was.

"Maya!" Rick stepped up. "Jayden's not leaving her own party."

"She's coming with me!"

"But, Mommy, I don't want to go. All my friends are here."

"Maya. Stop this. You're ruining her party." Rick was getting aggravated.

"I'm ruining the party?" she waved him off. "Jayden, get out and get your stuff." Jayden looked at me through tearful eyes.

"That's enough, Maya. You need to go!" I pointed toward the gate.

"You can't tell me what to do! Come on, Jayden."

"But, mommy!" Jayden cried. All the girls had crawled out of the pool and stood along the side watching with wide frightened eyes.

"I said, come on!" Maya yelled. Jayden flinched, startled by her mother's outburst. "She doesn't want you here, anyway."

"That's not true! You keep saying that, but Paige does like me. She did all of this for my birthday."

Maya's eyes narrowed to slits. Kerri shook her head and walked back over to the deck, giving our family space. Lyric followed suit, ushering the girls with her, leaving Rick, Mrs. Thompson, Loren and me with Maya and Jayden.

"Oh, now you're on her side. I'm your mother, Jayden. She stole your dad from us and now she's trying to steal another woman's man." We all looked confused. "That's right. I saw them at the diner together." Maya smirked like she had something on me.

Rick looked from Maya to me, then to his mother and sister. Something in me snapped.

This time, Rick was unable to grab me before I made it to Maya and grabbed her by the front of her shirt. Before I could shake her, Rick grabbed my shoulder and pulled me away.

He turned to Maya. "You need to leave now before this gets any uglier."

Maya's mouth formed an 'o' and her fingers were splayed across her chest. "Are you threatening me?" she gasped.

"Leave before I call the police. And Jayden's staying." Rick was adamant.

Maya's expression changed from shock to anger and back again. Huffing, she remained nose to nose with me. I stood taller, challenging her. She looked at Rick and then me as if she was expecting him to tame me.

"Out!" I yelled again, pointing toward the gate.

Maya looked at Loren and then Mrs. Thompson. Both looked back with expressions that warned her to heed my command.

"Humph!" Maya snarled, turned on her heels and marched out of the yard.

Once she was gone, the air in the yard seemed lighter. The party resumed but ended shortly after. Once all our guests were gone and the girls were finally asleep, I showered and hauled my exhausted body into bed. I hadn't said much to Rick because I was tired of him letting his rabid ex-wife run wild, infecting everyone with her wretchedness. He should have put a stop to her tricks a long time ago. I appreciated the bit of firmness he displayed with Maya today, but it wasn't enough.

Rick finally strolled in the room once I was wrapped snugly under the covers. I think he had purposefully avoided me. He crawled into the bed, weighing his side down with both his body and his frustration.

"Paige," Rick said.

After a moment, I turned around, acknowledging him through the dark.

"Who is this guy Maya saw you with?"

I rolled over, giving Rick my back and ignored him. Dealing with Maya had zapped my energy and my resolve. I didn't have enough of either to continue this conversation with Rick—

especially when I had no idea how to answer that without making things worse.

"Answer me, Paige."

"Now, you're letting her come between us in our own bedroom?"

Frustrated, Rick turned over, giving me his back.

I had no idea how much Maya had seen, but could only assume that if she did see Blair kiss me that day, she surely would have said so.

 yric

I TRIED my best to enjoy the task in front of me, but as excited as I was about getting my modeling school slash agency ready for its extravagant launch, I still couldn't keep my mind from wandering to thoughts of Cypher. He never responded when I texted him to let him know that Nate refused to meet with him. There had been an eerie quiet from him ever since.

Every morning before I left the house, I'd scan the property's security cameras to make sure Cypher wasn't lurking somewhere out there. I watched my rearview mirror more than the road as I drove into the city and even had a few near misses. Just this morning, I had to slam on my brakes to avoid smashing into the back of another SUV on the George Washington Bridge because I saw a guy that resembled Cypher. I watched my back, searching my surroundings before sticking my keys in the door both at home and at the school.

Sounds as simple as a phone vibrating or a door closing set

off my heartbeat. My new assistant dropped a book on the floor while setting up the reception area and I screamed as if I had just been shot. Cypher hadn't responded to the bad news yet, but I knew he would at some point.

I told my mother about it on my last visit. She told me to keep watching my back and that she'd reach out to some friends for assistance. Mentioning any of this to Nate was out of the question, especially now since things were looking brighter in our marriage.

Thinking about how well things had been going between Nate and me put a smile on my face. I decided to leave early and make dinner for him. Maybe I'd do much more of that when Nate and I had a baby. I looked at the calendar on my phone. I'd set an appointment reminder for the day my next cycle was to begin. Hopefully, it would be a no-show, meaning I was finally pregnant. The timing couldn't be better.

"Britney," I yelled from my office.

My overly excited assistant, who was so hungry for a career in modeling that she could have eaten me alive, bounced into my office. She was pretty, with large eyes and big lips that she'd just grown into beautifully. Now she was a stunning knockout who turned the heads of men, women and children as she walked down the street swaying her well-placed curves. Fresh out of high school with no aspirations for college, Britney knew her body had the potential to serve her well. She reminded me so much of my younger self, which is why I hired her over the other candidates. I planned to teach her how to use that body for good and try to help her avoid some of the mistakes I made. She had a rough edge and not only did I like that about her, I understood exactly where it came from.

"What's up, Lyric."

"Mrs. Delaney!" I corrected her.

Britney rolled her eyes. "Mrs. Delaney," she mocked me, dragging the end of my name for a few beats.

I gave her one of my 'don't play with me' looks.

Britney straightened up. "What can I do for you, Mrs. Delaney?" Averting her eyes, she shifted from one foot to the other.

"Let's call it a day." Her skeptical sideways glance begged me to clarify my statement. "Yes. We're going home!"

"Am I still getting paid for the rest of the day?"

I rolled my eyes. "Yes!"

"You feeling okay, Mrs. Delaney?"

"I'm fine! Now go before I change my mind."

Britney moved as if there were hot coals under her feet. "See ya!" She grabbed her purse from behind the reception area and headed for the door where she stopped short. "Do I have to come in tomorrow?"

I glared at her with twisted lips. She laughed and waved off her attempt at stretching my kindness.

"See you tomorrow, boss lady!" Britney flew through the door.

I pulled the silk curtains, blocking the view to the inside through the large glass storefront. It was obvious that this had been a retail space before Nate bought the place. The spacious storage room in the rear was now my office. The designer built a partition behind the reception desk, separating the space to create two designated areas. We planned to use that for open calls, classes, and rehearsals. With stark white walls, splashes of bright color, and wood floors buffed to a high shine, the school looked fresh and airy.

Once I completed this first call for models, I hoped to find a few gems to book for the launch event. Candy and Britney had already begun sifting through scores of headshots to pick out a few people to interview. I'd step in to make the final decisions.

I took one last look around to make sure I had turned off all the computers and lights. Stepping out onto Broadway after locking the doors to my very own business felt surreal. I never imagined this dream would actually come true. Instead of walking, I practically skipped around the corner to the garage where my car was parked. Rush hour hadn't yet begun, so getting through Manhattan and across the bridge happened quickly.

I stopped at the grocery store and picked up crab legs, potatoes, corn, and asparagus. Nate loved those funny looking stems. Before marrying him, I don't think I'd ever seen them before. Now I loved them too.

At home, I prepared the food to cook later, set up the formal dining room with candles and fine china, and then took a long hot bath. I called Nate to make sure he didn't plan to work late, and so I could gauge how much time I had left to make sure everything would be just right when he walked through the door.

Just like I'd asked him to do, he called me as he was leaving the office. By the time he wrangled rush hour traffic and pulled into our driveway, dinner was ready. I answered the door in black, sheer lingerie. Nate's eyes opened wide as he walked in. He sniffed and then sniffed again.

"Smells good in here. Who cooked?"

"I did." I took his coat and hung it in the hall closet. When I turned back, Nate was still standing by the door as still as a block of wood.

"What? You cooked?"

I swatted him. "Don't be silly. You know I can cook."

"Yeah, but it's easy to forget." Twisting my lips, I crossed my arms over my chest and pouted. Nate took me in his arms. "I'm just kidding, Babe." After a moment, he pulled back, holding me at arm's length. "What's the occasion?"

"I just wanted to do something special." Nate's perfect smile sent a shimmer down my spine. "Come on, let's go!" I grabbed Nate's hand.

"Where are we going?" He stumbled to keep up with me.

"Upstairs."

Nate growled, and I couldn't help but giggle. It reminded me of how happy we were when we first got together. I used to do all kinds of things to win him over. Show up at his office with long coats and nothing but underwear beneath them. We'd make love almost anywhere. The higher the chances of getting caught, the better the sex. One time his secretary almost caught us. I was splayed across Nate's desk with my legs wrapped around his torso. He'd stuffed my mouth with a scarf to keep me from making too much noise. Luckily, I had locked the door when I came in, knowing my intentions. His secretary tried the lock, but it was when she banged on the door, calling his name that we realized she'd been trying to get his attention. I jumped off the desk and closed my coat as Nate scrambled to get his pants back on and buckle his belt. With mischief laced across my lips, I smiled, opened the door, and sauntered right past his suspicious secretary while the scent of sex hung in the air. Our business was 'unfinished' which meant he was sure to show up at my apartment after work. I loved leaving him wanting more.

I pulled Nate into the master bath and turned on the shower. R&B music flowed through the speakers embedded in the walls. Nate's erection grew as I peeled his work clothes off piece by piece. Once he was fully naked, he slid his hand around my waist. I shimmied out of his reach.

"No. No. Not yet."

Nate looked frustrated. I turned him toward the shower, handed him a washcloth, and towel and told him I'd be back.

"You're not going to join me?"

I shook my head and walked out. Downstairs, I set the food on the table, placed the wine in a cooler, and lit the candles. By the time I got back upstairs, Nate was stepping out of the shower. I helped him dry off and handed him a pair of silk lounge pants to put on—no underwear or shirt.

Leading the way, I took Nate down to the dining room and we fed each other until we had our fill of food.

Wiping his mouth with the fancy napkin, Nate shook his head. "Mmm. That was delicious." Then he looked at me with lust twinkling in his eyes. "Now, what's for dessert?" Nate pulled back his chair and I sat in his lap.

Following his lead, I straddled him—chest to chest. We kissed until we could hardly breathe. Our hands roamed every part of each other's body. I rolled my hips and Nate groaned, grabbing my behind and pulling me closer to him. His erection grew under me—poking my center, causing me to shiver with longing, and then the bell rang.

I looked at Nate and he looked at me. "Are you expecting company?" he asked. I shook my head, eager to get back to where we had left off. Ignoring the uninvited guest, we started back at each other. The bell rang again.

I sucked my teeth. "Are you expecting someone?"

Nate shook his head. We went back to kissing and grinding our heated bodies against one another. The ringing continued, followed by knocking—no banging.

Nate let his head fall back against the back of the chair and rolled his eyes toward the ceiling.

"Let's just go upstairs and ignore whoever it is. They should have called anyway." Contrary to my expectations, Nate agreed.

"Let's go." He took me by the hand, leading the way.

We snickered as if we were two teenagers trying not to get caught by our parents, but stopped short when a voice outside the door yelled my name. I froze. Had Cypher become that bold, I thought at first, and then realized it was a woman's voice.

Nate's face grew serious and he started in the direction of the door. I pulled his arm.

"Wait!" I didn't know who that was or what to expect. Cypher could have been out there with the woman yelling at my door.

"There could be an emergency." Nate shook me off and continued toward the door.

I couldn't move. I wanted to follow Nate to see who it was, but my feet had forgotten how to walk. My heart pounded and my hands became clammy. This had to be a trick that Cypher was behind. Everything shifted to slow motion as I watched Nate peek out the window and look back at me confused. He didn't recognize the person standing on the porch, but I'd finally listened well enough to recognize the voice. I was no longer concerned about Cypher.

My heart quickened more even though life still moved at an oddly slow pace as I tried to process what was happening. My ears had become sensitive, magnifying every sound. The locks clicked as loud as gunshots. My heart resonated in my inner ear like drums at a live concert. The door crept open with an eerie resounding creak. Footsteps reverberated, bouncing through the large space. I remembered we were both in pajamas—me in sexy lingerie too revealing for anyone else's eyes—but I couldn't get my mouth to expel words in time.

"It's about time!" she said, walking right past Nate as if she were invited in. She looked around in awe and whistled. "Wow! I knew my baby had married well, but I never imagined this! You must be Nate." She dropped her bag on the floor and held out her hand.

"And you are?" Nate asked, looking completely confused.

My heart started beating even faster. I gasped for air.

"Justine!" She shook his hand excitedly. "Lyric's mom."

Nate turned toward me, but suddenly I could no longer see clearly. My vision blurred and when his voice filtered through my haze, I heard him say, "You're alive?"

CHAPTER 39

erri

WHEN MY PHONE RANG, I snatched it off the nightstand wondering who had the audacity to call me so close to midnight. It didn't matter that sleep had eluded me for weeks. It was still rude. Then I saw Camilla's number and sent the call to voicemail. I wasn't ready to hear her pathetic voice. She called again. I didn't answer the second time either. My phone chirped. It was Camilla again, but what she texted made my breath catch. I sat straight up in the bed and called her back.

"What do you mean, Riley's missing?"

Camilla sobbed, struggling to speak through her cries. "I've been trying to call Rick, but he's not answering." I could hear from the guest room that Chris was in a deep sleep. "It's Riley. She never came home from school. I thought she was with you guys because she was upset with me. Rick texted me to say that she wasn't there. Every time I called, she didn't answer and then my calls started going straight to voicemail. I called all her girlfriends and none of them has heard from her. Even they are worried that something might have happened."

By the time Camilla was done speaking, I'd tossed the covers back, flew down the hall, and was now at Chris' side with the phone on speaker.

"When's the last time you heard from her?" You would have never known that he'd been fast asleep seconds before.

"I got a text this afternoon asking if she could go to her friend's house after school. I told her she had to come home and do her homework first. I spoke to her friend and she said she hadn't seen Riley since after lunch."

I racked my brain trying to think of where Riley could be. "Is Riley still dating that boy, Trevor?" Chris's head whipped in my direction. His face was painted with a scowl, making it obvious that he was the only one that didn't know about Riley's boyfriend.

"No. She hasn't mentioned him in weeks."

"Who is this boy? Get him on the phone!" Chris barked.

"I already spoke to Trevor. He has no idea where Riley is either."

"Give me his number. Where does he live?" Chris marched to his closet and started pulling clothes off the hanger. He jammed his legs into a pair of jeans from the pile he created on the floor and tore a shirt from a hanger.

"She's not there, Chris. I've already spoken to his mother. Trevor called up some of their other friends and he has everyone else looking for Riley. He's worried too."

"Did you call the police?"

I could hear Camilla sobbing again. "No!" she answered through sniffles. "I really thought she was just acting out. She heard me talking about...what happened...with us...when I was on the phone this morning before she went to school. She blamed me for breaking up the family and stormed out. I thought she was just trying to aggravate me by staying out. But

RENEE DANIEL FLAGLER

even when we are at odds, it's not like Riley to ignore my calls or texts, and the fact that none of her friends have seen her has me really worried. I just know something bad has happened." Camilla broke down. "This is entirely my fault."

"Camilla! Calm down. Call the police. We're on our way." I looked up and Chris was fully dressed. "Go get dressed. I'll wake up Alisa."

I followed his orders, running to throw on something quick. Picking up the first thing I laid my hands on, I ended up in a pair of leggings and a cotton tunic. Then I slipped my feet into a pair of flats.

I met Chris in Alisa's room and helped get her dressed. She moved lazily with her eyes half closed. She managed to get her shoes on by herself and make her way down the steps. Chris went to start the car.

The ride to Camilla's was surreal. Chris rocked forward and backward and drove wildly, blowing stop signs and speeding through caution lights. He'd cut the time it took to get to Camilla's in half. She met us at the door. Putting our differences aside, I held her trembling body as she fell into my arms.

"We have to find my baby!"

"Did you call the cops?" Chris walked into the house, past Camilla, and got right down to business. "Don't you have the app that people use to find or track phones? Did you activate it? Where was she last?" Questions poured from Chris's mouth like water rushing from a fall.

"The cops are on their way. The app can't locate the phone unless it's on. All the calls are going to voicemail so the battery must be dead.

Chris put both hands on his head and paced. Alisa lay on the couch and I started making calls. I wasn't sure who to call or how they could help, but once I sat Camilla down, I needed to do something with myself.

I called Paige first. She asked if I wanted her to come over. I told her I'd keep her posted. Then I called Chris's sister and begged her not to tell her mother just yet, but I felt she needed to know. She told me she was on her way and hung up the phone.

The police finally arrived and took our report. I knew they were only doing their jobs, but they annoyed me with the loaded questions they asked, insinuating possible foul play on the part of any of us. From the disheveled, withered look of Camilla, I could understand where they were coming from. She still wasn't her old self. After this, I was going to call her sister. Camilla needed an intervention. Camilla used to take great care with her personal appearance. Even after finally going back to work, Camilla often looked like she'd just crawled out of bed. Her hair needed a good wash and her clothes hung on her as if they were still on the hanger.

With nothing more to do, I sat in awkward silence in the living room while Chris paced from one window to the other. I'm sure they felt as helpless as I did—probably more. Camilla parked herself at the kitchen table and rested her head in her hands. She'd stopped crying for a while. I watched as she eyed Chris, tracking his movements. Slowly she got up from the table, reached under one of the cabinets. She turned her back to us.

I knew what she was doing, but Chris was too preoccupied with his pacing to notice. By the time she fully twisted the cap and went to pour her first drink, Chris caught on to what was happening. Speedily closing the space between them, Chris was at her back. Camilla jumped, startled by his sudden presence. Clear liquid splashed over the top of the glass and spilled on the floor. Chris snatched the bottle of vodka from her hand and sent it sailing across the kitchen.

"This is what started all of this crap in the first place!" He went back to his post, pacing from window to window. Camilla wrapped her arms around her body and backed up against the wall. Then, burying her head in her hands, she whimpered. Chris sucked his teeth, leaving her to stew in her own anguish.

Closing my eyes, I took a deep breath and sat for a few moments, trying not to let this affect me. When I couldn't take it anymore, I found myself at her side, helping her to a nearby chair. She threw her arms around me and sobbed into my shoulder. I hugged her back.

"I want my family back. Please. I just want my family back."

Chris's phone rang, causing all of us to jump. "Yeah…we're at Camilla's…okay." Chris's short answers made me curious. He didn't bother telling us who was on the phone and I didn't bother asking.

"I can't sit here anymore." Chris's outburst startled us again. "I'm going to look for her."

"Chris!" I looked at my cell phone. It was almost two in the morning. I was about to tell him to just stay in case the police came back or called, but the desperate look he cast my way caused my words to jam in my throat. His eyes were red.

"What?" His voice was harsh.

"Nothing." I walked Camilla to the couch. "Call me immediately if you find her."

Without another word, Chris was gone, leaving me with Camilla—the crumpled mess that she was. She held on tighter, not letting me move even to get a cup of water. When I finally peeled my arm away from her, she followed me into the bedroom to check on Alisa and back into the kitchen to get water to wet my dry mouth.

I sat at the table to keep her from clinging to me. She walked the kitchen floor, pushing her limp wiry hair from over her eyes. She looked at me with that same guarded stare, and then looked back at the cabinet where she'd retrieved the first bottle of liquor. I glared back, standing, daring her to try it again. Chris was right. Her drinking had become problematic.

Camilla's shoulders slumped and she huffed. "Please, Kerri. I just need one drink."

Shifting my weight to one leg, I crossed my arms, daring her to try me. Shamefully, she looked down and walked back to the living room. I followed her. She sat and turned her back to me when I took a seat on the chair facing her. We sat there for a long while until headlights flickered across the front window. Both of us stood and ran to the door, hoping Chris had found Riley. Both of us were visibly disappointed when we saw that it was Chris's sister.

I opened the door for Loren. Camilla stepped back. Loren kissed me and stepped in solemnly and pulled Camilla into her arms. Camilla broke down again. After we reiterated to Loren the little we knew, the three of us sat in silence for a while. The flash of another set of headlights brought us all to our feet. It was Chris, but Riley wasn't with him. It was now past three in the morning and we still had no idea where Riley was. We couldn't help but cry when Chris walked back into the house alone. Camilla rocked back and forth, holding herself as she tapped her leg.

"My baby," she kept repeating.

Loren started praying aloud. The rest of us quieted, silently agreeing to every request she made of the Lord, hoping he'd be gracious enough to grant them. "Bring Riley home, Lord."

"Amen!" We all cosigned and returned to our silent positions —Camilla rocking on the couch, Loren at her side, me in the chair across from them and Chris at the window.

As drained as we were, no one dared fall asleep.

Four miserable, grueling hours had passed since Camilla's initial phone call before the police found Riley. We all piled into Chris's car and headed to the hospital two towns away from where the police said she was. They wouldn't give us much more information.

During the ride, my imagination ran wild. I imagined Riley

with tattered clothing and covered in blood. I cried all the way there. The four of us burst through the hospital doors. They directed us to Riley's bedside in the emergency room. Riley looked as though she was sleeping peacefully. I wanted to shake her awake so she could tell us what happened. I stood at the foot of her bed, rubbing her legs. Loren was next to me and Chris and Camilla were at the head of the bed. Camilla leaned her face against Riley's and her tears dripped onto the pillow.

The nurse's voice startled us. Behind her stood two officers. After introductions, we followed them to a small waiting room. It appeared that someone gave Riley the date rape drug. They were about to examine her. Camilla, Loren, and I all gasped at the word rape while Chris's twitching jaw and clenching fists revealed how he felt about the information. I moved to his side and took his hand.

The police officers explained that other officers in a squad car had spotted her stumbling down the street. She was barely coherent but managed to mumble her name. Those officers took her to the hospital since it was obvious that she was under the influence of something. She didn't have her cell phone, school bag or wallet, so they couldn't find an address or number to call. When Riley was finally coherent enough, the hospital social worker managed to get an address out of her. They contacted the local police and that's when they called us.

My heart felt like it would burst through my chest at any second. Camilla was crying uncontrollably. I'm sure that, just like me, they were trying to imagine what Riley had gone through. We stayed in that room listening to each other cry and breathe until they were done with Riley's rape kit.

Finally, we were able to see her again. She was awake but groggy. We took turns hugging her, kissing her, and whispering that all that mattered was the fact that she was safe. All she could do was cry.

CHAPTER 40

 aige

I COULDN'T BELIEVE I let the girls talk me into allowing them to make cookies on a weeknight. Flour covered the counter, the floor, and parts of both Scotland and Jayden's faces. I enjoyed myself too much to get angry, and the sound of their laughter made me smile deep down inside. Jayden had been with us for a week longer than she was supposed to be, but I didn't mind. I almost wished that we had full custody, but Maya would never go for that. Jayden was her carrot. As long as she was able to dangle her over Rick's head, she got whatever her heart desired from him.

This time, Jayden's extended stay wasn't the result of Maya's many antics. Maya was actually in the hospital getting her lap band repaired for the second time. It appeared that she had refused to stop overeating and making herself sick. Unfortunately, she experienced some complications and a procedure that should have been rectified in a short period of time turned into an extra week in the hospital. She never told us why she was going into the hospital, but we found out when the doctor called Rick regarding the complications. He was still listed as the emergency contact on her records and identified as someone with whom her condition could be discussed. She even identified him as her spouse on some medical forms. With enough to deal with, I tried my hardest not to let that get to me. However, my tolerance tank was running on fumes after these past few trying months. I wasn't sure how much more I could take.

I didn't want to leave my husband, but I deserved to know what it felt like to be a priority in my relationship. I wanted Rick to stand up for me just once. Despite all that I put up with over the years, the clock started ticking on our relationship when he questioned me about my treatment of Jayden. How dare he believe Maya's lies?

I shook my head and brought my attention back to the beautiful girls giggling in my kitchen. Jayden was sharing another nugget of gossip, filling us in on the drama of middle school. Scotland was fascinated by the stories of who liked who, who didn't like who, and which boy was the cutest. Jayden's stories were like a forbidden movie to Scotland's first-grade world. She couldn't help but giggle behind her palm when Jayden told of the time two eighth-graders were caught kissing in the stairwell.

"Yuck! They're nasty!" Scotland squealed.

Jayden and I looked at each other and laughed.

"You won't say that when you get to middle school!" Jayden acknowledged.

"Oh! Yes, I will." Scotland was adamant about her declaration as she placed lopsided balls of dough on the cookie sheet. "I would never kiss a boy!"

"You better not!" At once, all of our heads whipped in the direction of Rick's alarmed voice. I hadn't heard him come in the door. "What kind of conversation are you all having in here?" He looked at each of us skeptically.

I continued laughing while the girls both focused on meticulously spacing the cookies without saying a word. They wouldn't dare have that discussion with Rick, who continued looking back and forth between the three of us, apparently waiting for an answer. When he signed, I assumed he realized he wasn't going to get one. He put his briefcase down and walked to the fridge. "What's for dinner? Cookies?"

The girls finally released the laughs they'd been holding in. Rick and I laughed with them.

"This is why I love being over here. It's always so much fun," Jayden said and continued laughing. "Plus you let us make and eat cookies before bed!" she teased.

Jayden slid the cookies inside the oven and hugged my waist. Scotland followed suit. Rick stopped making his plate and looked our way. His expression turned from one of amusement to confusion.

"Okay, ladies!" I said, pulling back from the group hug. "Speaking of bed, when these cookies are finished, that's exactly where you're going—right after you two brush your teeth. Jayden, go get your sax and put it by the door. You have to be at school early tomorrow for band practice and I don't want you to forget it. I have meetings in the office and I won't be able to bring it to school for you like I did the other day.

"Okay!" Jayden bounced off and Scotland ran after her.

Rick put the plate he had just made in the microwave, watched the girls leave the kitchen, and then looked my way wearing that expression that always preceded a line of questioning. I wasn't up for an interrogation, so I left him in the kitchen and went to help the girls find outfits for the next day. I didn't go back into the kitchen until the timer went off.

"Come on, girls. The cookies are ready!"

They thundered down the steps. We pulled the cookies out

and the sweet scent of warm chocolate filled the room. I poured two cups of milk, knowing they'd want to eat them while they were still gooey and hot. All of us gathered at the table, where Rick was finishing his dinner and ate until we couldn't eat anymore.

After more laughter and silly conversation, Rick looked at his watch. "Okay, girls. It's eight-thirty." He used his stern voice.

The girls grumbled, but stood immediately, cleaned their areas and headed upstairs for showers.

"I'll be up in a minute," I said, filling the sink with warm soapy water to wash the dried chocolate from the cookie sheet and plate.

I felt Rick's eyes on me but continued to ignore him. I didn't feel like bickering tonight. I finished the dishes, wiped down the counter and stove in silence, and headed upstairs. After checking in on the girls, I took a shower and crawled into bed. It took a while before Rick came into the bedroom. While I avoided his unspoken questions down in the kitchen, I knew he wouldn't let me go to sleep without mentioning what was on his mind.

My shoulders tensed and I took a few deep breaths. He walked in slowly, taking contemplative steps. Rounding the bed on his side, he sat down and huffed. I waited.

"I just had a little talk with Jayden," he said after a few moments.

I wondered where he was going with this—especially since I expected him to start asking more questions about Blair. I had finally told him a version of the truth, that Blair was a trainer giving me information to help with fitness goals. I was careful never to actually mention Blair's name. Blair had become my sounding board. I knew it was inappropriate, but with the outlook on my marriage being dismal, I wasn't ready to let him go. I knew I'd be able to lean on him in case my marriage completely fell apart.

"And?" Now that I knew it wasn't about Blair, I was curious.

"She told me she never told Maya anything bad about you. It appears that I may owe you an apology."

"May?" My voice rose. Now I knew why he had watched so intently when Jayden and Scotland hugged me earlier. It wasn't until then that he realized Maya had lied about me treating Jayden badly. It didn't matter that he had witnessed me sacrifice so much since we'd been together. I didn't get any credit for adjusting my life to care for his child. I was the one who made sure she ate, helped her with homework, drove her to school, planned girl's days out, and loved her as if she were biologically mine.

"I'm sorry! I know Jayden loves you and loves being here. I guess I should have—"

"You should have what, Rick? You should have believed your wife in the first place? You know Maya is a liar!" I stood, unable to continue to share the same air as him. The room suddenly felt smaller. I needed to get out of there. Rick stared at me. His expression showed his regret. I shook my head. "You couldn't believe me when I told you the day you brought it up. You had to verify it with Jayden. I have never mistreated her." My voice cracked and I fought back tears. "If it took a conversation with Jayden for you to finally believe that I hadn't done anything wrong, then you have no faith in me at all. My word apparently doesn't hold water against Maya's. Why don't you just go back to her since she has all the power anyway?" I turned to walk out of the room.

I had lost so many battles in my marriage. I wasn't sure if I even cared about the war any longer. I just knew I was tired of fighting.

CHAPTER 41

 yric

THE PHONE RANG and I sat straight up in the bed. Initially, I thought the ringing was in my dream—rather my nightmare —since it involved me opening the door to Cypher standing on my doorstep. I grabbed my cell phone just as Nate jumped up, but it wasn't ringing. It was Nate's phone. I went from being nervous to livid in zero point five seconds. Who was calling my husband at two in the morning?

Nate sat halfway up in the bed, grabbed his phone, and answered with a groggy, "Hello."

I could hear the person screaming through the phone.

"Sweetheart, slow down. I can't understand what you're saying...Oh God! When...where...I'm on my way." Nate tossed the phone, threw the covers back, and jumped out of bed.

"Nate!" He didn't seem to hear me calling his name as he scrambled to put on the pants he laid across the chaise before going to bed. Nate looked scared. My heart lurched, then fell into the pit of my stomach. "What's going on?"

"Vivian. She's in the hospital. It's bad!" Nate rummaged around for his shirt.

"What happened?" Now I was on my feet looking for something to put on.

"She got hit by a drunk driver going the wrong way on the expressway. She's in critical condition. I have to meet the girls at the hospital. The police just left the house."

"The police?"

"Yes!"

I moved faster. I didn't like Vivian very much, but that didn't mean I wanted something bad to happen to her. I stepped into a pair of jeans and pulled a wrinkled sweater over my head before heading to the guest room to wake my mother. She and Nate had spent the past few nights staying up late getting to know one another. They were close in age and had a lot in common. I thought he'd despise her, but instead, he seemed to have become best friends with my mother. Over bottles of wine, they answered every curious question about one another. He told her all about Vivian and his twins and she revealed every detail about how she ended up in jail for killing the boyfriend who tried to rape me when I was a teen and now, she had been released for good behavior. She didn't mean to kill him when she hit him with the lamp. She just wanted to get him off me.

"What?" she grunted with her eyes still closed as I shook her awake.

"Ma! Get up. Something happened to Vivian. She's in the hospital." I continued shaking her.

Jerking away, she rolled over and burrowed against her pillow. "So what does that have to do with me?"

"It's bad, Ma!" She opened one eye. "Vivian is in critical condition!"

The other eye popped open and she sat up.

"What…" she yawned. "What happened?"

"I don't know. We're going to the hospital now. I just wanted to let you know we were leaving."

She swung her legs over the side of the bed. "Give me a minute. I'm coming with you."

Within ten minutes, the three of us were headed to the hospital. Nate had barely put the car in park before opening the door to get out. My mother and I had to trot behind him to keep up. The twins met us at the door. Sidney was hysterical. Sky's arms were wrapped around her trembling body. Nate took both of them into his arms. My mother rubbed his shoulder. I stood there not knowing what to do with myself.

When the hug-fest was over, Nate asked where Vivian was. Sky told him that she'd been taken into emergency surgery. He held both their hands as they headed back inside to the waiting area.

There wasn't anything we could do but wait. I finally mustered up the courtesy to tell the girls that I was sorry about what happened to Vivian, and I truly was. I was expecting them to suck their teeth or look at each other the way they do when I say something that they'd rather snub. Instead, both of them said thank you and even managed weak smiles. Nate introduced them to my mother. That's when they started to ignore me. Justine had a way with people. She kept them engaged and even made them laugh a time or two.

Sydney's fiancé showed up and for the next few hours, we paced, took turns nodding off in those uncomfortable chairs and checking in with the nurses to see if there were any updates. The pre-dawn solitude was chased away when the sun came up, bringing the bustle of more workers and patients. Finally, a doctor came to us asking for Sydney and Sky. We all stood at once. Hope filled the twin's eyes as they held onto one another. Nate stood behind them.

"She's in recovery," the doctor stated after introducing himself.

"Can we see her? How is she? Will she be okay?" Sky, who had been the composed one, blurted one question after the other.

"It's too early to tell. She lost a lot of blood and suffered tremendously. The collision was apparently head-on, pinning her behind the wheel." The doctor paused, pressing his lips together as if he didn't want to have to say more. Nate, Sydney, and Sky moved in closer, waiting desperately for the next word to fall from the doctor's mouth. "It appears that one of the broken bones punctured her lung. We're hoping she'll pull through. We've done all we can." He paused again. "If you'll give me a moment, I'll send a nurse out to bring you in to see her. Due to the injuries she sustained, the surgery, and the amount of pain both of these cause, she had to be heavily sedated so she can heal. She won't be able to respond."

Minutes later, a nurse came for Nate, Sydney, and Sky. I walked in right along with them. I needed to see for myself. I was already feeling bad about all the things I'd said about Vivian. As we walked, I took Nate by the hand. Sydney was in her fiancé's arms and Sky had Nate's other hand. The closer we got to where Vivian was, the tighter Nate held my hand.

Vivian was connected to several machines, with tubes going up her nose and down her throat. Several IV bags hung from a stand at her side. Lights flashed and a symphony of hisses dings and beeps rang from the equipment. Her right arm and leg were wrapped in casts. Cuts and bruises covered her face and the part of her arm that was exposed. Her breathing seemed labored.

Immediately, Sydney began wailing, burying her face in her fiancé's chest.

"Ma!" Sky cried. She reached out to touch her hand, being careful of her fragile state. Nate went to her side and rubbed her back. Sky turned to her father and cried into his shoulder. I felt like I didn't belong there, but I refused to leave. I was going to stay by Nate's side.

One of the machines began a series of piercing beeps, sparking other loud sounds. Vivian's chest heaved.

"Ma!" Sydney yelled.

Abruptly we were pushed aside by a flurry of staff rushing toward Vivian, calling out code blues and other lingo that I deemed to be crucial. They synchronized and started working on her, calling out terms that made doctors and nurses move even faster. One doctor started yelling commands. Someone else ran to Vivian with a crash cart.

"Get them out of here!" a registered nurse screamed. Immediately, a team of physicians and nurses tried to usher us out as calmly as they could.

Panic set in and Sydney yelled. "No. Ma! No!" Reaching toward Vivian, she tried to run to her, only to be stopped by another nurse.

Sky tried to go around the crew that slowed her sister down and was also stopped. "Ma!" she cried out.

"Vivian. No!" Nate bellowed at the same time the doctor yelled, "Clear!" and placed the pads against her battered chest, sending shockwaves through her broken body.

Even as they tried to push us out, I couldn't stop looking at Vivian. Seeing her body jerk and rise from the volts shooting through her made my breath catch. They did it again and then once more. More physicians came in as we were ushered through the double doors and down the corridors separating the waiting rooms from the recovery area.

Sydney and Sky wailed, their cries bouncing off the sterile walls, expanding down the hallway. Witnessing their pain made tears fall from my eyes. Nate looked numb. He held Sky as we stumbled toward the waiting area.

"Mommy!" Sydney yelled continuously. "Please, mommy!"

"Lord, don't let her die!" Sky moaned.

When we made it to the waiting area, my mother stood to her feet and took Sky from Nate's hands, hugging her tight. She wetted Justine's shoulders with tears. Sydney's fiancé rocked her in his arms. Nate walked to the window and stared out. I stood beside him, rubbing circles on his back. Nate turned, and the look in his eyes scared me. I thought I saw regret through his tears.

Soon after, the doctor came back out. With a shake of his head, a drawn countenance and deep breath, he told us what we had all been afraid of hearing. Vivian was dead. He offered the opportunity to come back to say final goodbyes. This time, everyone came in and what scared me more than the forlorn look in Nate's eyes was the way he wept over Vivian's body, apologizing and telling her how he never stopped loving her as if I wasn't even standing there. My mother looked at me but didn't say a word. I knew she had taken all of this in and I would hear from her later.

In the days following, Nate refused to eat or sleep. I couldn't get more than a few words out of him at a time. He hardly even spoke to my mother. I gave him space to mourn up until the day of the funeral, which was one of the most extravagant I'd ever seen, with musicians, chariots, and scores of people sharing stories about how wonderful Vivian was. The way those people spoke of her made me feel small and insignificant. Instead of being moved by their words of encouragement, I was jealous.

After the funeral, I expected Nate to begin to bounce back, not skip work and cry himself to sleep every night. I thought I was at risk of losing Nate to Vivian when she was alive, and I'd been ready and willing to fight for my man. However, it seemed her pull was more powerful in death than it ever was when she lived fifteen minutes away. How was I supposed to fight that?

CHAPTER 42

erri

AFTER A WEEK, we were only beginning to see traces of the Riley we knew. The girl who used to spend hours on the phone, texting her friends and being the center of her social circle had crawled into a cave somewhere, leaving behind a withdrawn teen in her place. The only good that came of this situation was the fact that Camilla snapped out of her pathetic existence and started acting like she was a living being once again, especially after finding out what really happened with Riley.

She and a few of her high school friends had planned to cut school together, but only Riley had successfully made it out and reached their designated meeting spot after grabbing a bite to eat. The meet-up was supposed to be at the home of one of her friend's older cousins who had just graduated from high school. When Riley arrived, the boy let her in and told her she could hang out in the living room until the rest of them arrived. The young man offered Riley a drink, and she couldn't remember anything after that besides walking the dark streets in search of home more than twelve hours later, and then being picked up by the police. Fortunately, the rape kit confirmed that she hadn't actually been raped, but someone had tried. Her underwear had been torn. The police assumed that even under the influence of whatever drug she'd been given, Riley fought her assailant. The authorities scraped the skin from underneath her fingernails to help find the person who had done this.

Chunks of time evaded her memory, but when Riley was able to tell us what happened, we had to stop Chris from going rogue on the young woman whose cousin slipped Riley the date rape drug. We filed charges and he was charged with attempted rape and endangering the welfare of a minor. The girl's parents apologized and offered to help in any way they could, but Riley and the young woman were no longer friends.

I knocked on Camilla's door. She opened it almost immediately and took the tray of Starbuck chai lattes balanced in my hands.

"Where is she?" I asked, following Camilla through the house.

"In the bedroom. Just like yesterday. She comes in, does her homework and lies in bed," Camilla said as she placed the tray on the kitchen table.

"We need to get her out of that somehow."

"I know." Camilla shook her head. "But how?" She pulled out one of the chairs, sat down hard, and rested her elbows on the table.

I studied the deep lines in her face, noticing that despite the worry, she looked better than she had a long time.

I sat across from her and studied her some more. We remained silent for several moments and then I stood to go check in on Riley.

"Kerri...wait."

I paused.

"Please...sit back down for a moment."

I sat slowly, cautiously, wondering what she wanted.

"I need to get this off my chest. With all that has been going on, we didn't have time to really talk. You know...just you and me. I think we need to."

I took a deep breath. I didn't want to talk to Camilla. I only wanted to be there for Riley and then get back home to the nice dinner that Chris promised to prepare in his attempts to return to a place of normalcy. Not that we had resolved anything at our home, either. Since Riley's disappearance, we had all just existed.

"I'm sorry. I'm sorry. I'm sorry. I can't explain what happened to me after Aaron's death, but I want you to know that I'm sorry. Riley was right! I ruined this family and I'm sorry for that. Not that any of it was intentional."

I wanted to walk out because I didn't know if I believed her.

"I love Chris," Camilla continued, and the hairs on my arms rose. "But not in that way." I exhaled the breath I'd been holding. "Chris is my friend, at least he used to be—he's my daughter's father. I care about him as a person who is important in my life, but not in any romantic way. I haven't felt anything like that for him since Riley was born. Getting married seemed like the right thing to do, despite the fact that we didn't love each other in a way that a married couple should. It's the same now, and I need you to know that. I have never made any kind of advances toward your husband since we divorced, nor has he made any toward me. Both of us love you too much. You may not believe it, but it's true."

I couldn't speak. A mix of emotions clogged my throat. I swallowed, but still felt a lump there. I wanted to believe her, she seemed sincere enough, but I was still angry.

"Aaron's death knocked my world completely off balance. I couldn't tell my nightmares from reality. The hole in my heart was swallowing me up. You were there for me every step of the way. What you and Chris didn't know was that I wanted to die myself." Camilla stopped talking for a moment. "I tried to." She paused again. "Riley, you and Chris are the reasons I'm still here. I drank and took sleeping pills just so I wouldn't have to deal with the reality of my fiancé being gone." Camilla started crying. "We should be happily married, enjoying our lives as newlyweds right now." She smeared her tears across her cheeks. It took a few moments to gather herself. I wanted to hug her but stayed put.

"Anyway," she finally said, "you're so important to my daughter and me. I'd never betray you. Since that horrible incident, I've tossed my sleeping pills. I could no longer deal with the hallucinations or seeing Aaron's face when he really wasn't there. I was on my way to getting better when this happened with Riley. That shook up my life once again. I couldn't imagine losing my daughter as well. I'm getting help now, and Riley, too. I hope you can find it in your heart to forgive me for causing this family so much pain."

I just sat there crying. Something deep inside me allowed me to believe her. Camilla reached across the table and took my hand. I let her, and together we sat there and cried.

CHAPTER 43

 aige

I THOUGHT we were going to the hospital to drop Jayden off so she could visit her mom. Imagine my surprise when Rick came back to the car less than fifteen minutes later to let me know that Maya was being released. I wondered what that had to do with me until he explained that he offered to drive her home.

I sucked my teeth, not offering any other response. Rick shook his head and disappeared back into the hospital as I continued to wait in the car with Scotland. My stomach growled and despite my hunger and looking forward to the lunch that we planned together at one of our favorite restaurants, my appetite vanished.

Almost a half-hour passed before Rick came back out with Maya being wheeled beside him and Jayden holding her hand. I sat in the car across the lot as if I hadn't seen any of them. Leaving Maya, the orderly, and Jayden at the entrance, Rick walked to the car, jumped in, and looked at me with pleading in his eyes.

"We're just dropping her off. She has no one else to pick her up."

I turned my head and stared out the window as he wheeled the van around to the entrance. Hospitals had plenty of phone numbers for taxi services. I kept that thought to myself.

When we reached the bay in front of the hospital's entrance, Maya cut her eyes at me. Instead of responding, I took a deep breath. I had already decided that her influence had gone too far. With Maya at the helm, this marriage wasn't working for me. Mentally, I'd been preparing myself to leave, despite the love I had for Rick. Without critical changes that were now long overdue, there was no way I could stay. I planned to tell Rick once Jayden had returned home with Maya. I didn't want to upset the house any more than it was while she was there. Her mother's health scare was enough for her to deal with.

Now that Maya was coming home, 'the talk' could now be pushed up on the calendar. The idea of telling Rick I was leaving was frightening. What would life be like without him? I closed my eyes and tried to regulate my breathing.

"Are you okay?"

I opened my eyes to find Rick staring at me. I hadn't realized that he'd opened my door.

"I'm fine."

"Are you sure?"

"Yes." I turned away. Looking in his concerned face jarred me. I wanted to cry but held back the tears.

Maya mumbled the entire time Rick and the orderly helped her into the second row of our minivan. Not once during the ride back to our house did she utter a single word in my direction. Yet, she moaned about her pain and complained every time Rick drove over a bump.

"Can you try to avoid some of these bumps? I'm in pain back here."

"Relax, Maya!" Rick looked at her from the corner of his eyes. His tightly set jaw revealed how annoyed he was at her ungrateful attitude.

She huffed and then moaned.

As if sensing the growing tension, Jayden jumped in and tried to lighten the atmosphere. "I'm glad you're coming home, mom!"

"Me too, baby! I'll need you to help me out a little for the next few days. Okay?"

"No problem. Me and Scotland made cookies this week."

"Scotland and I." I corrected.

"Oh yeah. Scotland and I."

"Say it however you want, sweetheart. You don't have to be bourgeois all the time, like Paige."

Once again, I closed my eyes and took several breaths. Rick's eyes were on me. I could feel them.

"It's okay, mom. It's the right way."

"Whatever, Jayden!" Maya snapped.

The remainder of the ride was fairly quiet, but the tension was like thick, noxious air.

"Why are we here?" Jayden asked when we pulled into our driveway. "I thought we were dropping mommy off."

"We are honey," Rick said. "We need to get your stuff for school. Mom wants you to come home with her now."

"I can't go to lunch with you guys?"

Rick sighed. "Mom wants you with her."

"I need you with me, Jayden," Maya snapped. "You've spent enough time with them. It's time to come back home."

"But I wanted to eat with the family."

"I am your family!" Maya's voice rose.

"Mommy, can Daddy just drop me off after we eat!"

"No!" Maya snapped. "Ow!" Maya groaned. "See what you made me do? Now I'm in pain."

"Sorry, mom."

I whipped my head around, shot Maya a snarl and looked over at Jayden. Dejected, she sat with her arms folded in her lap and head down.

"Jayden, we'll order your favorite dish and bring it by afterward, okay?" I tried to encourage her.

"O—"

Before Jayden could finish speaking, Maya jumped in. "She doesn't need you to bring her anything. Her mother is here now. What the hell have you been doing to my daughter to make her not want to be with her own mother?" Maya was huffing now. "Jayden you're coming home with me and that's it. I'll fix you something to eat."

I turned around and looked Maya directly in the face.

"What are you looking at?" she yelled at me.

I turned around and jumped out of the car.

"Paige!" Rick yelled and jumped out on his side.

My appetite had left and so had my tolerance. I opened the back door to get up close and personal with Maya. I wanted her to hear me loud and clear. I leaned toward her and she leaned back. My face and forefinger were inches from her nose. Rick was behind me.

"The kids, Paige!" Rick shouted.

I readjusted. It wouldn't have been good to tell Maya that I would kick her ass in front of our kids. "I'm done taking the higher road with you. You've got one more time to talk to me like I'm less than human and I swear I will—"

"Paige, please!" Rick pulled my arm. I jerked away.

"No one is trying to take your child away from you. You want Jayden to believe that we don't want her around. You want her to hate us like you do. But guess what, she doesn't." Maya snarled but didn't say anything. "And your lies can't change that."

Maya closed her gaping mouth and reeled in her wide eyes. "What...Get out of my face! I'm not a liar!" Maya sucked her teeth. "Rick! Take Jayden and me home now, but before you do, take a good look at your daughter because as long as this heifer is around," Maya tossed a thumb in my direction, "you'll never see her again!"

"Mommy, no!" Jayden cried out.

"Daddy! Don't let her take my sister away from me." Scotland screamed from the back of the car and started wailing.

"Jayden, go get your stuff now!"

"But mommy." Tears streamed down Jayden's face.

"Now!" Maya barked.

"Daddy!" Jayden called out to him.

I turned around to Rick and saw a look I'd never seen before in all our years of marriage. Though he hadn't spoken a word, his jaw was set tightly and his narrowed eyes were trained on Maya as if he was ready to pounce. His head tilted sideways. Instinctively, I took a step back.

"What did you just say?" Rick asked, as if her words were taking time to register in his mind.

It was like watching those dots on a computer go around in circles while the words 'loading' flashed above them. Once the message fully downloaded, Rick's fury came alive. In one swift motion, he pushed me out of the way and stood inches from Maya.

"Did you just say as long as Paige is around, I'll never see my daughter again?"

"Yes. I. Did. Humph!" Maya punctuated her declaration by crossing her arms over her ample breast.

"I don't think so." Rick's statement was so strong, so absolute, and uttered with so much bass that all movement stopped. The girls stopped crying and sat stark still. Both Maya and my head spun in his direction. "Jayden! Scotland! Go in the house now!" he growled. The girls ran inside.

"That's it! My wife..." Rick pointed a shaking finger in my direction. "has done more for Jayden than you have. My wife..." Rick stood up straight. "...has been there for our child when neither of us could be, and since the day she married me, she's loved and cared for Jayden even while putting up with all your bullshit. I take care of my child. I'm the one that provides for her, pays for private school, and makes sure she has a roof over her head while you sit on your behind. You haven't worked in years. I do it out of respect because you're the mother of my child, not because you're entitled to it, so don't *ever* forget that!" Rick's entire body was shaking now.

Maya's mouth hung open in shock.

"Now apologize to my wife or find another way home. Jayden is going to lunch with the family!"

Maya's mouth closed and she glared at Rick. "Why do I have to apologize to her? She jumped out of the car and got in my face."

Rick's only response was a glare.

Maya avoided his eyes and looked away with her head held high and her lips twisted defiantly.

"I told you to apologize to Paige or find another way home."

"Humph!" Slowly, Maya turned toward me and cut her eyes. "Sorry, Paige," she grumbled.

I was unable to move, still in shock by my husband's moxie, and proud of him for standing up to Maya for once. My level of admiration for Rick went from low red-alert levels to off the charts. He finally had my back. When Maya apologized, I smiled.

Rick pointed at her. "Don't ever threaten me again or you'll have a custody battle on your hands." Maya swallowed hard and said nothing. "Let's see who wins when you have no job, no money, and no place to live. I pay the bills over there!"

Rick took me by the hand. "Let's go get the kids."

Maya watched, unmoving, as we went in the house. Inside, we calmed the girls down and told them that Jayden would be joining us for lunch.

"Yay!" Scotland yelled. They hugged each other and smiled.

During the ride, Maya kept quiet all the way home. Being the consummate gentleman, Rick helped her inside. He took my hand when he got back in the car and held it all the way to the restaurant, throughout lunch, and during the ride back to Maya's to drop a happy Jayden off, and then all the way back home.

Back at home, he stayed close as if leaving my side would sever the bond that began to regenerate the moment he stood up to Maya. He waited until later that night after Scotland had been put to bed, to show me just how apologetic he really was. Rick whispered sorry as he made love to me, reminded me why I fell in love with him in the first place and won me over by promising how things would be different from now on — change that I needed to see to know if my marriage was salvageable.

CHAPTER 44

yric

I CAME barreling through the door, halfway excited and halfway scared to deliver the news. My mother was in the kitchen making a salad and Nate was in the family room staring lifelessly at the TV. At least he was out of the bedroom where he started spending the whole weekend. I walked over to him and kissed his lips. He didn't respond at first.

"Hey," he finally greeted after a moment.

"What time did you get in last night?"

"Around midnight." Nate spoke to me, but never took his eyes off the TV.

"Oh. Okay. How did the listening party go?"

"Good."

Moments ticked by, his attention still trained on the TV that he wasn't really watching. "Did you eat yet?"

"No."

I looked at the cable box. It was after one. I decided not to ask any more questions because I was tired of his minimalist answers.

Since Vivian's death, Nate hardly spoke unless it was necessary. He and my mom no longer sat up talking into the night on the weekends. I felt like I'd been living with a roommate rather than my own husband. The twins weren't doing well either. They'd often call, crying, and that would start the tears falling from Nate's eyes. I never addressed all those things he said as he cried over Vivian's lifeless body at the hospital. I figured I'd leave it for when he was done mourning. Mom never mentioned any of it either. I headed back to the kitchen.

"Hey, Mom." I kissed her on the cheek and looked at the salad she was spooning onto the two plates in front of her.

"Hey."

"One of those for Nate?"

"Yeah. He hasn't eaten yet."

She was taking better care of Nate than I ever had, but then again, other than sex, I'd never really known what it was like to take care of a man. They'd always taken care of me.

"I know! I just asked him."

I sat at the table and fussed with my acrylic tips, trying to figure out how to bring up my good news while my mom drowned the salad with blue cheese dressing and poured two glasses of sweet tea. I wondered if Justine would consider this news good news.

"Can you make me a plate too? We can join Nate in the den and eat with him. I think he could use the company."

"Okay. Take this to him." She handed me a tray with his salad and drink.

Nate was flipping channels when I returned. I handed him his plate with a smile. Even though I hadn't made the food, it felt good to give it to him. My mom was a caregiver by nature and I could see the bond that had built between them in the short time she'd been here. Maybe I could bring Nate back to me by showing him I could take care of him too.

"Thanks." He took the plate and turned his eyes back toward the television and his attention back to the remote. I stood close, but still felt far away from him.

My heart descended into my stomach. I walked back into the kitchen fighting tears just as my mother was about to douse my salad with all that fattening dressing.

"No! I want balsamic vinegar."

"Oh. Okay. It's in the fridge."

I grabbed the dressing, placed it on the tray and followed my mother into the room with Nate.

For a while, we all ate in silence.

Mom broke the silence when she asked how things were going at my modeling school.

"Actually, really good." I loved talking about business. "We finished picking our models from the open call and we're almost all set for the grand opening celebration. There will be lots of press. I invited every fashion blogger on the internet!" I laughed. No one else did.

"That's great, honey. Isn't it, Nate?" My mother tried to pull him into the conversation.

"Yeah. That's good."

I bet he didn't know what he was responding to but answered anyway. That was okay because I was determined to get him to come around. I needed my husband back, which made me think of my news. This was just what I needed to get Nate to focus on me and me alone once again.

"So…" I cleared my throat. "I found an apartment for you, ma. It's really nice."

Both my mother and Nate's forks dropped into their plates. Slowly, they peeled their eyes away from the TV and looked at me, and then each other.

I tried to ignore their stares and the guilt I felt because this had to happen. I needed Nate to myself.

"Excuse me?" My mother finally found words to use for a response.

"It's beautiful. Now you'll have your own space. We can go see it now if you'd like. It's yours when you're ready."

Justine pursed her lips and nodded. "Fine. Let's go see it." She got up and placed her unfinished salad on the counter in the kitchen. I knew she was upset. Eventually, she'd understand.

"Nate. Why don't you come with us?" I said. When he didn't respond, I added. "Please."

He got up and put his unfinished plate on the counter next to my mother's plate. "Let's go."

Justine went into the guest room and got her bag. Nate followed us out to the car and we drove to the newly built apartment complex.

I headed inside the model home that housed the agent's offices and asked to see the unit again.

"Back so soon?" the tall blond woman asked, excitedly.

"Yes. My mother and husband would like to see the place."

"Sure. I'll meet you over there with the key. You remember the unit number, right?"

"Sure do!"

"Great. Just give me a moment."

Back in the car, I tried to get my mother excited by pointing out all the great amenities on the grounds.

"See Ma, they have a pool and a gym."

"Um hmm."

Justine and Nate carefully inspected every crevice of the large duplex apartment overlooking a man-made lake in the rear.

"You can use the Benz until you get something else," Nate said when the agent showed us her garage.

"Thanks, Nate," she said with a little enthusiasm as we said goodbye to the agent and got back in the car. We were halfway home before anyone spoke again. "It's a beautiful place."

"You'll love it there, Ma!" I added, happy that there was finally some display of interest. I kept talking because the silence was prickling my nerves. "We have to go shopping for furniture. I can't wait to see how you decorate the place. You've always had such a great sense of style."

We made it home and as we got out of the car, I had been running my mouth so much I never noticed the envelope left at the door until Nate held it in his hands. Curiously he looked from my mother to me and back at the envelope.

"What's that?" I asked.

"It was taped to the door," Nate said.

"Who's it addressed to?"

"Me." Nate shrugged his shoulders and opened the door. "I'm trying to remember if I asked anyone at the office to send me anything, but I don't remember doing so."

Once inside, my mom kicked off her shoes and headed for the family room. I joined her in there, still talking about decorating.

My mother looked at me sideways and I stopped speaking. "I get it, Lyric. I'll take the place."

Squealing, I ran over to her and hugged her neck. "Thank you, Ma!"

"Just do the right thing by Nate. Give him a little time. Don't mess around and lose him. He's a good guy."

"I won't. I promise."

"We can go sign the papers tomorrow."

"Okay! I know you'll be happy there."

Nate walked into the room and just as I was about to squeeze him in my arms to celebrate the fact that we would once again have the house to ourselves he tossed that envelope on the coffee table.

"Do you want to explain these, Lyric?"

My head whipped in the direction of the envelope, and that's when I noticed the contents. My mother's hands covered her mouth and Nate stared down at me with contempt, demanding an explanation. Pictures on top of pictures showed me bare-breasted in thongs, cozying up to the steel pole in The Lion's Den, the strip club where I'd met Cypher. Other images showed me on the laps of various men or bent over showing my assets to a voracious audience. However, the picture that was sure to end my marriage was the time-stamped one of me entering the hotel room of one of Nate's former artists, Jay Collins, delivering the package that ended his career. Everyone knew he had been framed, but no one could prove it.

It was after Cypher plucked me from the ravenous club one night when my boss was yelling at me for not wanting to put out for one of his biggest customers. I was a dancer, not a prostitute, and I outright refused. He raised his hand to hit me and Cypher caught it mid-air before he could land that wide-handed slap.

Cypher told me I was too pretty to work at that sleazy club. I told him I had bills. He told me not to worry because he would take care of me and he did, until I got him upset. After he put me in his video, requests started pouring in. That launched my modeling career and I booked video after video. I was able to pay off all of my bills and have loads of money left over. That's also when I met Candy.

Cypher was like the music industry's mafia until he crossed a producer with enough power to blacklist him. He hadn't been able to secure a record deal since then. However, before his takedown, he ruined several careers, including one of Nate's company's biggest money makers, by planting evidence to a murder that he's still doing time for. Evidence that, unbeknownst to me, was inside of the package I delivered to his hotel that night. I found out when I told Cypher I was leaving him after he had hit me. He threatened to expose me for my part in framing Jay Collins. I finally escaped when Candy helped me move out while Cypher was away trying to reinvent his career. I moved down south and stayed hidden until Cypher appeared to get over me. Then I came back to New York and started my career again. After that, I met Nate.

I was on my knees, shuffling through the pictures, feeling Nate and my mother's eyes on me. It felt like a mirage. This couldn't be happening for real. Neither Nate nor my mother knew about those few dark years I spent stripping for a living. I told Justine that I had a regular night job. My mother shook her head. Tears rolled down her face.

"What is this, Lyric?" Nate's voice boomed as he grabbed the few images of me coming in and out of the hotel room that had been raided shortly after I left the hotel. "You had something to do with this?"

Tears sprang from my eyes as I tried to explain. I ran to Nate and attempted to hold his hand. He jerked away from me. "Babe, I didn't know. Cypher made me do it. I had no idea what was in that package. You have to believe me."

"And you had the nerve to ask to meet with him after knowing all of this. I can't believe you brought his name up in my house." His eyes held disgust as he stared down at me and shook his head.

"I didn't want to. He would have hurt me. You have to believe me, Babe." Nate snarled and walked away, stopping at the fireplace. He stuffed his hands in his pockets and huffed. "After that night in L.A. he showed up and said if I didn't help him get a deal with you that he'd ruin me."

"I don't know what to believe. You lied about your own mother. What else did you lie about?"

"It's true, Nate," my mother said calmly. "She came to me to figure out how what to do about Cypher. I even tried to send him a message to leave her alone, but that didn't work out well. He put my messenger in the hospital with a few broken bones."

RENEE DANIEL FLAGLER

Nate looked like he believed my mother. That gave me hope.
My tears blinded me. "He's dangerous. I've seen the things
he's done to people. I didn't know what else to do. He even
showed up here at the house! I told him you weren't interested
and I hadn't heard anything else from him since then. I hoped
he'd just leave it alone. He'll do anything when he's desperate."

"He was in my house!" That was all Nate seemed to hear.
Rage encircled him and he seethed. "You let that bastard in my
house?"

"Nate, I was scared."

He marched over to the table and picked up several pictures
tossing them. "What else don't I know about you?"

"Nate! Please."

"You need to leave! Keep the business and move into that
apartment with your mother."

"Nate!" He turned his back on me.

"Nate!" my mother called him this time. He turned toward
her, but her words caught because of the harsh look he cast her
way. "Please."

I ran after him. "You can't do this Nate. I can't leave!"

"Why not!"

"Because I'm pregnant!"

CHAPTER 45

 aige

"Hi, Paige."

Confused, I looked at the name displayed on my cell phone and then put it back to my ear. "Hello!'

"It's me, Maya."

Nothing ever rendered me speechless, but Maya calling my phone and actually saying 'Hi' in a way that resembled cordial did the job. You would have thought that I had suddenly become mute.

"I know…Hi."

"I'm on my way to drop off Jayden. I tried Rick a couple of times but he's not answering."

"Oh…okay." I was still looking for words.

"I'll be there in about fifteen minutes."

"Okay." My vocabulary was in serious need of an upgrade.

"Bye."

Maya hung up and I held onto the phone for a few more

moments before putting it down. Did that just happen? In all the years Rick and I had been together, I have absolutely never had a cordial conversation with Maya. The fact that she called to say she was dropping Jayden off instead of showing up at the door without notice, snarling a time or two and storming off, had me in awe. I couldn't imagine that Rick's outburst was the cure for her insolent behavior.

"Rick!" I ran through the house looking for him. "Rick!" Taking steps two at a time, I made it up the stairs in seconds and shot through the bedroom to the master bath. Rick was in the shower. The steam made the air thick and moist, making the entire bathroom look as though it was sweating. "Rick!"

"What's up, Babe?"

I took a second to catch my breath. "Maya." I panted. "She called to say that she's on her way with Jayden."

"Okay." It sounded like a question.

"Maya called *me* and cordially told me she was coming."

"Again…okay."

"What did you say to her?" I leaned against the vanity waiting to hear what Rick had to say.

"What do you mean?" Rick pushed the frosted shower door aside and reached for his towel.

"Maya was nice to me. This can't be a result of your flare-up in the car last week."

"We had a little talk."

I reared my head back. "Really. When? About what?"

Rick stopped drying himself for a moment and shook his head. "This week. I stopped by after work to bring Jayden money for a trip."

"What did you say?" I drew closer, curious about how this conversation went.

"Mostly the same things I said when we picked her up last week, but I was calm. You were right."

"I'm sorry. Come again." I put my hand behind my ear and leaned forward. "Did you just say I was right?"

Rick huffed. "Yes, you were right." Rick cut his eyes upward. I saw the smirk as he wrapped the towel around his waist and walked back to the bedroom. I followed closely on his heels. "All these years I held back, not saying what I really wanted to say to Maya and it's allowed her to take advantage. It gave her the upper hand and that was unfair to you." Rick turned to me and held my hands in his. "I thought I was keeping the peace, not realizing that I was making things harder on you and everyone else. I love and respect you, and don't ever think that I don't recognize the sacrifices you've made for Jayden and me. I'm sorry, and I promise you that things will be different from this point forward. It was on me to make sure you receive the respect you deserve. Will you forgive me?"

"Yes!" I bawled, tears dripping over my lip. I wrapped my arms around Rick and he lifted me in the air.

The bell rang and I ran downstairs to the door. I swung it open and Maya stood on the other side looking like a lost puppy.

"Hi Paige," Jayden practically jumped into my arms and Maya didn't say a word. "Where's Scotland?"

"She's still asleep. We were up late watching some silly movies. Unfortunately, I can't get those hours back in my life!"

Jayden giggled. "I'm here so it's time for her to wake up." She ran upstairs, screaming Scotland's name.

Maya handed me the bag she was holding for Jayden, avoiding eye contact. "Tell Rick to let me know what time she'll be back next Sunday so I can make sure I'm home."

"Most likely it will be late. There's a lot happening."

"Fine."

Maya stood there for a moment. It appeared as if she wanted to say more. I didn't close the door right away, giving her a chance. I was still in awe of the new version of her that I was now witnessing with my own eyes.

"Hey, Maya." Rick walked up behind me and placed his hand on the small of my back.

"Hey, Rick." Now she avoided both our eyes. "Call me before you drop her off next week so I can make sure I'm there."

"Okay," Rick replied.

Maya turned to walk away and Rick cleared his throat. She stopped, dropped her shoulders and slowly turned back around.

Maya looked at me and then looked away as she began speaking. "Paige." She paused again. "I'm sorry. I shouldn't have been so nasty to you. I appreciate the way you take care of my daughter. She's lucky to have you."

With that, Maya turned and made quick steps to her car. I realized my mouth had been hanging open when Rick gently pushed my chin up and smiled. Right there in the open door, he pulled me to him and kissed me.

Maya's tires screeched as she pulled away, bringing me back to real time.

"Yuck!" Scotland's little voice squealed. I hadn't noticed that they'd come downstairs.

"Ewe! Get a room!" Jayden taunted.

"I already have a room, several of them." Rick waved his hand around. "I own all of them, in fact, because this is my house!"

The girls ran off giggling as Rick chased after them. I watched, laughing, as he caught Scotland. She squirmed on the floor like a worm while Rick tickled her. Leaving her breathless, he ran in search of Jayden who screamed to the hills when he caught her, too.

I had the proof that I needed to know that my marriage could work. My husband had my back. I went to the bedroom, picked up my cell phone and texted Blair, thanking him for being there when I needed him, but letting him know that I could no longer be in contact with him. The next thing I needed to do was change my gym.

After that, I sat on the bed listening to Rick and the girls laughing as they rumbled through the first floor. The sounds that filled my home to the joists made me smile, and I never wanted them to stop.

CHAPTER 46

 yric

I WOKE up panting and sweating. It was another nightmare about Cypher. The room was dark except for the time glowing in white digital numbers on the cable box.

I felt for Nate. He was still there. He hadn't kicked me out. After my announcement, Nate wanted proof that I was pregnant and made me take a pregnancy test in front of him. He even took off to come to the doctor with me. This baby was coming right on time, possibly even saving my marriage.

Unable to go back to sleep, I tiptoed out of the room and headed downstairs and sat in the den without turning on any lights. I texted Candy. To my surprise, she was awake, so I called her.

"Hey. How's it going?" she asked. Her voice was soft and filled with concern.

"I'm still here." A few beats ticked before I added. "I had another nightmare."

"That's why you're up, huh?"

"Yes."

"Trust me, Lyric. It will all work out somehow. As much grief as I give you, I don't want to see you and Nate's relationship fall apart. You guys are like Ken and Barbie. He's handsome, you're beautiful and you're living just as well as that plastic heifer! Now you're going to have a beautiful baby. Y'all give us girls hope!"

Candy was always good for making me laugh. I rubbed my belly. It was still flat since I was still in my first trimester. There weren't any visible signs of a life growing inside of me as of yet. "Too bad I don't feel like I'm living a perfect life."

"Girl. We all have issues. If Barbie's smile wasn't molded with plastic, that chick would probably be in tears! The struggle is real, honey!"

I laughed loud that time and then looked toward the steps. I didn't want to wake Nate or my mother.

"Mom moves into the apartment today. Nate took the day off to help manage the move."

"Nate's going to move something?"

"Girl, please. All Nate will lift is his finger to point to where things need to go."

"Ha! I hear that. He's too rich to lift more than a finger. I don't blame him one bit. Is your mom excited?"

"She is now." I shifted on the couch, getting more comfortable.

"Good!"

Candy and I talked for about an hour until I started yawning. We got off the phone and I went to sleep right there on the sofa. The sun was up when I felt my mother's hand on my shoulder.

"Hey!" I stretched my arms and twisted the kinks out of my neck.

"You want breakfast?" Justine asked.

"Sure."

"Go wake up Nate so he can eat."

I took my time getting up the steps. I wanted more sleep but needed to get moving. Shaking Nate gently, I told him to get up.

He looked disoriented and then came out from under sleep's haze.

"Ma's making breakfast."

I started towards the bathroom. Nate called my name. It didn't have the angry clipped tone I'd become used to since that envelope arrived on our doorstep. Nate had gone from a constant state of mourning to being angry all the time. However, this time he said my name in a gentle tone that he hadn't used with me in a while.

I stopped and turned back toward him slowly. "Yes, Nate."

"Come over here." It was a command and I obliged. He swung his legs over the side of the bed, sitting up. "Sit." He patted the space beside him.

I sat down.

Nate blew out a heavy breath and remained silent for a few beats. "Listen." He placed his hand on my bare leg. "I checked things out. I know now that you were telling the truth about Cypher, but what I don't like is a liar." I cringed internally. "This baby is our second chance."

"Nate, I'm sorry! I won't keep anything from you ever again." I grabbed my husband and kissed him until he fell back on the bed. I was lucky that family was so important to Nate.

I'd missed his affection. Climbing on top of him, I covered his face with more kisses, letting my hands roam his body until his lower parts became rigid. When he wrapped his arms around me, I felt my anxiety melt away. I had my husband back. Unleashing all the pent up passion from the past few weeks, I took my time making love to Nate, wanting to hold onto these moments forever.

We held each other tightly as he drove himself deep into my

walls. I knew it wouldn't be long before we both exploded. As much as we both loved sex, we'd been deprived due to all the strife we'd experienced lately. The delicious ride to euphoria overwhelmed me, bringing me to tears. Nate's eyes were closed and he had tucked his bottom lip into his mouth, pinning it down with his teeth. His face was twisted into an excruciatingly pleasurable expression. Just looking at him made me shudder.

"Nate!" I shouted. Not caring if my mother heard me on the lower level. "Nate. Nate. Nate." I chanted, as a slow burn started in my core, causing me to quiver as the fire expanded through me. Nate held my hips and pulled me down on him with more fervor, grunting with every thrust.

"Oh!" escaped Nate's lips between grumbles and then he exploded. His body growing rigid as he convulsed against me.

That fire sprang through me. My muscles convulsed, suctioning the life flowing from his erection. Nate's back arched hard. An earthquake rumbled through my body just before I reached my own peak, which sent me sailing through space and time. I collapsed against Nate. He wrapped his arms around me.

I whispered. "I love you. Nate."

He whispered back. "I love you too, Vivian."

I sat straight up—stunned. I glared at him. Nate was still caught up in his rhapsody. Eyes closed, instinctively licking the proverbial deliciousness from his lips, Nate laid there completely sated, oblivious to the fact that he'd just called me by his ex-wife's name.

I watched him as tears fell from my eyes and stained his bare chest. I was pissed, debating whether I should call his mishap to his attention or let this go since we were finally getting back to where I wanted our marriage to be. I'd just gotten my second chance, so I swallowed my anger. I knew he still loved her when we got married, but I figured I'd win him over. After all, he walked down that aisle with me, didn't he? I did win, didn't I?

He's still here. Eventually, her memories would fade and lose their hold. I hoped.

I got up and headed for the shower and attempted to wash away the disdain. After a while, Nate joined me in there, still clueless. He slid arms around my waist from behind and then caressed my breast, which to me now felt more like groping. It made me feel dirty—in the same way those raggedy men in the strip club used to. I pulled away.

"What's wrong?"

He looked confused when I turned to face him. "You called me Vivian." I snapped at him.

Nate scrunched his face. "No, I didn't?"

"Yes, you did!"

"Babe."

I turned from him, finished up and left the shower. I was going to stay with Nate, but I had to find a way to win him over from Vivian's ghost.

We dressed and headed downstairs for breakfast. Mom noticed I was upset. She shook her head at me. Nate's attitude seemed just fine. After we ate, my mother left to pick up some custom made curtains she'd ordered before the movers arrived. She wanted to put them up when she got to the apartment. Nate told her to take his sports car since it was the first in the driveway. That way she wouldn't have to move the other cars.

When the doorbell rang shortly after, I ran to open the door thinking it was her and she'd left something. I swung the door open and Cypher pushed his way in!

"You thought you got rid of me, huh? Sent your dogs after me again. How'd hubby like the package I sent? He'll like the next one even more!"

I screamed, expecting Nate to run into the room at any second. When he didn't, I started calling his name, frantically wondering where he was. I'd left him in the kitchen when I answered the door. Where could he have gone? My heart palpitated. Sweat ran down my spine and my mouth went dry.

"Your man just left. I saw him pull out in that nice little Ferrari. There's no one here to save you, baby girl."

Cypher hadn't recognized my mother behind the wheel of Nate's car, but where was Nate? I couldn't control my breathing. I panted and trembled. I knew firsthand what Cypher was capable of doing. My imagination took off. Maybe Cypher wasn't alone and whoever he was with had gotten to Nate. I hoped Nate wasn't hurt or dead. Why wasn't he answering me?

"I should beat your ass for not keeping up your end of the deal. Apparently, the pictures weren't enough. I'll teach you not to mess with me!"

Cypher grabbed me, backing me up into the banister. He raised his hand to strike me, but the gun clicking at the back of his head stopped him mid-motion.

Behind him, Nate cracked his neck and said, "I would rethink that if I were you."

Cypher released me and held both hands in the air. I melted onto the floor in relief. For a moment, Cypher just stood there, breathing hard as if he was thinking about making a move.

Nate must have sensed Cypher contemplating. "Like I said, brother, think again. I wasn't always a businessman, so don't try me."

Cypher's shoulders dropped. He knew it was over. The sounds of sirens grew out of the distance. Nate kept the gun on Cypher and slowly walked him back toward the door. I prayed Cypher wouldn't try anything stupid. I didn't know Nate in his early days, but I'd witnessed what a fearless businessman he was. He was comfortable in the presence of anyone from hardcore rappers to elite professionals. I had already assumed his edge was homegrown. I didn't doubt for a moment that he'd do whatever was necessary to protect his family especially his unborn child.

I was still on the floor. Nate tilted his head in my direction. "Get your mother on the phone and let her know what's going on. Tell her not to come back until we call her. I don't want her walking up on this." I followed Nate's orders.

Cypher tried to run when the police pulled up. I guess he assumed Nate wouldn't shoot him in front of them, but they caught him. I ran to Nate and wrapped my arms around him. He held me tight.

The movers came soon after the chaos was cleared. On our way to my mother's new apartment, we stopped by the precinct. Cypher also had an outstanding warrant for assault to add to the trespassing and attempted assault charges that we were pressing against him.

Now I could really be free — well almost. We had our house to ourselves so Nate and I could work on our marriage. Cypher was no longer a worry. All that was left was to free my husband from the clutches of his broken-hearted memories.

CHAPTER 47

 erri

"Wake up."

I fluttered my eyes and opened them to Chris's lips connecting with my forehead.

"Here." Chris handed me a tray with egg, bacon, and grits. He took the orange juice and placed it on the nightstand.

"Oh!" I pulled myself up and rested my back against the headboard. "Breakfast in bed?"

"For my special lady!"

"Thank you!" I hugged him, not wanting to kiss him with my morning breath.

"Plus, after last night's workout, I figured you'd need this to replenish your energy!"

I tossed the pillow at him! "You're naughty!"

"And so are you!" He raised his brows and then winked. "Thanks!" Chris headed to the shower as I chowed like a hungry ox on my delicious breakfast.

I shook my head at his quirky comments, but they brought our passionate night back to mind. Alisa and Riley had stayed with Camilla last night, so we had the house to ourselves. We'd spent the past few months working on finding our way back to happy and used our rare time alone to consummate our reconnection. There probably wasn't a part of the house that we didn't make love in except Alisa and Riley's rooms.

Camilla had been spending a lot more time with both girls since school let out, and she was getting better every day. Our relationship was permanently changed, but we were okay. The girls were our common ground. Riley was returning to her old self and the jerk that tried to rape her was behind bars. She'd become more protective over her little sister.

When Chris got out of the shower, I was still sitting with the empty tray on my lap, reminiscing about all that happened this past year.

"Hey, lady! You need to get dressed. We have to pick up Camilla and the girls on our way to the park."

"What time is it?" I put the tray aside and stretched.

"A little after ten." Chris sat on the side of the bed to put on his socks.

My eyes bulged. "Ten!" I tossed the covers back and bolted out of bed.

"Yeah." Chris looked confused. "We have time. It doesn't start until noon."

"But the planning committee was supposed to be there at nine to setup! Oh! My goodness!"

I stumbled around the room in search of my cell phone and finally found it in my bag. I had less than twenty percent battery life left and more than five voice messages and tons of texts. I called my co-chair to let her know I overslept and would be there ASAP. Then I called Camilla to make sure that she and the girls would be ready to leave the second we pulled up.

Chris watched in amusement as I raced around trying to get

ready. We were back to our normal routine of me rushing around while he anticipated my needs. I ran into the shower and yelled for him. He tossed a washcloth into the shower for me, which I'd forgotten in my haste. He didn't have to wait for me to ask. When I got out, my phone was connected to my charger and I was up to at least thirty percent battery life. By the time I finished getting dressed and made it downstairs, he was waiting in the car with my bags in the back and the AC on high.

We swooped over to get Camilla and the girls and made it to the park by eleven-thirty. Fortunately, our team had taken care of everything and assured me not to worry. The food had been delivered. Balloons marking our territory within the park swayed in the breeze. The registration area was prepared and staffed, ready to receive attendees and distribute wristbands and t-shirts. The DJ's were setting up the music. Various sections had been designated for games and the band shell was all ready for presentations.

The hot sun beat down on us as people started to show up for the Brimming Nest Family Fun Festival. We worked against the heat to make sure everything ran smoothly. Chris found a table for our family and Camilla worked with me behind the scenes.

I spotted Paige, Rick, and the girls leaving the registration table and ran over to them. We hugged. I embraced Chris and the girls and then froze. Paige smiled knowingly and threw in a quick little smirk just for me.

"And who do we have here?"

"Hi!" Maya held out her hand. "Kerri, right?"

"Yes!"

"Nice to see you again." Figuratively, my jaw was on the ground.

"Nice to see you. Enjoy the picnic." I looked at Paige one last time and she opened her eyes really wide. "Follow me. There's a spot right by my table."

I was surprised to see Maya, but it all made sense. If anyone could help get a blended family in one accord, it was The Brimming Nest.

As we approached the table, I gave Chris a look, letting him know I had something to discuss with him later. He and Rick exchanged man-hugs before he planted a friendly peck on Paige's cheek. Maya greeted everyone and sat down.

Before I made it back to the kitchen, I spotted Nate. I headed in his direction knowing that Lyric wasn't far behind. Someone was calling my name so I told Paige to show them where we were all seated. I headed over to the executive director of the organization to work out a few last-minute changes to the itinerary and went back to greet Nate and Lyric.

As usual, Lyric looked stunning in a flowing halter dress. However, there was something different about her. Her skin looked flawless and bright.

"Hey, Chicca!" She reached for me.

"It's been so long!" I pulled her in for a tight hug. "Wait! What did I just feel?" I put my hand to her stomach. You couldn't see it through the dress, but I definitely felt a little bump when I embraced her. "Lyric! Are you pregnant?"

With a brilliant smile, she twisted in delight. "Nate and I are having a baby," she sang.

"Oh!" I screamed and hugged her again.

Paige got up and hugged her too.

"I can't believe you kept this from us," Paige said. "May I?" she asked, holding her hand over Lyric's belly. Lyric nodded and Paige rubbed her stomach.

"I wanted to surprise you. We haven't seen each other all summer!"

"Goodness! You're right," Paige said, covering her mouth.

"It's been a long time," I added, counting back to before the drama that hit my life."

"We have to catch up. So much has happened," Lyric said.

"We need a girl's day. Let's do it before the summer ends," Paige said.

"The summer is already ending. My girls start school in two weeks!" I added.

"Let's set a date today," Paige said.

"Where's Camilla?" Lyric asked.

"She's over there." I pointed to the area where the food was set up.

"Let me go and say hello." Lyric checked in with Nate before going over to chat with Camilla.

The executive director officially kicked off the picnic. The girls joined other kids their age to play games. Maya made herself busy chaperoning the girls. The men all ended up playing cards and Paige, Lyric and me did what we do best, talk, laugh, scream and gossip just a little. Lyric suggested we spend a weekend at Nate's home in the Hamptons. We promised to make plans for the next summer. Each of us was making our way around a brand new sense of normal, whether we liked it or not.

ACKNOWLEDGMENTS

Kerri, Lyric, and Paige have been hanging around in my head since 2013. They took their cues from the real world, where sixty percent of American households represent blended families. Shout out to you if you are part of a winning blend yourself. Each of them came to this journey with a few surprises and I, for one, enjoyed each crazy, unexpected turn. My hope is that you did too. If you did, tell a friend.

To God be the GLORY!

As I sit here on quarantine lockdown with more time on my hands than I know what to do with, I can't help but think about how blessed I am despite what's happening in our world. I'm so excited to have finished book number seventeen! Eight of those books have been published under my name, Renee Daniel Flagler. The other nine books are romance titles written by my alter ego, Nicki Night. This journey has been nothing short of amazing. Nicki hijacked my publishing life for a few years and wrote those eight books like rapid fire, crafting stories centered in love and building a name for herself. I'm excited for her... well me. She's got more to come. Well, let's just say that we've got more to come. Stay tuned in.

There's so many people to thank, so let me get started. First, my Lord and Savior, Jesus Christ, through whom all things are possible. He's always first. I'm eternally grateful for all the doors

He's opened for me. Next up, my fabulous family who never considers it robbery to share me with my passion for writing or my addiction to community service. My hubby/homeboy, Les, is my backbone, and my babies, Lil Les, Hollywood, & Suga Mama are the reason I take every breath. The Daniels Clan has always been my rock. Thank you for your unwavering support. To the rest of my friends and family, thank you for being *you* in my life. To my author-sister-friends, where would I be without our fun, friendship, and commentary? Tiffany L. Warren, Victoria Christopher Murray, ReShonda Tate Billingsley, and Lutishia Lovely, thanks for being my girls. To two women who paved the path and always answer my calls, Brenda Jackson and Beverly Jenkins, thank you, and I love you ladies dearly. To my editor, Cindy Draughon, my new partner in editorial crime, thank you for your patience and expertise. To the family, friends, readers, book clubs, and all of you dope VIPs (that's you because you're Very Important People to me) who have been down with me on this journey for years, I love y'all to life!

Up next, *The Arrangement*. In the meantime, meet me on the corner of Facebook and Instagram.

Ciao fabulous,
  Renee

4.3.2020

BIO

Renee Daniel Flagler is an award-winning writer, adjunct professor and speaker who is passionate about inspiring women and youth to pursue their passion and purpose. Renee is the author of several novels. She also facilitates writing residencies and develops literacy curriculum for grades K-12. Her poetry has appeared in *Ink & Voices* and *Spirit Harvest*. Renee received an MFA in Creative Writing from The College of New Rochelle and was the recipient of the graduate program's inaugural Creative Writing Division Award for Excellence in Writing and Commitment to the Profession. She is an advocate for empowering youth by influencing literacy in the United States and abroad. Renee resides in New York City where she currently lives with her husband and children. Visit Renee at ReneeDanielFlagler.com.

www.ingramcontent.com/pod-product-compliance
Lightning Source LLC
Chambersburg PA
CBHW020910200626
46814CB00001BA/258